Contents

Editorial

Well, that was stressful. Welcome back. Sorry we're a bit late. Small matter of our publisher imploding.

In April of this year, the Editorial team had just collated submissions and were about to select the final work for Issue 17 when we learnt that all was not well at Freight Books. The precise details are not clear to us, and lawyers are involved so it is probably best if we keep our counsel. What we do want to make clear, however, is that the *Gutter* Editorial team are eternally grateful to the faith, vision and technical expertise of all at Freight Design and Freight Books for everything they have done to help make this magazine a success over its first sixteen issues. Had it not been for Freight's support, energy and infrastructure, *Gutter* would have not been able to achieve its current profile and reach. Also, as none of us are designers, it would have looked much uglier...

We now enter a new, exciting chapter in the *Gutter* story. It's been a tough couple of months, but we are really happy that *Gutter* will be carry on as an independent cooperative with art direction continuing to be provided by Davinder Samrai. We really appreciate all the support we have received from so many quarters and we are delighted that *Gutter* can carry on playing an important role in Scottish writing, and bringing you the best new prose, poetry and reviews.

Being an independent cooperative brings greater freedom – and comrades, we are delighted to be officially worker owned and run – but it also brings fiscal challenges. We'd therefore be incredibly grateful if those of you who are keen to regularly support the magazine could take out a subscription via our website. A subscription purchase returns us almost double what we would receive for a copy that is sold in a bookshop or via Amazon. As a non-profit organisation, all the money goes straight back into promoting new writing. And if you happen to know any rich philanthropists, please point them in our direction. Unfortunately Mme Liliane Bettencourt didn't leave us anything, but we still think We're Worth It.

We have some exciting plans for the years ahead. Meantime, on 28th November we are hosting another party as part of Bookweek Scotland at Mono Café Bar, King Street, Glasgow, and we hope you will come along, catch up with old friends, meet some friendly new faces and make the night as big a success as last year's event.

We would really appreciate the help of you, the reader, in spreading the word that *Gutter* is back and here to stay and helping us relaunch in style in the New Year.

Regardless of the details of what transpired at Freight Books, the result represents a setback for independent Scottish Publishing, as well as a personal disaster for the authors and staff involved.

With the recent move of Saraband's Head Office to Manchester, the year 2017 could potentially see Scotland lose two of its most dynamic small publishing houses. The reasons are complex, but it does serve to illustrate the continuous precarity of making books in Scotland.

One thing hasn't come to pass, however: in our first issue in February 2009, we pinned our hopes to the belief that there was still a market for high quality, printed books. As we have said somewhere before, "ye cannae giftwrap an eBook", and the much vaunted death of the printed word has yet to arrive. Sales of printed books rose by 7% in 2016 – so the question is how can small publishers capitalise on that sustainably?

We hope that part of the answer lies in good ideas and quality writing, and that is why we will continue to seek out the best new work we can find from Scotland and beyond, and strive to give it a readership. We, and the writers whose work features in these pages, thank you sincerely for reading *Gutter* and we hope for your continued support over the months and years ahead.

Right, enough navel-gazing – to the work! Welcome to the Crime and Punishment issue (perhaps a little apt, given the intrigue that has surrounded us recently?) We are dead chuffed to offer you a new story 'Quiet City', by the reliably splendid Louise Welsh. This comes hotly followed by Lin Anderson's fascinating insight into the genesis of her forensic scientist, Dr Rhona MacLeod. We then have further dubious behaviour from Scott McNee's crossbow-wielding boy scout on p023, and Graeme Smith's cannibalistic dental patient on p076. There's some chib action from G Armstrong on p151, while Saraband author Claire MacLeary makes her *Gutter* debut with Phil, the autoerotic home-shopper in 'Centre Ville' on p148. But it's not all knives, crime-scenes and ball-gags, there's some gamekeeper-baiting rural suspense too in Fiona Rintoul's new story 'The corvid liberator' on p094.

This year marks the centenary of many of the most gruesome battles of the First World War, and that was clearly foremost in the minds of many of the poets who submitted for this issue. So much so in fact, that the second poetry section of this issue (beginning page 079) is entirely devoted to poetry of conflict, loss, displacement and war. It includes new work by our new Makar, Jackie Kay, focussing on Sassoon and Owen in Craiglockhart, as well as writing on a less well known and more distant front, with Marjorie Lotfi Gill's account of events that involved her grandmother on the Iran-Azerbaijan border, and which legacy still resonates in the ever-unfolding horror show in Syria, one hundred years after the Sykes-Picot agreement.

This thread of jingoism deconstructed continues through Hugh McMillan's '364 BC' and Stephen Keeler's 'National Day' to Martin Malone's 'Phoebus Apollo', before being brought to the present-day dystopias of Trump America and Brexit with Jim Ferguson's 'the fallen and the missing' and 'rhythm of political heart-break'.

Elsewhere, other poetry highlights include *Gutter* debutante Elizabeth McSkeane's playful found poem on ScotRail (p034), Anne Hay's concrete poetry (p038), a found piece from New Jersey poet David Crews (p031) as well as new work from those other east-coast (Fife & the Lothians, that is) stalwarts Brian Johnstone, Jim C Wilson and Ken Cockburn.

For those of you who share our belief that more poetry in translation will help save the world, you could do worse than to read our Reviews Editor, Calum Rodger's fascinating conversation with French poet Benjamin Guérin and translator Andrew Rubens on p101.

We hope you enjoy this delayed issue, and thank you for your forbearance over the past few months. In particular, we would like to thank our contributors for their patience during this period of limbo. As a durty wee treat for you, somewhere within these pages lurks *Gutter's* first sex scene in a while. We're not going to tell you where it is, so you'll just have to thumb frantically...

Thank you for reading, and buying *Gutter*, and can we cordially remind you that a subscription makes an ideal late Christmas gift for that errant niece or nephew in your family.

Quiet City

Louise Welsh

It is long past midnight in the city. The orchestra has gone to bed. Even the brass players are tucked safe between their sheets, dreaming brassy dreams. Central Station's metal grills are long since slammed shut. Trains lie dormant in dead end sidings, their destination boards blank, carriages dark. The subway shoogled to a halt, hours ago. Now busy rats swim noses up, whiskers dry, in the underground streams that trickle through its tunnels, black, black, black beneath the ground.

The gallus, strong-legged girls who tottered across cobbles, arm in arm, wearing high heeled ankle-breakers, now glitter their pillows with makeup, breath sweet as bairns (if bairns drank vodka and Red Bull) building up their strength for the morn's autopsy of the night that is not yet past. The *Naw she never*! and *Ach he didnae*! and *Wait till you hear what she...*

Their boys are sunk in snores. One dreams his hand was run over by the night bus and it is louping right enough. Soon it will wake him. Soon, but not yet. These are the in-between hours, when revellers are almost all abed, and the working day is still blissful time away.

Taxi ranks are deserted and only a few black hacks patrol the streets of the city centre, their, *For Hire* signs glowing like golden tickets. Even the slip of waning moon has deserted the city for a berth behind the cloud. It is a dark night, despite the sodium lights and glowing shop windows where shop dummies stand frozen.

Or did that one just move?

No, they are as still as the City Chambers. Still as the security guard snoozing at the reception desk within, still as the marble staircases that lead to silent meeting rooms – all business done. Still as the grave portraits of provosts past that line the landing walls.

Outside a fox trots across George Square, keeping close to the flower beds, full of kebab, ready for some foxy business. A woman sits on a bench. She has seen the fox before, seen more than she likes to let on. Two policemen cross Jeffrey Street, bright in their high-vis stab vests, and she slips away before they can ask her if she is alright. She passes the statue of young Queen Victoria, who is crowned and sitting side saddle on a horse pointing onwards with her sceptre. *All right for some*, the woman thinks. She wishes she had the strength to ride into battle, but she has no horse, no sword. She reaches into her coat pocket and lets out a sigh, no cigarettes.

It is the watch hours of the night and the city is quiet. Cars slide along the motorways that scar its centre, headlamps shining, as if there had never been and will never be again traffic jams, treacle slow, slow as blood forcing its way through hardened arteries. It is quiet, but the business of the night is not quite over. Mini cabs ferry lone men away from quayside flats whose addresses the drivers know well. These were meant to be the new executive districts. *Luxury Apartments* the billboards cried as the new streets in the sky grew from building sites, busy as frontline Dubai. But that bubble burst and now downsized pensioners lie awake, calculating negative equity and trying to ignore the *ping* of the lift as it announces yet another gentlemen caller for the pretty girls across the hall, who are always home, always home.

They are nervous on the way there, the lone men, silent on their way back, no eye contact, no chit chat, but prone to tipping well. Sometimes they remember the view from the quayside buildings, the city laid out in lights like a backdrop to a New York movie, but this is not New York, and they are not actors.

Up on Jamaica Bridge a man leans against the parapet, smoking a cigarette and thinking about life, the Clyde slides by below, oil black, indifferent. On the south side of the river the City Mortuary is sunk in shadows, though something moves within. The Sheriff Court glows squat and just; all of its edges sure. Ducks sleep, two by two, in the tall grass that line the riverbank, a lonely heron stands on one leg, head tucked beneath his wing. If birds could dream, then he would dream of a mate.

It is too early in the year for the flutes and trills of the dawn chorus, but soon the blackbird will fly to the top of a chimney pot to sing out his territory and Kingfishers will skim the river, flashes of impossible blue. Soon, but not yet.

It is still night and the blue and pink shimmering on the water are the neon lights of the Riverside Casino. Inside the gamblers have murdered time. But each new day is a resurrection, fresh chances and old debts. *6am* the roulette wheels sing. *You have until 6am, and then all bets are off.*

The Humane Society Boat is tucked safe at its mooring. Tomorrow it will patrol the river, but for now there is no one here to dip the oars if someone should decide to turn the quiet night into a roar of ruptured eardrums and bubbling air.

Beneath the bridge, rags stir and a youth mumbles in his sleep. There are no dreams for him.

The man standing on Jamaica Bridge flicks the end of his smoke into the air and watches its glow sail into the dark. It dies before it reaches the water. He shoves his hands into his pockets and begins the walk home. A helicopter clatters above, training its searchlight onto Glasgow Green. And the man thinks to himself how these machines can sink like a stone, sink like a stone.

A CCTV camera turns to watch his departure. And in a bright fluorescent room the operator leans back in her chair and takes a swig of cold tea.

'It's alright,' she tells the police patrol she had alerted. 'I thought he was a jumper, but it looks like he's away home.'

A female officer radios, 'Roger that.' And the two person patrol turns course for a cheeky wee burger van they know. 'I shouldn't eat this kind of rubbish' she says. 'I'm training for the marathon.'

'Best thing for marathons, burgers.' Her partner says. 'A little of what you fancy...'

She shoves him and he laughs. The policeman would like to put his arm around her and tussle her close. He is tired of chasing scallywags and getting his meals from burger vans. His dreams are the same ones the heron would have, if birds could dream. A mate, a tidy nest, some chicks...

Their radios burble news of a screaming burglar alarm and the patrol change direction again.

Not far away in Washington Street, two men are swearing as they carry boxes out of the Pentagon Centre. They're only taking what's rightfully theirs they tell each other. Failed businesses, failed marriages, defaulted mortgages and unpaid bills have brought them here. The burglar alarm blares and one of them shouts, *GO GO GO!* They scramble into their van and race west, laughing as they realise that no one is following them. But they have failed at burglary too. Every move has been captured on camera. Soon will come the knock at the door, the steadying hand cupping their heads as they duck into the police car, arms cuffed behind their backs. Soon, but not yet.

On the edge of the city, people snug in bed, some alone, some tucked in the lee of warm backs and warm bums, falter in their sleep and dream of earthquakes, the Clydebank bombing, the house that fell, the rumble of beer kegs rolling into cellars' depths. And outside a convoy makes its way towards the Rosneath Peninsula, steady as a child carrying an overfull glass of milk. Careful not to spill a drop.

A retired warehouseman, kept awake by thoughts of *how to manage, how to manage*, draws the kitchen curtain back and stares down at the convoy rolling by. *Aye, that would put pay to a world of problems*, he thinks. And though he wants his grandkids and beyond, to live out their spans, the thought that everything could be gone in a flash cheers him. *Mushrooms for breakfast* he thinks. And smiles at his own joke.

'Come to bed, Bobby.' his wife calls and he goes to her.

'We'll manage.' He whispers as he burrows in beside her.

'Why would we not?' She says.

And for the moment, the difference between their pension and the price of fuel and food recedes. 'Aye,' he repeats, 'Why would we not?'

Out in the back court, in the gloom of the bin shelter, Alec the cat, who sat pretty all day on a blanket on the radiator, has caught a mouse. He lifts a paw, lets the mouse run three quick steps and then flattens his reach against its back. He lets the wee creature squirm, then releases the pressure and watches it run. This time he snags it by the tail. Alec the cat, who dines on Sheba and salmon cuts and tins of line caught tuna, is not hungry, but there is something about this game that makes him lick his lips. He'll make a present of the eyes to his mistress and not care that she calls him a cruel beast.

In the city centre, street cleaners have washed away the detritus of the night before. The business mob who will soon crowd the streets, will have no clue, that here someone dropped their poke of chips, or here a carton of noodles. Here was a broken shoe, here a broken bottle, a broken nose, a broken romance.

The tins, jars and boxes are almost all unpacked in the one-stop-shop supermarkets and the shelf stackers' thoughts are turning towards home; the bed that must be delayed until the kids are up and dressed, the university essay set to one side. A student wonders if webcam work might suit her better. Three pounds a minute the advert said, just for wiggling your arse in your own sitting room. She shares a flat with three other girls and isn't certain of her arse's charms, but the last time she handed an essay in late her tutor said, she should prepare for the day when she enters the real world. She looks at the ugly brightness of the supermarket aisle and wonders; *is this the real world?*

Night is almost over, the prelude to the day almost done. Early morning office cleaners pack the tools of their trade, the mops and buckets, the cloths and dusters, away and pull on their coats. Posties heft their sacks onto their backs. The free newspaper stands are fully stacked. Bus drivers swing their buses out of the depot. Trains rumble at platforms and then get on their way, *no delay, no delay, no delay, no delay.*

The streams of traffic are slowing on the motorways. Shining necklaces of car headlamps stretch East and West, edging through the ghosts of tenements, where whole families were born, raised and died. SPEED KILLS the overhead signs say, and more than one motorist rolls their eyes and thinks, *Aye, chance would be a fine thing.*

The grey dawn brings rain, a gentle smir at first, soft and smeary; damping hair and faces, running wetly off windscreens. Alec the cat leaves his present on the doormat and then slips through a neighbour's open window, Alec the cat burglar, his fur jewelled with raindrops. The drizzle builds into a downpour. It falls on the school run and harried commuters, batters car roofs and valiant cyclists, hisses against the Clyde.

But Glasgow is not a city where rain stops play. Engines are revved, radios turned on, drilling commenced, scaffolding unloaded; CLATTER. The noise of day is underway. It is now, and the quiet city is over.

Forensic Fact meets Forensic Fiction
–character versus authenticity in crime novels

Lin Anderson

My series featuring forensic scientist Dr Rhona MacLeod runs to twelve novels with the latest, *Follow the Dead*, published in August 2017 during the Edinburgh International Book Festival. However, I didn't set out to write a forensic crime series when I penned the first book, *Driftnet*. My late father was a Detective Inspector in Greenock and one of his fears was that that he might turn up at a scene of crime to discover the victim was one of his three daughters. When I contemplated writing such a scenario, I had no idea who that person might be, and what their connection to the victim was.

Whilst a teacher of Mathematics and Computing Science, one of my best Maths pupils at Grantown Grammar School, Emma Hart, went on to study forensic science at Strathclyde University. This was well before C.S.I., when few people had heard of the subject. When she returned to Carrbridge, our home village, she talked with great enthusiasm about her course.

Remembering this when beginning *Driftnet*, I decided, on the spur of the moment, to make my protagonist both female and a forensic scientist, although for me the fact that the teenage victim looks so like her, that she thinks he may be the son she gave up for adoption seventeen years before, is the dramatic premise of the story. She quickly finds out he's not, but the guilt Rhona harbours because she gave her child away, makes the murder of the young man more personal, and fires her determination to discover where her son is now, in tandem with finding the killer.

Thus I made Rhona a forensic scientist by chance, before I knew anything about the subject, and I have always thought of her as first and foremost a woman, who happens to be a forensic scientist, just as William McIllvanney said Laidlaw was a man who just happened to be a policeman.

Crime novels, like many novels, are all about character. A long running series even more so. Your readers will forgive you a plot or a setting they weren't too keen on, but they don't like you to mess with *their* characters.

Having made Rhona a forensic expert, I then had to learn about it myself. Emma, who inspired Rhona, helped me with the first book, but then she moved to work in forensics in London. So I signed up for a Diploma in Forensic Medical Science at Glasgow University. Along with fellow crime writer Alex Gray, we sat among over sixty professionals - mortuary assistants, police officers, pathologists, social workers and anyone who might have to give evidence in court. And guess who always had their hands up? Yeah, the pesky writers. I made great contacts and friends during that course and have called on their extensive expertise throughout writing the series.

So how do we marry forensic fact with forensic fiction? First of all, there must be a valid reason to choose to feature forensics in your story. It should for example further your understanding of character, their actions and the fallout from them. It must give us some insight into a character or the crime, or both.

Remember Locard's (forensic) principle of 'Every contact leaves a trace'. That applies to physical forensic evidence, but also arguably psychological forensic evidence. Why someone does something is as significant as how. And it's important to remember, this is not a textbook you're writing, but a living breathing human story, so you must find a way to weave the science into the story in a way that engages your readers.

In reality, the investigation of a serious crime involves hundreds of police officers and science professionals. As Ian Rankin has said, our fictional characters are the representatives of that huge team. Making a fictional team too large would dilute the characters in the story. Since the reader enters the story via the protagonist and stays with it mainly because of their interest in them, that would defeat our story. The most important thing is to make your readers care about your protagonist and what happens next.

There are many branches of forensic science and many specialisms. I chaired a group of forensic specialists a couple of years ago at Harrogate Crime Festival. Their areas of expertise covered soil forensics, arson, maggots, facial reconstruction, forensic archaeology and forensic pathology. At previous events, I've been partnered by fingerprint specialists, SOCOs who process a crime scene, forensic scientists and a forensic criminal psychologist.

The field is vast and expanding. So why choose to use it in your story? And if you do decide to feature forensics in some manner, which area of forensics do you choose and how do you apply it?

My own books arise from an opening scene that has occurred to me in a very visual manner. When I write these scenes, many of which contain the actual murder, but not all, I have no idea who did it or why. I have no plan or outline, and no idea of the ending. Not everyone works like this, but I do. Anne Cleeves explained at an event I did recently with her at Aye Write that she does the same... she approaches the story like the reader, never sure what will happen next.

I know that my protagonist Rhona will visit the scene and study it forensically. She will attempt to read what has happened there (the context), similar to a detective, although she has the added skills to view below and beyond what's visible. The scene itself will dictate the area of forensics prevalent in the story. To illustrate this we can look at a selection of the most recent books in the series.

None but the Dead

When human bones are unearthed on Sanday, Orkney, the grave must be excavated meticulously in a place where the wind doesn't allow a forensic tent to stay up and daylight is short. Soil layers can only be properly discerned in normal light and the weather is closing in. Rhona is an expert in buried and hidden bodies and she, with her assistant's help, excavates the remains, but she also uses the help of a forensic soil specialist in the hunt for the killer and a forensic anthropologist who reconstructs the skull, although we don't meet them in person. Sanday has no police station, is inaccessible in poor weather, a mobile signal is rare and there are no CCTV cameras, so none of the usual tools to help catch a criminal. But, as in all small communities, people know your business. And, the soils of Sanday can tell the tale of exactly where you've been.

The Special Dead

A young woman (a practising Wiccan) is found hanged behind a curtain of Barbie dolls, which are set out in patterns of nine, a key number in most religions, including Wicca. The patterns and the manner of her death are therefore subject to forensic psychology as well as strict forensic examination. In this case Professor Magnus Pirie, a criminal psychologist is involved. His knowledge of symbolism, witchcraft and forensic psychology is vital to understanding the context of that murder and the ones which will follow, as is Rhona's minute forensic examination of the body and the dolls.

Paths of the Dead

A young man is found dead inside a neolithic circle outside Glasgow, his body displayed in a ritualistic manner, and a stone in his mouth with the number five scratched on it. When the next victim is found in the Ring of Brodgar in Orkney laid out in a similar fashion, this time with a stone scratched with a four, both the *modus operandi* and signature of the killer leads to an expectation of three more deaths. (Forensic psychology in action again). A link between the victims is found via their participation in an ARG, an alternative reality game. The game play takes place across Scotland at neolithic sites. So criminal psychology, forensic geology (via the stones which are not local to the area the bodies are found) and cyber forensics are all involved.

Follow The Dead

The latest Rhona book, out in August 2017, opens on top of Cairngorm in a blizzard. Any death on the mountain is treated as a crime scene, and it is usually the Cairngorm Mountain Rescue service who are there first, so they must secure the scene. Determining how and why people die on the mountain, especially in very low temperatures is forensically very difficult. So in this case, the forensic pathology of determining death at -15 degrees plays a big role, as too does the expertise of non-forensic people like the rescue team.

It's all about context. That's why a forensic scientist may spend up to twelve hours with a body in its surroundings before removal to the mortuary. Once the body's been moved you can't get back to the original scene, so nothing must be missed. The study of the body *in situ* tells us as much about Rhona as it does about the victim, and the perpetrator.

Because I approach the story like a reader, I'm never sure what areas of forensics I will end up using. I research as I go along, and often what I discover affects the story. For example *Final Cut*, book six in the series, has the discovery of a skeleton under trimmed branches in an area of managed woodland. The idea for this came while walking through the woods in my home village of Carrbridge, where such heaps are common. When they rot down the layers give information about how long they've been there. Incidentally, it was listening to a lecture by Professor Lorna Dawson, an expert in soil forensics, about worm action in soil that developed the idea. I had originally planned to have some glass unearthed in the soil below the skeleton. I knew glass was very good forensically, but in my research I discovered that stained glass was even better, the chemicals used for the colours being particular to each manufacturer. So coloured glass becomes important to the story. If I had planned the story in advance, I might well have missed this.

My last piece of advice is to do your research well, but don't try to use it all. And often it is the anecdotes people tell you that make forensic fiction feel authentic. Dr Jen Miller, who says she thinks she is Rhona MacLeod, told me that she sits with the body to write up her notes, because it's the only peaceful place at a crime scene. No one wants to be in there with her, and it's her way of paying her respects to the dead. I loved that story, and of course Rhona does exactly the same.

A Scratch on the Record

Jenna Burns

At 7:03pm on the 4th of November, Helen Davidson's car hits a patch of black ice. She screams and turns the wheel with all her might, but the car still spins and spins. She mounts the pavement, killing Nathan Smith instantly. He had been walking to his work, a night shift on the till at the corner shop. No-one will miss him, but Helen kills him all the same.

Except, that's not what happened.

~

At 6:32pm, Helen clocks out of her shift at 'the office'. There is of course a more specific name for the company she works for and her precise role within it. But, like most people stuck in stories, she *hates* her job and simply refers to the whole damn wretched thing as 'the office.'

Her neck and back ache from sitting at a desk and typing all day. She heads to the car park and tilts her neck to the right, a pained satisfaction filling her as it *click-click-clicks*.

'Ooh, stiff are you love?'

Helen turns. Roger- a typical co-worker character, naturally- leers at her. His tie still bears a stain from last week's Chinese takeaway.

'I could loosen that up for you. Fancy a little – *massage?*'

In the slight pause between 'little' and 'massage', he actually holds up his hands and wiggles his fingers. It might have been funny if it wasn't so disgusting. Helen supposes that if she squints very, *very* hard she might be able to convince herself that he has just made the Attractive Scale. She could throw him her car keys and they would drive to 'His Place' and they would make the most passionless love on his collapsing sofa. Just to shake things up a bit, you understand. She smirks at the thought. How very *American Beauty*.

Except, that's not what happened.

~

At 6:47pm, Helen trips on the third step up to her daughter's 'flat'. Do not be mistaken: the internal inverted commas don't signify that her daughter's 'flat' is *not* a flat at all. She most certainly *does* have a flat, with doors and carpets and everything else you'd expect in such a dwelling. Helen simply uses said inverted commas because this is how her Going Out For Coffee Friends talk about their own children's 'digs'. Helen, of course, has not yet grown out of the fact that her daughter is not a student anymore.

She can already smell her daughter's sickly vanilla air-freshener. She screws up her nose. Helen does not know it yet, but this might be the last time she ever sees her daughter.

~

At 6:47pm, Helen almost trips on the third step up to her daughter's flat. She rights herself with ease, and continues her ascent. Yes, her nose still twitches at the pungent smell of vanilla, but she says nothing. She raps on the door. Her daughter answers with a wide smile, and they chat a little. Helen is told that Plans have already been made so, no, Mum, I'm sorry, I can't make it to dinner, some other time, I'll make it, promise!

And, that's more than fine. They give each other a last hug goodbye and say 'I love you.'

Except, that's not what happened.

~

At 6:49pm, Helen barges into her daughter's unlocked flat. She shouts and rages at how irresponsible it is to leave one's door unlocked. Her daughter emerges from the shower, still dripping wet, and scowling.

Helen is told in no uncertain terms that her daughter will not make it to dinner. She leaves with one last slam of the door, and does not come back.

And then, Helen starts her fast and furious drive home.

~

Nathan Smith could be Anybody. A brother, a son, a lover, a loner. Perhaps he was thinking of some grand thing when Helen's car crushed him. Perhaps he would have saved the world. But, in today's dull reality, the last thing he thought was more likely to be some cheesy pop song stuck in his head.

Except, that's not what happened.

~

Nathan Smith watches on with a strange, sick fascination. It is as if he knows what is going to happen before it *really* does happen. He sees Helen Davidson's car swerve on the black ice, and spin and spin like some grotesque top. She mounts the pavement and he leaps out of the way. Superhuman with his leaps, that boy.

She cannot brake in time. Helen's car slams into an inconvenient wall. Her neck snaps, and she dies instantly.

Nathan shrugs and walks on. He does not want to be late to work. Someone else is bound to have heard that palaver. They will take care of it. Naturally.

Except –

?

Genesis

Shane Strachan

In the beginning they thought it was a heart attack that Peter had suffered at his new job a few days before, but it had turned out to be angina. The doctors said it had been caused by a bad diet and stress, and Peter's mam was sure that the stress was due to his second wife leaving him. He thought it was probably the years he'd had to put up with her beforehand and the loss of his fishing boat not long after. He'd been the skipper of it for over twenty-five years and had spent about a third of his life out at sea. Now he spent his days lifting things in a warehouse on the outskirts of Aberdeen. Sometimes he'd lift them with his flabby, hairy hands, like tools and boxes from a conveyor belt to a lorry; sometimes he'd use a forklift, carrying oil machinery and iron beams from one end of the warehouse to the other. Three months in and he'd ended up in Aberdeen Royal Infirmary.

Compared with the image of cramped hospitals that came to mind when he read about one the paper, the ward they had put him in was fairly quiet. Of the four beds in the room, only two were taken up: himself and an old man in the bed across from him. Sometimes the lack of any other folk seemed a bit orra, but he was glad to get peace and to be able to wander about more of the room. It meant he could open and shut the windows whenever he pleased, especially when the sun managed to break through grey cloud outside and the room became stuffy.

The other man never said a word. He'd either be sleeping – his liver-spotted, white-haired head poking out from the blanket – or he'd have a Bible propped up in his two hands covering all of his face. He said nothing to the nurses and nobody had been in to visit him.

Peter, on the other hand, had had two visitors so far: his mam and dad had been the morning of the day before. They'd brought him a newspaper, a bunch of grapes and sparse conversation.

A day later, he was still picking away at the fruit as he re-read the sports pages, until all that was left were two black grapes dangling from the centre of the little tree. The rest of them had made his teeth furry and his tongue dry.

As his eyes grew tired of reading, he heard a faint tapping noise at the window. Without looking, he knew it was the seagull. It had come to the window a few times over the course of the last two days. The first day he'd ignored it, having been scunnered with the things whenever one flew at him in town or when he returned to his newly-washed car after a hard day's work to find it clarted in birds' shit.

This one was different though. After it chapped at the window, its eyes seemed to enlarge like a needy dog's and it stuck its beak through the open gap as though it was a beggar's empty palm.

It was on the second day that Peter had caved. Boredom had set in with laugh-a-minute in the bed across from him and nobody showing face during the afternoon visiting hours. He'd placed a crisp down on the windowsill and the bird had raxed itself as far as possible until the crisp was in its beak, before slowly retreating. It gnawed away at the crisp on the window ledge and then took off into the air, five flights up from the ground below.

And here it was, back again for a third day running. Peter lifted the paper up off his belly and folded it away. With the grape bunch in hand, he crept over to the window and plucked the last two off the stem before placing them down on the wide windowsill. After he lay back down on the bed, he watched as the gull made a clean swipe of the first one and then gripped awkwardly onto the second. Its beak pierced through the purple skin and clear juice spilled out over the sill.

Once it had flown away, Peter turned and faced forward. The old man had been watching the whole thing. He swiftly turned a page of his Bible and held it back up in front of his face.

Peter was grateful that his daughter was visiting him that evening. His mam and dad had told him she'd be in as soon as she could after getting the train up from Glasgow where she studied.

He thought about trying to get more rest until then, but that's about all he'd done the past two days. He should have taken a book when the wifie had come round with the trolley that morning. He always meant to read when he was at home, but there was never the time. He would never have chosen the Bible like the other man had; he'd read enough of that in his time. He'd been dragged to church by his parents, his first wife and, lo and behold, his second. He needed to start moving in different circles, start meeting different types of women.

Thinking back, the only times he could remember reading a book from start to finish was when he read to his daughters. He remembered how the eldest, Ruth, would insist he re-read the stories with bad parents and wicked stepmothers until the spines were cracked: Hansel and Gretel, Snow White, Cinderella – all the ones that made her feel like a lucky girl, that made her love her daddy.

The nurse came into the room and headed over to his bed. He made Peter sit up and unbutton his shirt, before checking his blood pressure and heart rhythm. As the young man listened to the beat, the stethoscope felt ice cold on Peter's chest.

Everything seems fine to me. You'll still need to stay in a day or so more just to make sure it remains regular, but there's nothing to worry about right now. How've you been feeling today?

Aaright, aye. Still a bit wiped oot, but okay, Peter said as he buttoned his shirt back up.

There was a tapping at the window as the nurse updated Peter's chart.

Not again. That bird's been coming back and fore to that window for months. We really need to phone in some sort of pest control.

Peter looked over at the gull. It turned its head to one side and, through a beady yellow eye, looked back at him.

It's nae a bother really. It's kinda rare to see een so tame.

Yeah, the nurse said flatly. Right, thanks for that. I'll let you get back to resting. One of our cardio experts, John, will be in to see you tomorrow morning.

Okay, ta.

The nurse went across to the old man, who pointed up at the curtain rail as the nurse neared him. The white curtain was promptly pulled shut around the sides of the bed.

Peter listened hard, but only the nurse spoke.

He lay his head back down and watched the bird pace the window ledge. It tapped at the window once more before turning away and flying off.

Peter fell asleep.

He woke up a few hours later to find himself dammert at the sight of the room. As he started to see the familiar in the beds and machines around him, he realised his daughter was sat on the chair by his bed.

Hiya, he croaked. Hoo lang have you been sitting there?

Ruth looked up from his paper. She brushed her dark curls off her pale face to speak.

About ten minutes. She looked down at her gold watch: this year's birthday present from him. Yeah, just the back of seven. It's quarter past now.

Ye should have woke ma up.

I didn't want to disturb your sleep.

Och no, the visiting time only lasts sae lang.

She looked back down at her lap and folded up the paper.

I can't stay too long anyway. I've got to meet a couple of ma chums in town.

Well, that's aa the mair reason why ye should have wakened ma.

Yeah, but I didn't want to scare you. She sighed as she put the paper back onto the bedside table. So how've you been? You coping with the food?

He sat up and rubbed his eyes.

I'm okay, he yawned. I've nae been aeting much. Food's one of the things that's caused this trouble in the first place. But the stuff I've heen has been aaright I suppose.

That's good. She crossed her trousered legs and folded her arms.

Their conversation went on like this for a while longer, lapsing into silence every now and then. During one silence, he reached over to pour himself a cup of water on the bedside table. Dull pains started shooting through his chest and he placed a hand on it.

You okay?

He didn't reply.

Dad, you okay?

He lay back down.

Aye, he panted. It's just palpitations. Nae nithing to worry aboot.

Her eyes welled up and she hid her face away from him.

Darling, it's nithing.

She started to sob quietly.

This is all my fault, she said as she wiped at her face.

He would have laughed if it wasn't for the pain.

Dinna be daft! Fit ye spikking aboot?

From behind her hands, she shook her head. He wanted to reach out and rub her shoulder, but was too feart to move about again.

I've caused you all this stress dad. She looked him in the eye as her jaw trembled.

Rubbish. Hoo could you think that?

She shook her head again and some curls spilled onto her face. Her voice broke off into a whisper as she replied, Beth left you because of me.

Fit ye on aboot?

I told her about when I was little. What you did.

Peter's heart thumped hard. He looked over at the man in the bed across from them. He was sleeping.

Nae this again Ruth. Ye were telt nae to bring this up again.

I haven't, she wept. She folded her arms and looked down at the floor. It was about a year ago, when we weren't speaking. I was out and Beth was in the same pub with folk, and I was really angry with you over that whole car thing and had a drink in and I... I told her. I knew the next day I shouldn't have. I knew I'd done the wrong thing, but I thought she'd maybe forgotten.

Peter said nothing so Beth continued.

But then she asked me about it the week after. She said she was scared to leave you and Emily alone together and I told her to not worry and to just forget about it. I said it had only happened when you used to drink too much. I said you'd never do it again, but she wouldn't listen. And then the next thing I knew, she'd left you.

He looked up at the curtain rail above them.

Ye telt her a pack o lies.

Ruth inhaled sharply.

Dad, I'm not going through all of this again. You know what you did.

I ken fit your mam telt ye to say I did.

Dad, stop it.

I wish you'd fucking stop it, he spat.

Dad! She'd stopped crying. She was angry now: the Ruth he was used to.

She stood up and put her jacket on.

Far ye gan?

I'm not staying, she said. I thought you'd maybe listen this time, but I'm only making things worse.

Aye, ye're right enough there.

She shook her head as she left the room.

He closed his eyes and tried to take deep breaths. His heart ached and his hands shook. He waited for them to stop trembling before reaching out to pour a full cup of water. He drank it in one go, lay back down and wiped sweat from his brow.

The old man coughed and Peter looked up to see that he was awake and once again hidden behind his Bible. This time though, he began reading aloud.

...they shall move out of their holes like worms of the earth: they shall be afraid of the Lord our God, and shall fear because of thee. Who is a God like unto thee, that pardoneth iniquity, and passeth by the transgression of the remnant of his heritage? He retaineth not his anger for ever, because he delighteth in mercy. He will turn again, he will have compassion upon us; he will subdue our iniquities; and thou wilt cast all their sins into the depths of the sea.

Peter felt crushed. It was as though the man's booming words had indented themselves onto the four walls around him. As he stood up and pulled the curtain shut around his bed, he felt his face burn.

He sat down and gripped onto the blanket. He remained like this, staring into space, until he could hear snores coming from behind the curtain. He felt himself relax at the sound. He got in under the bed sheet and put his head down.

He'd been dreaming that he was drowning in a sea in the middle of a wild storm when he jolted awake the next morning. The cardio specialist, John, was at his bedside. He was a tall, fit man with a full head of greying hair.

Now, before I check everything again, I've got some questions to ask about your general level of fitness and your diet. So, shall we start with the diet?

Peter sighed as he sat up. He realised his breakfast was sitting on the bedside table: a small bunch of grapes and a yoghurt. He spooned the yoghurt pot empty as he told John what must have been a horror story for him to hear. It wasn't much better for the fitness either: sitting in a wheelhouse and shouting orders down at your crew whenever there was hard work to be done could never have constituted as exercise. It hadn't been much better when he'd been at home, for then it was a stool and an order at the bar instead.

After he'd finished writing down some notes on a piece of paper, John didn't ask anything more. He took out a blood pressure monitor and Peter swiftly rolled up his sleeve. John took a reading, tutted and then read through the previous notes on the chart.

I'm going to be honest with you, Peter. If you don't change the way you're living your life, you're going to die a lot sooner than you should have to. For some reason, your blood pressure and heart rate have gotten worse overnight and it isn't looking good. I would like to think the monitor is playing up, but I'm not going to fool either of us.

Peter nodded his head.

Right, I'd better head along. Take it easy and you'll get home sooner. You'll start a new life when you get out of here. Fruit and vegetables, exercise – the lot. He hooked the clipboard back on the bedrail. Oh, before I forget...

He lifted his paperwork up off the end of the bed and pulled a book out from underneath.

The old fellow you were sharing a room with asked me to pass this on to you. Maybe it'll be of some use.

Peter looked up and saw that the bed across from him was empty now. He took the Bible from John and put it down on the bedside table.

Thanks, he said. See ye later on... hopefully. He started to laugh. John shook his head as he walked out the room and Peter stopped chuckling.

Alone, he looked over at the Bible. He imagined it exploding as he opened it up, bits of his body flying into the air, splatting across the walls.

He snatched the book off the table and spun it around in his hands. A dank smell rose up from it: that foostie stench of old, yellowed paper that always reminded him of churches. He opened it at the first page and a small scrap of paper fell out onto his leg. It read,

¹ John, chapter 1, verses 5-10

He didn't want to have to see the old man's words from the night before, if that's what it was. He flicked through to the correct book and scanned the pages. To his relief, there was nothing about worms and seas. He found the five verses and read what was there.

⁵ This then is the message which we have heard of him,
and declare unto you, that God is light; and in him is no
darkness at all.
⁶ If we say that we have fellowship with him, and walk in
darkness, we lie, and do not the truth.
⁷ But if we walk in the light, as he is in the light, we have
fellowship with one another, and the blood of Jesus Christ
his Son cleanseth us from all sin.
⁸ If we say that we have no sin, we deceive ourselves, and
the truth is not in us.
⁹ If we confess our sins, he is faithful and just to forgive us
our sins, and to cleanse us from all unrighteousness.
¹⁰ If we say that we have not sinned, we make him a liar,
and his word is not in us.

He snapped the Bible shut and threw it across the room. It hammered against the wall and fell down onto the bed where the old man had lain. How come he'd gotten to go home? He'd come in a few hours after Peter, and now he was already away. It made Peter feel like he'd been sitting in a restaurant watching as all other customers were served while he was ignored.

There was a tapping at the window.

Peter didn't bother to look over at the gull. He lay back down and faced the wall opposite the windows. As the tapping continued, he placed a pillow over his exposed ear so that he no longer heard it. He closed his eyes so that he couldn't see. All he had to endure was the feeling of the sheet wrapped around him and that sorehead that called itself life.

As he lay there, he thought of one of the books he'd read to Ruth and Emily when they were toddlers: *The Hungry Caterpillar*. He imagined himself as the caterpillar trapped in a chrysalis, waiting for rebirth; he would escape from this prison and transform his life like John had said – stop being a fat, hairy caterpillar and start flying.

He laughed into the pillow, laughed until he cried. He sobbed the pillow wet and kept going until he was asleep.

The room was in darkness: night again. He remembered that the nurses had tried to wake him and that he'd waved them away with his eyes still shut. A cold breeze was coming in through the window. He turned and looked over his shoulder.

The seagull was there with its feathers ruffling in the wind. It turned its head and spotted Peter looking at it. It began tapping on the window again then stuck its head in the open gap. It made a small screeching sound that made his skin crawl.

He got up out of the bed and stood for a second to find his balance. He took the small bunch of grapes that was still left from breakfast and walked slowly over to the window.

The bird leant back as he climbed onto the windowsill and stood up. After finding snibs at either side of the window frame and clicking them open, he pulled the window further up above the bird's head. He knelt down and stared at it. Slowly, it turned its head from side-to-side to look at him with both eyes.

He plucked off a grape and threw it out into the night. The bird turned and looked downwards. He kept throwing more past its head, but it refused to budge. Once he was down to the last two, he gave up and placed them on the sill between himself and the gull, both grapes still attached to the stalk.

I'm sorry, Peter cried to the bird. I'm so sorry.

The bird leant in tentatively and pulled the stalk out onto the ledge with its beak. Taking the very last of what Peter had left to give, the bird turned away from him and flew up into the darkness.

Mallaig Sprinkling Song

Scott McNee

Alex waited until the others were sleeping, or as close to sleeping as they could manage in the tent's greenhouse atmosphere. About half an hour after the chatter came to a halt, and about fifteen minutes after the background noise from the leader tents fell away, Alex slipped out of his sleeping bag and crawled out under the canvas and into the cold. The grass was cool and dry under his feet, and made as little sound as a comb passing through hair. He stood still for a long time, adjusting his eyes to the country dark, the maze of tents and guy-ropes, and the distant silhouettes of other scout troops going about their nightly routine.

The sky had opened. Looking up had a dizzying effect – a vortex of stars swirled and beckoned like a dive pool. You couldn't see stars back in Shawkirk – not many, at least. Wherever Alex stood, he was the single fixed point in endless shifting depths. Alex pulled a long forgotten word from biology class, ran it through his mind – *abyssopelagic*. His hair was wet at the roots from the gorge walk earlier in the day, and droplets of water dotted the tent canvas at the first sign of a breeze. He imagined how he must have looked in a mirror at this moment – pale skin wrinkled and glistening, golden hair pinned and blackened by the moisture; a tall, powerful creature in the mirror writhing, exposed.

He walked at an ordinary pace, striding over tent pegs with feigned importance. He knew from experience that looking as if he was meant to be up and about would disarm anyone who happened to notice him. Prowling around was just going to get him dragged back to a bewildered troop and a junior leader overjoyed to have another chance to lecture. *I'm meant to be here.* Besides, he was heading towards the toilets now. That was where people would assume he was going, and in a way it was true.

The toilet block sat elevated at the perimeter of the camping ground, next to an open field that did not seem to be owned by the activity centre. There was no path. A single circular yellow light hung between the male and female doors – Alex's midnight sun.

He stopped at the base of the hill and turned around. Satisfied he was alone, he cut off to the side and slid belly-first into the thick weeds that grew under the perimeter fence. He pulled himself further under, dragging his entire weight through by dirt-smeared hands. He felt the early dew diffuse through his t-shirt, and wriggled himself back around until he was facing the toilets once more.

The crossbow was where he left it, nestled in a dip behind a rotted fencepost. *Here's one I made earlier.* He and Simon argued over the use of the word 'crossbow' to describe the contraption – Simon claimed it was, in essence, a slingshot. He was technically correct, but Alex always won these things. Besides, he always tried his best to make it look like a crossbow. The base was a thick wooden cross, haphazardly nailed together. The vertical shaft had been shaved at one end, to allow the horizontal guard to sit lower than the launcher. A thick collection of rubber bands stretched back over a series of notches on the stock. They had invented them a few summers back, bored in Shawkirk, for sniping wasp nests from a safe distance.

This particular device had been crafted during an unsupervised stretch at the campfire that week, while leaders and troop members alike wasted their time at some sort of dance. Alex had been glad to avoid it. Back in Shawkirk, he would have had to attend something like that, and smile and joke with everyone like it was actually enjoyable. At scout camp however, there was no pressure. Scout camp had the right amount of *fuck all happening*. And of course, he couldn't go wandering too much in Shawkirk. The schizo lady at number 9 had flipped her lid when she saw him crouched in the rose bushes. *Why the fuck was she even up at 2am?*

Alex took the clothes-peg from his pocket and snapped it over the elastic, drawing it out of the notch. He balanced a stone on the flat of the wood. Here was where the design faltered – it demanded a disciplined balance. They had experimented with various solutions to hold the ammunition in check, but each experiment had ended in disaster, often with snapped elastic jumping directly for eyeballs. Alex gripped the back of the peg, releasing the band.

The midnight sun groaned as the stone thudded into its surface. The light's protection was plastic where he had hoped for glass. He spent several more shots testing the strength, though a couple went wide, either scattering against the whitewash or simply vanishing past the toilets without a sound. He lowered the crossbow and sucked his cheeks through his teeth. Soon, his head lowered too, and he lay motionless in the grass, waiting.

He could not make a guess at how much time had passed when a silhouette began making its way across to the toilet block; a spindly shadow puppet cutting across his landscape. Its sudden appearance was alarming – his static image wrenched back into reality. He focused on the lanky figure, saw how it loped with the awkwardness of a foal and felt reassured of his control over the situation. He brought the crossbow to his face. The shadow puppet skidded under the light, became a momentary blaze of colour, then disappeared inside the building. A secondary light illuminated the doorway.

Alex readjusted himself and fired. He let the sound of impact on plastic reverberate before hitting it again. Sound carried.

The shadow puppet peered around the doorway. Alex readied himself. Once the puppet had finished peering into the dark, convinced itself of safety and tottered back into the toilet, Alex shot the light again. The figure came out flailing, and began tearing its way across various campsites, to a rising mutter of complaints. At one point, Alex heard the familiar twang of a loose guy rope, and then, fainter, the dull impact of a tent peg hitting the ground. *This guy must be all limbs.*

In the midst of this chaos, a second figure had started up towards the toilets, but Alex had been lucky enough to see where she had come from. Megan was in his own troop, and while he was not a great believer in faction loyalty, he felt that even in the savage rules of scout camp, messing with a girl on her way to the toilet at night could be considered something of faux pas. He ignored her and rolled onto his back. She was whistling a hymn from school, that he heard fade into the sound of his breath. *And fill me with living water.*

It was while he raised his palm in front of his face, blankly contemplating it against the stars, that he noticed the leech nestled in the crook of his elbow.

Alex was impressed. The gorge walk had been hours ago, and waist-deep at its most treacherous. Since then he'd been running, leaning over campfires, rolling over and over in his sleeping bad and now the grass – and here it was. The leech had been through a spectacular ordeal and clung on, unnoticed. Alex prodded it. The slimy exterior had dried slightly, and Alex figured the creature was near death.

It wriggled.

'Hello,' said Alex.

He didn't think leeches had eyes. He wondered, if it could, what a leech understood of its prey. *Probably nothing.* The leech swam through a long dark, clinging to titanic, heaving clumps of flesh where it found them, gorging until it died. Alex plucked it from his arm, a little surprised at the force with which it held on. He wondered if he had torn its head off. He knew that could happen to ticks when you pulled at them. He was, he thought, probably attracting ticks now – a sluggish white banquet nestled in the grass.

'Are you dying?' he asked the leech.

It was still wriggling, but pressed between his finger and thumb the movements seemed far too erratic to be merely responsive. Alex turned it over lengthways and bit the fat little animal open. He wondered how much of the resulting squirt of blood had been his own. He dangled the ragged carcass over his head and thought that it looked a little like a burst water balloon. Whatever else had come with the blood tasted foul. He flicked the spent leech away, back into the dark.

He rolled over and spat, twice. He worked his jaw, wondering if he ever had a reason for doing the things he did. The nearest tents seemed to have settled again – it was as if the shadow puppet had not only disappeared, but been retroactively erased. And then the voices started up again. They came from a fair distance, and Alex was not sure if it was indeed his victim at the head of the group, waving torch beams across the countryside, illuminating and tarnishing everything in their way.

Shit. He had not thought of this. How the shadow puppet had managed to rouse what looked to be at least six others was beyond him. Perhaps he'd inadvertently sparked a ghost hunt of some kind. All of the boys he had seen had been too old for that, but he knew the lack of streetlights and billboards had a way of working on the imagination.

They walked past him first, heading for doorway. Their torches exaggerated them – throwing shadows under flesh and carving ordinary expressions into bulbous, shifting masses.

'I telt ye twice, it's gaunna be the motor.'

'The motor? What's there a motor in the fucking showers for Dazza?'

'The thing that keeps everythin runnin, the lights and the water and that.'

'Those are all run by different things you fucking goon.'

'Aw the mair reason there's a lot of noise.'

'Shut it,' said a third voice. This was the shadow puppet, identifiable by his height and excessively long, gesticulating arms. He reminded Alex of a spider he had once skewered with a pencil, and the random, gawky movements it had made when he had begun pulling its legs off.

'Maybe we've got to go in for it to work,' one said helpfully.

Alex's body began to work against him. This was progress in a way, because he didn't tend to regret his actions until afterwards. Even so, he couldn't help himself. He reached for the crossbow. The six were standing in a loose circle; arguing, pointing, mythologizing. Alex listened to their theories develop, from the plausible if poorly described 'motor theory', to the surprisingly accurate 'wide cunt chucking shit' to the bizarre 'ghost paedo' hypothesis.

Alex lined up his shot and smiled for the second time that night. The shadow puppet was facing him, underlit and grotesque. Once Alex was satisfied with his positioning, he drew back the bands. Something loose in the back of his mind began to mutter about the need for an escape plan, but he was too excited to do anything about it now. His hands were shaking, and he compensated by partly resting the crossbow over one arm, though this meant he had to cock his wrist at an uncomfortable angle. His breathing came ragged.

Technically, he missed. When the boy doubled over with a screech, Alex was exhilarated at his own talent, but slightly disappointed that the boy came up clutching his ear. He had been aiming between the eyes. *Apples and oranges.*

'Fuck was that?'

'You alright Ian?'

Ian the shadow puppet buckled slightly with each step. 'Slingshot or something I- Christ. Is it bleeding? Someone check if it's bleeding.'

There was a pause. 'It looks okay,' someone lied.

Alex wished he could have seen it up close. He hoped he'd taken a chunk off, though he doubted the crossbow had that kind of power. More than anything, he wanted to take another shot, but two of the hunting party had already begun walking down towards the fence, casting their torches low and searching. One of them was keeping a hand to his forehead – tentatively, like he was merely looking into the sun instead of protecting himself.

Movement at this point, Alex thought, would just draw attention. Even so, the thick grass couldn't mask him from torchlight, and he thought about how he had been so proud of his luminescence earlier that night. As he watched them stumble closer, he snapped the rubber bands silently. He didn't want them finding it and turning it against him. The shadow puppet, or Ian, was being helped over. He actually had one arm over his friend's shoulder, like Alex had shot his knee out or something. *What a pussy.*

'Motor running, christ.'

'It wis sensible at the time.'

'You were just being a prick Dazza, admit it.'

'Quiet,' said the foremost figure. He had begun to narrow his search area, swinging his light across smaller and smaller distances. Alex imagined he could feel the heat from the beam nuzzle his flesh. Sooner or later the torch-wielder would realise that the blond dead grass brushing the fencepost was in fact the tip of a stranger's head.

Every thought of Alex's concluded flatly with the word *run*. Attempting to wriggle under the fencepost and dashing for his tent was sure to end in disaster. On the other hand, running deeper into the field, while likely to put him ahead of his pursuers, threatened the dark unknown of the countryside out with the grounds. He blinked slowly, made eye contact with the searcher.

The other boy was slow to understand the sight. Then there was a gaped expression forming into the words 'what the fuck', and Alex pressed his hands to the dirt and pushed himself up and back into the field, twisting around and letting his feet catch the fall and turn it into a sprint. The ground was softer than at the fence, and his body trembled constantly in a rapid balancing act, heels teetering over numerous concealed holes. Indeterminate shouting came after him, and when it came to a sudden halt he knew they were over the fence and focused entirely on the chase.

His back ached. Any unexpected height decline in the field jarred him all the way up to his cheekbones and made it feel like his eyes were about to launch out before him. The deeper he went, the higher the grass whipped at his body until at one point, deep into the run and lost to all but the most basic thoughts, he became aware that it was slicing at the thinner material of his t-shirt under his chest. Nettles clung to his socks like the leech before them.

His throat and chest felt congealed and they were still after him. He could hear them, much in the same state as himself – panting, slowing and yet oddly steadied. Alex chanced a look to his left and tried to judge where he was in relation to the grounds. A clump of trees progress alongside him at the edge of the field and he was headed for them before he realised.

Someone shouted, and throwing his head to the side Alex glimpsed his hunters and fancied that there were fewer of them than before. When he looked back ahead, he raised his arms defensively, seeing the fence rise unexpectedly before him and leaped before he could judge the distance.

Technically, he made it over. His ankle cracked against the fence, a sound he would remember for the rest of his life, and he knew before he hit the leaf and root-strewn dirt that he had broken it. He landed on his chest, hard – and while the wind rushed from his chest his body registered the broken ankle. Alex squeezed his eyes shut, forced the tears to the surface and hissed. He had not felt anything like it since the car accident that had caused his back problems a decade before.

He didn't dare look at it; not that he could. Even with his eyes adjusted to the dark, the woods were nothing more than varying shades of black. He had begun to fear that his eyes really had dislodged until he saw the faint outline of his hand when he touched it to his nose.

'He's… gone in there, I saw him jump.' Their words came to Alex in a blur, pain clogging his senses.

'Made me drop my torch, where is he?'

He had to move. Mobility, previously a chore, seemed a luxury. They would find him again, with or without their torches. He dug his hands and one good foot into the ground and began crawling. *Cunts.* He was coming back for them at some point. The bad leg trailed behind him, jittering up and down when it hit another tree root, each incident causing yet another stop. It sounded like they were climbing the fence. *Cheating cunts.*

The ground became softer the deeper he went into the trees. *When I'm better I'll –fuck.* The leaves rustling under his body began to squelch, and soon each grip of the terrain meant seizing a fistful of mud. Alex pitched to the side, exhausted.

'Fuck am I going in there.' Shadow puppet. 'I think I need first-aid.'

'Get him tomorrow, can find him I bet.'

'The fuckin motor, I mean Christ…'

Their arguing grew painstakingly distant. Alex pulled himself into a seating position and leant back against a tree, wet bark chipping off into his hair. His clothes were smeared with everything the countryside had to offer. His back protested, aching in a familiar spot. He looked up at the sky, and found it obscured.

It was a long way back to camp.

Supervet

Alex Howard

This cat is on wheels.
A postage stamp

of golden down
has vanished from his flank

harvested by glistening
chatter-knives.

This is new kind of scent-marking:
a microchip.

Numbers now bubble up
through his skin

like steam from an Icelandic geyser.
His rescuer is thin

hunt-eyed, blue-dressed –
a windswept sapling of trembles.

New lives are about to begin.

Road Kill

Brian Johnstone

There's nothing left
            but a pus
    of flesh and muscle
    cartilage and bone
                fur
that took
    the wrong step
    at the wrong time
fleshed
    the hub cap of some 4x4
with life
    lived in the ditches
hedgerows
    round the boundaries
of fields
    that rubber
    thumbs its nose at
    the glint of metal
                passes
as it's passing this
                indifferent
        to light

Purple Martin

David Crews

Sterna hirundo 8 in (20 cm). Fairly common swallow that hawks insects on the wing at high altitudes performing dramatic acrobatic flight patterns. Our largest swallow. Males a dark blue-black. Can be heard chirping low, sometimes garbled. Song rich and guttural. Will skim lake and pond surfaces to scoop water with lower bill. Long distance migrant. Travels from Great Lakes and upper coastal regions of U.S. to Gulf Coast, Central and South America. Highly sensitive to abrupt changes in weather. According to the North American Breeding Bird Survey numbers declining by over 1% per year between 1966 and 2014. Greatly affected by the European starling and House sparrow, both invasive species to North America, that steal nesting cavities. Roosts together in thousands, nests almost exclusively in birdhouses. Native Indians known to have hung gourds for martins before Europeans arrived. First reported sighting sometime after 1492.

Angela, Gazing at the Stars

Elizabeth McSkeane

It's after midnight. Angela can see
the Milky Way. It wasn't a bad fall.
She toppled over, how? She can't recall
exactly what she's doing, lying here
at this hour. Yes. The washing that the home
help put out earlier. It looked like rain
so Angela just thought she'd. Not again.
They're always telling her she mustn't roam
around at night or get up out of bed
unless she has to. What got into her?
The devil. *You can do it. Try!* A whisper
made her. At least she hasn't knocked her head.
This time she won't pull the alarm, the one
she wears around her neck, if she bothers
them too often they won't come, the neighbours
must be sick of her. The night's quite warm,
it's four hours, maybe five, before the dawn
comes. Meantime, it feels good to see the stars
again. She knew them all, once. Venus, Mars.
The wind is up. A shower's coming on.

Angela Wonders About Emptying the Commode

Elizabeth McSkeane

It's not the sort of thing you can ask
just anyone to do. The home help takes
it off no bother but she's paid to plus
she's got kids. There's the carer but she makes
a fuss about it even though she used
to be a nurse. The neighbours bring in tea
and sandwiches. It's not that they'd refuse
to do the rest but they're not family
and most people only want to go so far.
No one lets strangers see them in that state
it's not the thing. The sun is up, the air
is thick, the nurse should be here soon. Long wait.
No flies around today it's just as well
with any luck she won't notice the smell.

Glasgow Central

Elizabeth McSkeane

The train now approaching platform four
is the nine-o-six to Glasgow Central.
The next stop is Troon.
We are now approaching Troon.
(Change here for services to Kilmarnock).
This is Troon.
  This train is for Glasgow Central.
The next stop is Barassie.
We are now approaching Barassie.
This is Barassie.
  This train is for Glasgow Central.
The next stop is Irvine.
We are now approaching Irvine.
This is Irvine.
  This train is for Glasgow Central.
The next stop is Kilwinning.
We are now approaching Kilwinning.
This is Kilwinning.
  This train is for Glasgow Central.
The next stop is Lochwinnoch.
We are now approaching Lochwinnoch.
This is Lochwinnoch.
  This train is for Glasgow Central.
The next stop is Howwood.
We are now approaching Howwood.
This is Howwood.
  This train is for Glasgow Central.
The next stop is Milliken Park.
We are now approaching Milliken Park.
This is Milliken Park.
  This train is for Glasgow Central.
The next stop is Johnstone.
We are now approaching Johnstone.
This is Johnstone.

This train is for Glasgow Central.
The next stop is Paisley Gilmour Street
      Paisley Gilmour Street
      Paisley Gilmour Street
We are now approaching
Paisley Gilmour Street
(Change here for stations to Weymms Bay and Gourock
and connections to Glasgow Airport.)
This is Paisley Gilmour Street
      Paisley Gilmour Street
      This train is for Glasgow Central
The next stop is Glasgow Central.
We are now approaching Glasgow Central.
Please mind the gap when alighting from the train.
This is Glasgow Central where the train terminates.
Please ensure that you take your luggage
and belongings
with you.

It's hard to care about football

Alex McMillan

It's hard to care about football when your
Old man is dying and Indonesians
Die in the streets outside
The taxi windows. It's hard
To keep up with who everyone is and
Who's winning and losing their job
Next and all the love and hate and their chants when
Really the players don't change only their
Shirts do it all mostly looks
The same as it did 20 years
Ago except now Match of
The Day lasts 300 hours a week and everyone cares about these
Millionaires and
Billionaires
And the adverts telling you this one – this
One – is the big one, none of the big ones before
Were as big. But when you don't
Believe, you and your
Old man, that there's a lot
Else
To talk about
You find a way to care
About football

Playground snippet (circa 1972)

Alan Macfarlane

Geez the baw
Nuht
Geezit
Nuht
Geezit
Soorz
Smine noo
No it's no
Aye it iz
Yirno getnit
Geezit orull bah-ur yih
Geh affit ya choob
Yoor claimed yabass
No amno
Aye yir
No amno
Yoorgettna tankin
Ahl tellma Da
No yillno
Aye ah wull
Ma Da ull bah-ur yoor Da
No eelno
Wull
Wullnay
YoorDazzapoof
No eezno
Iz
Eezno
Anneewerz yerMumz dressiz
No eediznae
Aye eedizz
Diznae
Dizz. Noogeez the baw
Nuh

Concrete Poetry

Anne Hay

has	rec ntly	und rgone	i spection
to	deter ine	t e level	of cor osion
of	its	rei forc ng	bars.
Poems	of the	sixties	are in danger
of col apse	and may	require	rem val
fr m	ant ologies	on groun s of	health and safety.
We	favo r	the use of	renew bles
suc as	bamboo	and	rammed earth.
Initial	tests	g ve rise to	optimism.

We are currently exploring graphene, suited to modern poetry due to its high tensile strength and ability to adopt any form.

On the motorway flyover

fallen

fading
      bouquets
            hang
like
      the drooping
            corpses
of
    martyred
          raptors
strung out
      to scare
          others.

All Things Bright

Jim C Wilson

Again she wiped the toilet bowl
until it shone, hard, white and cool
as marble – a monument. Her sole
aim as a wife was Spotlessness. She'd
buckets and brooms, cloths and creams,
an armoury in her years' crusade
against all dirt.
              In private dreams
she soared astride a throbbing Hoover,
displaying her standard, a bright
yellow duster. Germs fell and knelt
at her feet in awe.
              All sunlight
was banished from her house
(it made the carpets pale). And all must
be neat in case of guests.
              Her spouse
obeyed her commandments: not to vex
her, he ate with care, wiped his feet
and folded *everything* away. Sex
was unthinkable when the sheets
were fresh, uncrushed and taut. While
he snored, she pored over her chores,
exulting silently. A thin smile
in the dark inched over her lips;
her house, the fruit of her labour,
was now Just So. Then, barefoot,
and draped in cotton polyester
of the whitest washday-white,
she'd glide downstairs to behold
her world, clean, stark and cold
as a church at dead of night.

Ghosts

Ken Cockburn

This room was once my study
where I returned from summer
road-trips cooling into autumn
and translated dreams through a harsh winter.

By spring you so disliked what
you called the clutter and scoring
through in red everything I wrote
the way you said I cut myself off in here.

When I moved we emptied it
of content and now it's your spare room
where you keep momentoes
and whimsical eBay buys.

Shadings on the long wall recall
the flatpack bookcases I filled and cleared
while the print of the pegged shirt you liked
hangs there empty as ever.

I see you've put my last book
on the mantlepiece. I think sometimes
I'd like to clutter up your life again
but I stay elsewhere.

Play In A Day?

Jim C Wilson

(A double tetractys, acknowledging Bert Weedon's
best-selling book on how to play the guitar)

In
order
to make friends
I learned guitar:
'Home On The Range', 'Jingle Bells', 'Drink To Me
Only With Thine Eyes' (slowly strummed in D).
And I remained
a lonely
solo
act.

Prospect

Jim C Wilson

Beyond this
whirlpool —
calm sea,
green fields,
blue hills
and, in the air,
vague birds.

The Plot

Brian Johnstone

A neighbour pushed me away so I wouldn't fall
in the pit. Then my mother came and asked
me questions I wasn't able to answer.

Evidence to the Yahad-in Unum
group, Paris, July 2007

He's stared at the plot for fifty years,
known what it could not tell,
gone easy with mattock and hoe
for fear of disturbing something
he'd not recognise as his own.

The earth cracks in the summer heat,
grows weeds amongst the stubble;
turns uneasily beneath the snow
that melts to run-off, mud; brings flies
to swarm above the root crops, corn.

They're growing now: a few potatoes,
a patch of maize, above the mouths
he'll never have to feed but planted,
with a gun held to his back,
not deep enough to harvest anything

but silence in the face of questions, needs.

Commitment

Judith Kahl

The only thing that I have
continued to pursue to the point of obsession
for my entire life
is Nutella.
I buy one jar and I eat it all.
Some people do yoga first thing in the morning.
We all need rituals.

If I were to get a tattoo
it would have to be a hazelnut.
Aesthetically pleasing as well as
comforting and symbolic,
a daily reminder to myself that maybe
I am capable of love.

This Be The Soup

Ian Newman

I've just got right my father's soup,
Three parts broth and two parts gloop -
First, buy in a cheap ham hock,
Boil three hours to make the stock.
Next add carrots, grated, sliced,
Potatoes, turnips, peeled and diced,
Lentils, barley, onions, leek –
All the more to make it so thick
You can spread it on a slice of bread -
And that's what you eat when you are dead.

My father sang when we were young,
In eldritch tones while making fun,
Whenever you see a hearse go by,
It's a reminder that you're going to die
And a tune about the wee cock sparrow,
Less memorable than bones and marrow.
The worms crawl in, the worms crawl out,
They go in thin and they come out stout.
And older now, he asks disapprovingly
Why I have such a lingering morbidity?

I've inherited more than simply soup.
When drunk I walk with a familiar stoop.
The young man at the churchyard gate,
He saw two corpses staying out late.
It's something primordial - he'd say vocational -
Something subtle in the educational
Discourse - we recognise our compulsions,
A meeting of our disrobed destinations.
They put you in a long white shirt
And cover you over with rocks and dirt.

Is this what Larkin meant about his dad?
And churchyards and the walking dead?
A serious stew with comical flavours,
A soup mix of twitches, tics and behaviours,
Different yet the same. The one remove -
Our beliefs - of which we each disapprove.
The young man to the corpses said,
Will I be like you when I am dead?
Yet I approve the singing of his song
For life is all too short – but art is long.

Wasp

Ian Newman

Once, in the shadowed collars of a tree
I saw a wasp devour a caterpillar.
And bringing this to mind now stirs
More sickly childhood memories—

A dead chaffinch burst open
Slowly under a bicycle tyre—
A lone baked bean rudely spat out
And floating in a cup of milk.

Yet these images are hazier
Than those yellow mandibles,
Zoomed in and sharply focussed,
Slicing and sucking at the juice.

For a time I thought a wasp
The most evil of insects—
Somehow bees are friendlier,
Their ethics to be admired—

For what good are wasps to us?
An entomologist's response
Would be they serve a purpose—
A loaded term if ever there was.

What purpose the painful throb
Of a last gasp sting in September?
What purpose the angry squadron
Emerging from a mashed up paper nest?

What purpose this pest upon our bins,
Feasting on the rotten goodness
Of chip pokes bloodied by tomato sauce,
Of spilled and stickied fizzy drinks?

This hive mind, this intelligence
Is attracted to human waste—
It's true that form follows function,
For they are what we don't eat.

Yet in the grubby murder on the branch
I had merely a quantum involvement,
My observation unaccompanied,
Just this once, by guilt or shame—

Instead, that childlike combination
Of revulsion and curiosity – even then
I knew that all nature feeds upon itself.
Who am I to judge the morality of bugs?

Elegy

i.m Kenny John Nicholson, d 17.2.1968

Helen Nicholson

feadag, feadaige (n, m)
    a plover
    a flute, a whistle
    the third week in February.

feile, feile (n, f)
    an oration
    a prayer, an entreaty
    the lowing of deer.

an sàs (adv)
    hooked
    in custody
    embedded, as a needle in cloth.

sùgh, sùghan (n, m)
    juice, sap, moisture
    sense, meaning
    dearest object, darling
    huge receding wave.

Jus tae put ye in the picture,
I'm still livin in the same flat in
Glasgow's East End and it's still
where I do ma wee bits n bobs
of furniture restoration. Wee
workshop in the hoose saves on
the travelling expenses, bus fares
and the like cause I couldny afford
the private jet even if there wiz a
handy runway on Duke Street.
As it is we still have the privatised
First Bus to aid travel at low speed
through this wonderful
Metropolis of Glaswegia.

Pine-Box-Jig Revisited
Jim Fergusson

Pine-Box-Jig Revisited
(extract from From the Diary of a Scottish Hippy)

Jim Ferguson

Monday, March 13th 2017

Well, here we are again, as the auld Revered I M Jolly might have said in laconically miserable tones that filled us with laughter back aboot 1980. Wee Nicky [Nicola Sturgeon: First Minister of Scotland] has this morning set us oan the road to indy ref #2. I welcome this news. Nothin like a bitta politics to get the blood circulating wae a wee bit mer Gallopin Gay Gordon's in the tank. And talking of wallopers what ever happened to Gordon 'I've put an end to boom and bust' Brown? Probably aboard a private jet to Raith wae a face like fizz at the prospect of another Scottish indy ref.

Jus tae put ye in the picture, I'm still livin in the same flat in Glasgow's East End and it's still where I do ma wee bits n bobs of furniture restoration. Wee workshop in the hoose saves on the travelling expenses, bus fares and the like cause I couldny afford the private jet even if there wiz a handy runway on Duke Street. As it is we still have the privatised First Bus to aid travel at low speed through this wonderful Metropolis of Glaswegia. The buses are of course operated by one man, nae Conductresses, nae Conductors, just the one man, in a wee plastic box. Exact fare required, no change given and certain to catch any cauld or flu from the close breathing proximity of your fellow travellers. The generosity of Glaswegians is legendary after all. And while I'm digressing here, I should mention that my last book *The Pine-Box-Jig Involves no Dancing* has nearly sold out of its original print run. A lot of folk have asked me why I called the book 'The Pine-Box-Jig Involves no Dancing', so here's a wee explanation jus in case yeezaw huvny worked it oot awready. I work a lot wae wood, I'm fond of pine, a pine box sometimes means a coffin. Aye a coffin, ye got that? A jig is in this case is a dance. Ye know dancing a jig an aw that. If you're doing 'The Pine-Box-Jig' you're dead. In other words there's no dancing after you're dead, unless you believe in an afterlife of some kind but ah don't. 'The Pine-Box-Jig Involves no Dancing' can be re-stated then as THERE IS NO DANCING AFTER YOU'RE DEAD. Which was in some ways a metaphor for what I thought life would turn oot like here in Scotland if we voted NO to independence in indy ref #1. And here did we no jus go and dae exactly that. Life didny get that bad really but we're still livin wae the effects of the Banking Crisis and the Austerity Budgets, and Cuts to Public Services that the newish Tory Prime Minister, Theresa May, has carried on from the original Austerity of the Con/Lib coalition government led by David Cameron and some other Lib Dem dude who's name escapes me at the moment and probably will for eternity.

Aye… there wisny much celebrating in the streets of Raith after the NO vote either, not much gloating of the doom merchants. No dancing after we'd voted for Scotland's death, so to speak. It was business as usual but life was quieter and less interesting. Until Cameron put his Brexit referendum plan into motion. Then we had to put up wae a couple of months of weird brands of British Nationalism being flung at us from aw corners of The Mainstream Media or the 'msm' as trendy folk now call it… A lot of the media is quite modern, like TV, tweets, mobile phones and laptops but the message was again from the Battle of Waterloo. Johnny Foreigner had to get the chop. And chopped did Johnny get. At least in England, and in the Wales tae. But no in Scotland or Northern Ireland. Anyway, as with EVEL, that's English Votes for English Laws, it turns out that English votes give us Scottish and Northern Irish laws as well. And that's very handy for lovers of the United Kingdom but shit for anything to do with mainland Europe, or Scotland or Northern Ireland, or probably even anybody anywhere except England. Clear as crystal? Aye?

*

An interesting thing this morning, or the day, or whatever it is in terms of passing time, was that Wee Nicky had Theresa May by the proverbial political pubics. Politically speaking that is… Of course I have no desire to infer anything ataw about the state of Mrs May's pubis, what it is, is, that Wee Nicky had her mer off balance than Jeremy Corbyn has ever managed since he became UK Labour Party leader. Aw that time waiting for an actual socialist to become Labour leader and when he gets there everybody pure ignores him, insults him and he gets almost nae coverage or air-time in the msm. Politics is a fickle gemm indeed. Time for a doobie. Foam and feathers ya tadgers. Mer anon.

Thursday, March 16th

The strangely bat-like vampire-woman and UK Prime Minister Theresa May invited public school boy and alleged TV journalist Robert Pest(on) roon tae hur bit fur a chit-chat. Fur some strange reason the topic they chose tae focus oan was indy ref #2. Imagine my surprise when vampire and arch Unionist May said 'Now is not the time.' Apart frae a well known aversion tae mirrors there's nae proof Mrs May actually is a vampire but we've aw been thinkin she is fur quite a wee while noo. Anyways, Peston, a man who is capable of growing a very dubious moustache, performed his public duty and sent Mrs May's message right oot intae the public domain wae barely a question asked. He took the role of Renfield to May's Draculé Drella wae a superb servility for which he huztae be highly commended. It was aw aboot timing and choreography. Mrs May is saying no to a Scottish Independence referendum at any time afore she's got the

Brexit negotiations completed. As UK PM she has the power to say naw to the naughty Scottish Parliament on all constitutional matters. According to May, this is not the time to divide the Union. Cause right noo she's too busy dividing another Union, the European Union. Meanwhile in the Ho-Netherland Region of mainland Europe the far right only won 15% or so of the vote in their general election. They're a democracy and allow fascists to stand for election, which is very tolerant. We do the same; it's interestin how far right fascist policies are now called 'populist'. What the fuck is that aw aboot? Oh aye, and on Woman's Hour [BBC Radio 4] they were warning young aspirational women against recreational drug use. It can lead to very dark places ... like vampirism and a desire to be the Prime Minister of the United Kingdom. Both of which are very dark places indeed. Well done Woman's Hour, pass the disco biscuits please, why don't ye. To get back tae timing and choreography, Peston's chit-chat wae Mrs May was broadcast at the same moment Wee Nicky was being questioned in the Scottish Parliament aboot indy ref #2. Coincidence? I dinnae well hink sae! May was getting her vampire fangs intae wee Nicky's potential air-time, coverage blah blah blah, I bet the Whitehall Mandarin Oranges were up aw night thinkin up the phrase, 'Now is not the time.' In the parlance of the recreational cocaine user, May wis hooverin up Wee Nicky's lines afore they were even oot on the air-waves. Don't Boggart that joint ma frein, pass it ower tae me. Dooby dooby doo. Mer anon, ya tadgers.

*

The weather is mild the noo, 10 degrees C on average but still windy with light rain. I canny wait for summer...

Friday 17th March
Spent a couple of hours gluing the drawers of rather elegant mock-Victorian Tall Boy. Great stuff. In the process I was wont to ponder the concept of 'Constitutional Crisis'. I discovered little new. As the no too long deid Davy Bowie wance sung 'So much has gone and little is new...'

Tis the day of Saint Patrick as well and huvny as yet downed wan pint o Guinness never mind enough furra free T-shirt or a daft hat. The Gaels and Scots and the Irish are said to be heavy drinkers, along with the Russians, the Poles and some other folk as well, whoever they ur I canny remember ... You rarely see politicians inebriated on TV. Or anywhere else for that matter. Poor auld Liberal Charlie Kennedy was killed by the strain of hiding his alcoholism. He liked his whisky it's rumoured. He shoulda stuck on the beer, much less damage. Whisky is a serious business, it has aw the qualities of a class A drug, and then some extra wans that we don't like to talk aboot cause it involves a poo in yer troosers when ye only expect a tiny wee fart. Or worse still, a poo in yer bed. Oh, the horror, the horror. The DTs is positively romantic by comparison. It's enough tae geeyi a heart attack. Moving swiftly on: The Chancellor of the Exchequer is in fact PM Theresa May's long lost brother. A lot of folk don't know that cause it isny true, but they do seem remarkably similar, he's like a male version of her. When Gordon Brown was Chancellor he was never anything like a male version of Tony Blair. Same thing with Osborne and Cameron, they were similar but both distinctly public school boys. There was maybe a slight whiff of transvestism that you never got with Blair and Brown: but Mrs May and her Chancellor, they're swapping claes and fashion tips every morning ower breakfast. And good for them cause it makes for more joined up government. I mean sexuality is a spectrum rather than a series o fixed points. The world is fluid, it's no glued, unlike those drawers I just repaired.

Do ye ever wonder what's really gaun oan in your mind when yir no looking? I mean how can yi know, if ye don't know, ... know? Know whita mean? naw, me neither. Think I'll pop doon the local furra sneaky Guinness, nae whisky mind ye, sends me aff ma heid that stuff. Mer anon ya tadgers.

Tellyi whit's nice, St Patricks day oan a Friday, pity they couldny make it oan a Friday every year. Good Friday is always oan a Friday, so why no St Paddy's always oan a Friday anaw. Dooby dooby dooo....

*

I'm gonny take a long bath in a wee while, for personal hygiene and relaxation at the same time... two burds anaw that... should be nice. Reminds me of the fact that some folk from Edinburgh refer to Glaswegians as 'soap-dodgers'. To be honest I find this a smidgin offensive cause I'm a man of habitual ablution, and they're no exactly the crème de la crème when it comes to the ablutions themselves. We Glaswegians rarely give the populace of Edinburgh much thought, never mind in depth consideration of their correct use of soap. It would seem that they like to think they're in some way superior which is perhaps why 25% of children there attend private schools. A Scottish state-education isny good enough for them, snobbery is a vile thing. Somebody should tell them.

*

The reason the Chancellor of the Exchequer was in my mind a lot was cause he recently announced 'his' budget. He planned to raise a lot of revenue from the self-employed by increasing their NICS [National Insurance Contributions] which was in direct contradiction to the government's election manifesto of 2015. The upshot was a lot of his own team privately protested and he withdrew his proposal leaving a 2 billion pound hole in 'his' budget. Said hole does not concern him, what's two billion here or there? Anyways, some TV reported said, 'George Osborne once had an omni-shambles budget but it appears this budget is a mega-shambles'. Que sera sera... Smoke and mirrors, foam and feathers... 'all that is solid melts into air.' Bath time noo.

*

I'm so clean I've lost weight by virtue of shedding micro-organisms. I took a book of poems wae me into the bath. The poems were written by my former accountant and he sent me copy through the Royal Mail. Way back, when I first started as a self-employed furniture restorer George did my accounts for me. I paid him fur dayin it right enough. Noo he does poetry. I enjoyed the poems, a great read and funny. He writes under the name George W. Kolkitto or some such thing, his real name's George Walker, if yur gonny huv a pen name it might as well be exotic, I'm sure he knows what it means. Anyways, aw the poems happen oot at Castle Semple Loch, and they got me thinkin aboot humans and evolution and aw kindsa things including mortality. It occurred tae me during my bath-time musings that humans are basically an optimistic species over all. We can see our defects and improve things. Of course improvement isny always improvement, it gets called 'improvement' when it's really environmental vandalism. The phrase environmental vandalism for some reason brought to mind the haircut of The Donald Trump, President of the USA, and leader of the so-called 'free-world'. The Donald, as he's known, presents himself as a fairly simple capitalist with likes and dislikes. There's no grey with him, everything is golden like his hair or deeply black. Things that are golden like his hair include, guns, lots of money, the US military, the doors to his penthouse at Trump Tower, the right to choose not to have a health insurance plan and inner-city ghettoes where he rents out property. Inner-city ghettoes where he doesn't rent out any property are deeply black, other deeply black things include, Muslims, Mexicans, government funding for the arts, and scientists who 'believe in' climate change; so that's nearly aw scientists and poor people are deeply black too. So how does a basically optimistic species elect a leader who sees the world as such a scary place; by amplifying fears and dangling a selfish kind of optimism through a mass media he pretends to despise. President Trump, like Nigel Farage in this country, was pumped through every media outlet like he was only interesting person on planet earth. Never has any American Presidential Candidate received so much free publicity. He didny even have to bother buying aw that much advertising. He is truly the President for unfettered cronie capitalism. Very deeply black indeed in President Trump's book are liberals like his poor brother who inherited the Scottish gene that brings on alcoholism and allegedly drank himself to death. Strangely Mother Trump hailed from somewhere no too far from poor auld Charlie Kennedy. Makes yi wonder eh. See what happens when yi go furra bath ... The bathtub is a deeply thoughtful place, that's why they always want us tae take showers noo-a-days, ye don't have time to think in the shower, yur in n oot, the bath is a very different tub of tatties. And aw this oan St Patrick's Day, the Patron Saint of Booze. Pass the Hooch. Dooby dooby doo.

Tuesday 21st March

Martin McGuinness died the day. He was an IRA man and former Deputy First Minister of Northern Ireland. His objective was a united, independent, non-sectarian Ireland. Of course the British had created serious problems in that department when Arthur Griffith and Michael Collins took the 26 counties deal back in 1921. The Irish had to negotiate with Lloyd George and Churchill, two men not known for giving up anything in regard to British Imperialism and racists to the core. The inherited history of Ireland is no easy thing to live with: Cromwell, Plantation and god knows whatever else the British were up to made everything difficult in Ireland for many a year. Divide and divide and divide was the British tactic, and then, having sown the seeds of chaos, become the voice of 'civilisation'.

Of course, no aw British governments are the same, but you'd think noo that they've no really got an empire anymore they'd be a bit mer humane, but that's no as easy an assumption as it seems. Politics is better undertaken by peaceful means. As long the interests of the British establishment are unthreatened they'll be peaceful, but they still pop-up everywhere with their whining, quasi-racist, right wing economics and politics: pleading their case as the voice of reason, rather than admitting their historical crimes and the ugliness of their Austerity views. It's like Nigel Farage is meant to be a man of the people. Is he fuck, he's a racist merchant banker. A right wing baw-bag and there are many more like him in and around the Tory party. I'm glad there's peace in the six counties. The 70s and 80s were a truly miserable time. Many suffered and that suffering on all sides has to be respected.

Only the psychotic want war. But I'm only a furniture restorer so what do I know aboot what motivates war mongers? Fuck all in truth. Though I suppose you can only take so much punishment before you try to fight back. And World War Two is problematic in that opposing Hitler was probably the right thing. World War Two was a necessary evil. But Iraq, Afghanistan, the Falkland Islands, surely no the same kind of questions ataw ataw. Jesus, I'm super serious the day. Think I'll make a pot of soup afore I disappear up my ain arse. Anyways, that's maybe why we should have a written constitution wae a clause aboot active citizenship and participation, then the professional politicians canny just make it aw up as they go alang, like the UK has done for the 310 years since the Act of Union. That unwritten constitution has be finished wae at some point surely. I'm for a Scottish Socialist Republic. Indyref #2 puts that on the table. No more working class Tories and no more greedy middle-classes, let's get something right for wance. Okay so Indyref #1 was a set-back, but that's no reason no tae get in aboot it again. Finally dismantle the British

Empire and get a new future, a socialist future on the go. Otherwise we'll aw be in Trump world. Thems yer tawtees. We can huv a social wage instead o the wasteful, stigmatised, demoralising UK benefits system. We can really build public housing, lots of small scale projects, no more Easterhouse or Castlemilk disasters wae nae shoaps or pubs. Cheers the noo. I'm right hungry, so am ur.

Ashloaning

Rob Currie

Ashloaning is a road in a village
with pre-fab houses
more cars than parking spaces
immaculately kept gardens
(unless it's a house with kids, then, the lawns are overgrown, with bikes thrown
down and muddy shoes kicked off by the doorstep)
satellite dishes on every wall
(unless it's an old person's house, like Anne Beck, who lives for *Fifteen to One* and
therefore doesn't need Sky).

Ashloaning is a cul-de-sac with bungalows
and slowly every house is being roughcast in pink or yellow or amber gravel
double-glazed windows are being installed
the roundabout at the play park has been removed for safety reasons
the streetlight outside Irene McLeod's that flickers all night and never gets fixed
no matter how many phone calls Watty Drummond makes to the council
starlings every spring
and the sound of crow-scarers every autumn in the surrounding fields of hay and
rapeseed that make my nose itch
the back fields where we'd sit on freshly rolled bales and kiss for the first time
where we'd go with stolen whisky from my granny's dusty cabinet...

Have you ever been in a room with a family member, like a granny, or even an aunt
or uncle, it doesn't matter, and it's a room you've known for years, a room where you
crawled on the swirling brown carpet when you were a baby, with a sofa where you had
your nappy changed, and a corner where the Christmas tree you helped decorate every
year since you could hold a bauble went, twelve years of the same ancient ornaments, and
the drinks cabinet full of those bottles that haven't been touched since your granddad
died, and you're in this room that you've known for years with your granny, which could
be your aunt or uncle except, no, it's your granny, and the question is, have you ever been
in a room with her and realised you don't have the faintest idea who she is?

You know *stuff* about her like her age, which is seventy, and her phone number,
which is Denholm two-eight-four, and you know the way she treats people who come to

her house, and the way she never washes a mug, just rinses it, and her favourite Denby mug has a layer of tea-staining on the white inside, and you know the way your dad looks to the sky when somehow she always manages to phone as he sits down for his tea, and he says to your mum, 'just leave it,' but mum answers anyway, and so you know some stuff, yes.

But you're standing in the wood-panelled living room with the painting of gulls swooping through crashing waves above the electric fireplace, and *Countdown* is on and a man with thick glasses and a receding hairline is saying, 'one from the top and five small please, Carol,' and your schoolbag is heavy with your gym kit and you've just stopped in on your way home because that's just what you've always done, every school-day pretty much since primary school, because this is before you stopped stopping in, and you're standing there, and she holds your shoulders to pull herself up to kiss your face and you suddenly realise,

you've been raised to love your family members, and of course you do that, and you love them without question and you suddenly realise,

that this has left you with a lot of questions.

And although she's told you about parts of her life, and you know that she had diphtheria as a child, that she was shot at by a crashing German plane during the war, that she travelled the country on a motorbike when she was a teenager, that her favourite word is 'cellar door,' even though it's technically two words, although you know these things you wonder when she first fell in love, when was her first kiss and who it was with, when did she get drunk for the first time, when did she first smoke, did she ever do drugs, when did she last cry, has she ever had her heart broken?

And this thought, all of this thought races through your heart in the time it takes her to kiss you on the cheek, and she has known you your whole life, and you have known her for a fraction of hers, and she must have hopes and dreams like you, like everyone must, and you have no idea what they are.

Ashloaning sounds like the pine tree branches that threaten to fall in the wind empties in sticky Safeway bags as Anne Beck clinks down to the bottle bank the growl of dad's motorbike as he comes home from work and thunders up the road and

Ashloaning looks like a line of light
shining between the bottom of the door and the bedroom carpet
and a boy's head on its side peering through
watching adult feet and trying to understand the words.

Blackwaterfoot

Iain Maloney

They had crossed the Kilbrannan Sound by late morning; the sun striking the three kayaks and flickering on the swell gave the sea the glint of a silver trout. Jason took the lead south, following the west coast of Arran, keeping them a decent distance from the shore, close enough they could reach it if the sea took against them, far enough that he didn't feel in its orbit. Sitting in his one-man island, his gear stored watertight and only the splash of Malcolm and Eddie's paddles behind him, he could let the strain fall overboard. He didn't so much drown his sorrows in the firth, as make them walk the plank, cannonballs tied to their feet.

Well, all but one.

Malcolm caught up with Jason and grabbed the end of his kayak, pulling alongside. 'Avast. Prepare to be boarded unless ye have a bottle of rum!'

At least he didn't do the accent. Ever since they'd seen the news report about Somalian piracy and David Miliband's statement on the TV in the pub in Inveraray Malcolm had been shouting, 'Shiver me timbers' in a non-specific African accent.

'I've got some Jaffa Cakes you racist fuck.'

Eddie drifted in alongside Mal and they lashed the kayaks together, let the current edge them south, passing Jaffa Cakes across their makeshift raft. Eddie stretched down the bow of the kayak, his lower back still giving him a bit of jip. Usually by the third day all the kinks had been pulled and pummelled out but it was taking longer. Age catching up and that camp spot Jason had picked hadn't helped – all those hidden rocks that only made themselves known slowly, an ache in your sleep that grew. He'd have to get back to the running, the swimming. He'd let his fitness slip over the winter; the endless stretch of dreich mornings and one too many whiskies at night with his marking.

'Glad you came?' Mal echoed his thoughts, waving the last biscuit under his nose.

'No, it's just the way I'm sitting.' Eddie looked over at Jason, his eye on the horizon, as always with them but somehow separate, same as he'd been at school. Away with the fairies one teacher had called it, and Jason had been 'Fairy' for the rest of his school days. It took a stint in the army to get most people to drop it. Yet Eddie took Jason's distance as implied superiority. He'd been the one that spoke about leaving, about travelling the world, about there being more to life than fucking Dingwall, but thirty years later he was still there, a street away from the house he'd grown up in, but still with that air of having one foot out the door. 'How about you, Jason? You glad you're here? We're sure glad you could make the time.'

A pained look briefly sailed across Jason's face. 'Sure.' He took the empty Jaffa Cake box from Mal and stowed it. 'I'm not convinced the weather's going to hold. If we're going to camp at Blackwaterfoot we need to get a shift on.'

They pulled up out of the water just as the first drops fell. Mal had picked a quiet spot around the headland, a bit north of the village. Few people on the west coast had a problem with wild camping as long as you tidied up after yourself, but it was always better to keep out of sight if you could. With an empty golf course between them and Blackwaterfoot, they should manage to avoid a run in with some poker-arsed busybody.

Jason lay in his tent, his copy of Treasure Island open on his chest, the last of the shower pattering out on the canvas. Bloody Mal had ruined the book for him, Long John Silver's west country accent replaced with Mal's black-and-white-minstrel version of East African. Every trip they did, five or six times a year, he took a Stevenson with him, the stories perfect for the setting. He should've taken Travels With a Donkey in Cevennes. He was, after all, travelling with an ass.

Did Eddie know? His dig out in the Sound about 'making the time', was he reading too much into it?

When Melanie texted him to say Mal was planning to go away over Easter weekend they'd immediately made plans, a B&B near Tongue booked, cover arranged at work, John agreeing to manage the restaurant and bar for double time and the next week off. He'd been packing when Mal called.

'Fairy! Get your gear out of mothballs, we're going away. The forecast is good, Eddie's free, and I'm itching to get out on the water. What do you say we do Kintyre and Arran this time?'

'I can't Mal, some of us have to do real work.'

'Real work? You don't even cook anymore, just get others to do it for you. And you call me the capitalist. Anyway, I was in your place for lunch and John was bumping his gums about having to work all weekend.'

'Liquid lunch was it?'

'A glass or few. New client, a resort up the coast. They liked my design for the one near Crieff. Big contract. Big. Called for a glass or few. So you in?'

'For a drink?'

'For kayaking. Eddie's in.'

'I don't know, Mal. I've got a lot on...'

'What's so important it would trump kayaking with your mates? Is it a bird? Is it? Bros before hos, Jason, thems the rules.'

He couldn't think of anything Jason would buy and the truth wasn't an option.

Jason got his phone out and texted Melanie. Missing you. Outside a tent unzipped. Footsteps. The sound of someone pissing and a sigh of relief. Mal. She replied instantly, You too. Leave him, he wanted to write. Pack your bags and I'll tell him. There's a key under the third plant pot from the left at the back door. Pack your bags and come to mine. We can make it work. Instead he texted a colon and an open bracket.

The squall passed leaving the kind of sunset you could sail off into. Eddie collected driftwood and got a fire going while Jason dealt with the rations. After school he'd joined the army believing their promises of seeing the world. Instead all he'd seen were the insides of kitchens and mess halls in Britain, Germany and, latterly, Bosnia. He'd got out at the earliest opportunity and took over the lease of The Crofter, a former working man's club that he'd turned into a bistro that got mentioned in the Sunday papers. He was capable of so much more than two tins of beans and sausages over a fire but this was supposed to be his weekend off. He should be eating scallops with Melanie not watching her increasingly tubby husband pour whisky into plastic camping cups. He shared out the bowls, took his cup from Mal.

'A toast,' Mal raised his cup, the smoke from the fire obscuring him for a second as the wind shifted. 'To Alba Hotels for signing on the dotted line, making me the happiest architect under this bruised sky.'

Jason was next. 'To our Lord Jesus Christ who died so that we might have a long weekend.'

The wind whipped up the fire, spraying a wave of ash across the sand. Eddie raised his cup a third time. 'To us, to you, Mal, for organising this trip and to you, Jason, for choosing, as Mal delicately put it, bros before hos.'

In the sinking light, the flitting smoke, the fierce glow of the flames, Jason wasn't sure whether Eddie really did wink.

Eddie took the dishes down to the shoreline and rinsed the remnants of sauce into the dark water. Jason was still sitting on the sand playing with his phone. Mal had a first generation iPhone and Eddie was waiting for the 3GS to come out in a couple of months before taking the plunge. Jason however was hanging on to his Nokia like a hippy to vinyl. Eddie shook his head. Jason was clearly texting Melanie.

Eddie and Melanie both taught in Dingwall Academy, her physics, him geography. It had been at the staff Christmas dinner at the end of last term that she'd let slip enough details for Eddie to piece together what was going on. Since then he'd sat on the knowledge, unsure what to do with it. Mal may not be the most attentive husband but he loved Mel in his own way – a financially generous way - and had since she moved to Dingwall from Glasgow after her graduation. He shook water off the spoons and watched Mal dance around the fire to the Rolling Stones coming from his iPod and tiny speakers. For all his size and bluster, there was still a small boy in there. The news would crush him.

Mel was an adult and free to make her own mistakes. If she wasn't satisfied with Mal and got whatever she was missing from Jason, then it wasn't his place to judge. He wouldn't be the one to split up Team Mal and Mel.

But then there was Jason. The three of them had been mates since primary school yet he was sitting there, drinking Mal's twenty-five year Macallan while texting his wife. That wasn't on. It just wasn't.

<Can't believe I'm eating beans with him when I could be eating scallops with you.>
<That's not all you could be eating.>
<Don't! That B&B had a huge bath. I had all these plans…>
<Tell me.>
<Now?>

<I'm here by myself with only his wine cellar and the TV for company. This is my holiday too. I demand some excitement.>
<You're filthy.>
<And you love it. Details! So we're in this bath and…>
<And I start kissing your toes, one at a time, then your foot. I run my tongue up your calf…>

'Hey, you boys having a swim?' Eddie dried off the dishes and repacked them, pulling his towel from his pack. 'Mal? Before you put too much of that whisky away?'

'Aye, good point, don't want to fall overboard.'

'Jason?'

Jason put his phone down and peered at Eddie. The hard fire against the black sky made it difficult to see him clearly. He rubbed his eyes and stood. 'Aye, sounds good. My shoulders are stiff from today.'

'Out of shape?' Mal patted him on the stomach. 'Come on soldier, drop and give me twenty!'

'More likely you're stiff from being hunched over that phone.' Eddie pulled his shirt off and took a step towards the sea. 'You're like a fucking teenager, or a… fucking Golem hunched over with it in your palm. My precious. Gonnae leave it for a bit? Bros before, eh?'

'Aye, sorry,' Jason grabbed his own towel, kicked his crocs off.

'You going to tell us about this bird?' Mal stepped into the shadows, dropped his shorts.

'Dunno. Don't know if it's serious yet.'

'Seems pretty serious to me,' Eddie said. 'Look, you guys go on ahead, I'm going to take a shit.'

'Trowel's in the thing,' Mal pointed towards his Kayak. 'Make sure you go far enough this time. All through last night, the stink of your turd wafting over Skipness.'

Eddie waited until he was sure they were in the water. Lit by the fire his movements had to seem plausible. Under cover of returning the trowel to Mal's box he got hold of Jason's phone, tapped into the contacts, his back to the sea, quick as you can, changed an A to an E, and E to an A. He checked the sent folder, <…my fingers exploring…>, deleted all the messages, same in the inbox, then turned the phone off and dropped it on the sand close to the fire.

'Hell of a shit! What did you eat? I hope it's at least six feet down.'

'Aye, buried treasure for Tony Robinson.'

'Arr, X marks the spot!'

Eddie dived into the chilly water and pulled a few hard strokes feeling the tension in his lower back stretch out, his shoulders warming with the rolls. Over the Sound west-southwest, the lights of Campbeltown glowed like fireflies, the lighthouse on Davaar sweeping warnings into the night. Bobbing in the water he turned in time to see Jason towelling off as he walked back to the fire, picking up his hot phone in a panic, switching it back on. He'd assume the heat had caused some sort of malfunction, would wonder which drunken idiot had kicked it as they walked by. He'd see his contacts were still there, see his messages had gone. He'd text Mel, compulsively, openly, honestly, perhaps even erotically. Somewhere in Malcolm's tent, maybe in one of his shoes, his phone would beep, would flash out in the dark, a warning.

Eddie treaded water, warm and cold patches trailing by him, as the tableau played out, the ridge of Arran like a dinosaur spine against the purple sky, the beach a stage for a tragedy. From here it didn't look real, wasn't something he was part of. He could float, secret in the dark, his betrayal hidden as Jason's played out on Blackwaterfoot beach, and in the fall out there'd be pieces to pick up.

Rasmie Gengs Furt

Hannah Nicholson

Furt (adv.) out-of-doors. [E. forth: in the open] (from Shetland Words *by Alistair and Adaline Christie-Johnston)*

The morning that Rasmie Ratter made the decision that shook his life up had started like any other. It had been a lovely summer morning, unusually bright even for the time of year. The sun had shone right into Rasmie's bedroom window, penetrating his thin beige curtains and projecting onto the walls, highlighting the lurid shade of ochre that they had been painted with. Rasmie woke to this, but he didn't immediately get out of bed. He lay there for some time, staring at the off-white ceiling as he often did, thinking about what he was going to do today and wondering which of his family members would bring his shopping to him that afternoon. They hadn't needed to get him much, just the staples – milk, bread, and a couple of tins of meat for the cat. If it wasn't for his cat – Filska, a name which had described her well in her youth – he would have been a hermit as well as a near recluse.

Rasmie Ratter had always been a man who preferred his own company. Even in childhood he had been relatively solitary, preferring to spend time on his own than with the other pupils at school, or any of the other members of his scout pack, or the neighbours who were around his age. It wasn't that he didn't like the other children – most of them were actually pleasant enough, and they did try to befriend him, but he wasn't one for interacting and it eventually put many of them off. He had left school at fourteen with no notable qualifications, and managed to find work in a fish factory, but other than this he rarely left the little but-and-ben crofthouse where he had grown up unless he absolutely had to. To him it became like having his own little castle, and the land that made up his parents' croft was the kingdom.

Other than his job, he was interested in woodwork and metalwork, and often he spent a lot of time in the workshop he built himself out the back of his home, carving things such as tables and chairs, and mostly keeping himself to himself. That wasn't to say that he didn't see anyone – other than his work colleagues, he was close to his family, and he continued to live with his parents. Despite his advanced age, Rasmie's father still drove, and it was up to him to take his wife and son where they needed to go. Sometimes it was just to the local shop, sometimes to Lerwick for other things, or even to different parts of the island for day trips. When his father died, the day trips stopped as neither Rasmie nor his mother could drive. When she died, the trips to the shops and to Lerwick also stopped. After this, Rasmie took early retirement from the fish factory, and the frequency with which he left his parental home gradually dwindled, until eventually he was never seen going past his front gate.

Between the money his father left him, the sales of the animals from the family croft, and his fish factory pension, Rasmie lived comfortably enough. He relied on his siblings to do the outside duties for him mostly. He had been the third of the four Ratter siblings – his older brother, Johnnie, and older sister, Brenda, still lived in Shetland, while his younger sister, Tamar, had moved out to New Zealand some years ago. She sometimes stayed with Rasmie when she returned for a visit, mainly because he now had the extra space, but also because she got nostalgic for her childhood homestead. While Rasmie generally didn't mind – he'd always been close with his siblings – he still enjoyed having the place to himself. The little croft house was his castle, and the land was his kingdom, and he ruled it as he liked.

On this particular day, when Rasmie had finally tired of lying still and staring up at the ceiling, he finally stretched and got out of bed, then went to shower. As always, he spent more of his time in there contemplating rather than washing. He always had his best ideas in the shower, and previously in the bath. The house no longer had a bath, though. They'd had to rip it out and replace it with the shower after his mother had the operation for her new hip. The shower was more accessible for her in these circumstances, and the chair she had sat on while using it was still fixed to the wall, another memento of her.

Rasmie got dressed and went to fix breakfast. Filska greeted him when he entered the kitchen, slithering around and between his calves. As always, he fed her first – a mugful of Whiskas in her plastic pink bowl – before he put on his porridge oats. From boyhood, porridge had set him up for the day.

Once he had finished his breakfast, he sat back in his chair and gazed out of the kitchen window. He never got tired of the view. After miles and miles of lush, green grass – now devoid of sheep, cows or any other livestock, and thus allowed to freely grow – the North Sea was fairly visible just on the horizon. It was a beautiful sight on a day like this, but even when the weather was at its most typical – namely coarse, windy and grey – Rasmie still found it quite pleasant, although perhaps not as soothing. He still preferred to watch it from inside the house, though.

He was drifting off into his own thoughts when the sound of the phone ringing snapped him back into reality. He dashed through to the living room and answered it before it could ring off.

'Hello?'

'Ah, Rasmie, du's up!' Bertha's booming voice rang into his ear and he had to hold the receiver a short distance away from it.

'Yea, coorse I am,' he said. 'Why wid I no be?'

'Weel, du keens me,' thundered Bertha, 'I juist haed tae mak sure. Is du still needin de errands brought tae de?'

'Oh…yis please, if du could,' he replied. 'Whit time'll du be alang?'

'I'll likly be aboot eleven-ish,' Bertha told him. 'Is yun aa at du's needin'?'

'Fir eanoo, yea. Cheers Bertha, see de den.'

'Nae buddir, Rasmie. Cheerio!'

She hung up, and Rasmie put down the receiver and scratched the inside of his ear. As sisters went, he felt fortunate to have Bertha, but she was loud and at times overwhelming.

Just as Rasmie was making his way back to the kitchen to clear up after himself, there came the familiar sound of the letterbox clattering, and the soft thud of the mail hitting the welcome mat. Rasmie went to pick it up. He didn't get much mail these days, usually just bills and bank statements. He didn't bother with the internet, believing himself to be too old for such rubbish. Last time Sheila had come to visit she had commented with delight about how she could get something called 4G on her mobile in Rasmie's house, and what a random part of the isles it was to have such a thing set up, but this of course meant nothing to him. Amongst today's post, though, was a letter with Rasmie's address in handwriting. How queer, thought Rasmie. He so rarely got personal letters, although when he did it was very pleasant – most people nowadays insisted on emailing things, or even using that Facebook thing that his nephews and nieces banged on about. Rasmie didn't understand the internet, or its attractions. He barely even watched his television. He preferred the phone, or face to face interaction, and it did his head in when the family came around and the young ones had their faces buried in their mobiles. So needless to say, he opened the letter with great enthusiasm – but his face fell when he saw what was inside.

Rasmie inhaled, and then exhaled. He certainly hadn't been expecting Sheila to invite him to the wedding. It was possible that she simply wanted him to be acknowledged, but to him it was still a bit of a waste. He looked at the RSVP card that had arrived with the invite. It asked for the food selection for each of the three courses, if he had any allergies, plus if he would need the bus going back from either hall on either night? The thought of boarding a bus frightened Rasmie. He'd hated getting on the public one with his mother after his father had died, but this would be a coach, full of guests, a number of whom he'd never have met. He felt ill thinking about it.

He set the invitation down on the worktop and sat at the table, wringing his hands. He was fond of all of his nephews and nieces, but had been particularly close with Sheila when she was a child. She had spent a lot of time visiting the house and helping her grandparents out with the croft on weekends. She'd had two cousins whom had married before her, and he'd found it so much easier to turn those down – although it helped that one wedding was in New Zealand. This was different.

Still unsure, Rasmie decided to go out to his shed and work on his latest project – the set of bookshelves he was planning to gift to Sheila and her husband-to-be, John-William. He hoped it would clear his head and that he'd be in a better space to make a decision.

So he set to work on the shelves, and sometime later he heard the familiar sound of Bertha's Range Rover come roaring into his driveway. He set down his tools and left the shed. Bertha clambered out of the driver's seat, opened the back passenger door and foraged for the shopping bag containing Rasmie's messages. Rasmie heard the other front car door slam, and Sheila came walking around. He greeted her and her mother warmly.

'Come you in, lasses,' he replied, 'an I'll fix you baith a cup o tae.'

'Dat wid be splendid,' Bertha declared. 'Am parched!'

Rasmie took his bag from his sister and the three made their way in.

Anyone who didn't know Bertha and Rasmie would never have thought they were siblings. Bertha was tall, broadly built and extroverted. Rasmie was small, slender and meek. Despite this, they remained close, even more so since Bertha's husband, Malcolm, had passed away from a heart attack four years prior.

Rasmie set the bag containing his shopping down on the table, put on the kettle, and rummaged in his wallet for money, handing a crisp new £10 note to Bertha when he located it. She handed him the change.

'So,' he asked her, 'whit uncans wi you da day?'

Bertha and Sheila looked at him quizzically.

'Did du no get it, Uncle R?' Sheila asked.

'Get whit?' Rasmie tried to act innocent but was fooling neither of them.

'Fir da love o Christ, Sheila,' Bertha blared, 'did du no see da invite lyin apö da worktap yundir?'

'Oh, yun,' Rasmie said gravely. 'Yea, am seen it.'

'Weel, is du comin?' Sheila asked.

Rasmie shuffled uncomfortably in his seat and looked down into his lap. Usually he didn't mind silence but this one was proving awkward. He could feel the eyes of his sister and niece on him – Bertha's were harsh and demanding, Sheila's more vainly hopeful.

'Come on noo, Rasmie,' Bertha said in the firmest voice she could muster. 'Du's no' gjaan' tae let wis doon dis time, surely?'

Rasmie tried to look away from his sister and caught Sheila's eye in doing so. She looked genuinely hurt.

'I...I doot no,' he said meekly.

'But I wis hoopin,' Sheila interjected, 'at mebbe du wid gie me awa?'

Blindsided, Rasmie tensed up. Now he felt even worse for planning to say no. He thought of all the times he'd had with Sheila when she was young. When she'd wiped out on her first shot of her granddad's quad bike and broken her leg, he'd been the one who comforted her as they waited on the ambulance. He'd also helped her to carve little wooden boats, and one Christmas he'd made her a nativity set that she'd kept with her all her life. She'd even taken it away to university with her, and she now kept it in the house she shared with John-William.

'Kin de bridder no do it?' he asked her.

'He's an usher,' Sheila told him. 'I mean, I'll no get de tae do a speech or onythin – he kin do yun, or Uncle Johnnie. But if du could get me doon da aisle, I wid love dat.'

The look of disappointment crossing her face was more than Rasmie could bear. He curled his toes and closed his eyes.

'Aright,' he replied, 'I'll do it.'

He opened them again and saw that Sheila's face had lit up. She ran to him and threw her arms around his neck, kissing his cheek.

'Splendid!' she exclaimed. 'I canna wait.'

Rasmie smiled tightly and nodded.

'Weel den,' Bertha said, 'yun settles it. I'll be alang dis comin Settirdee tae pick de up an get de fitted fir a suit.'

'A suit?' Rasmie said faintly. 'But I hae a suit.'

'Yun owld thing?' Bertha snorted. 'Du's no wearin dat tae Sheila's weddeen, du'll look lik somebody at belangs tae naebody! We'll get de a new een.'

'But I'll hae ta geng tae toon!' Rasmie exclaimed.

'Weel so bloody whit?' Bertha retorted. 'Hit's aboot time du guid past yun fence!'

Again, Rasmie could feel his toes curl. But there was no going back now.

That night he lay in bed, wishing he'd not agreed. But then he remembered the childlike look in Sheila's eyes as she had asked him, and he managed to reassure himself that he was doing the right thing. All the same, he found himself dreading Saturday.

The week flew in a little too quickly for Rasmie's liking, and on Saturday Bertha arrived at his house at nine o' clock sharp and practically bundled him into the car. The plan was to get him a suit for the menswear shop in the Toll Clock Shopping Centre, then they would go to a café for lunch before heading back home. Rasmie spent the whole car journey gazing wistfully out of the window, dreading the experience. He disliked Lerwick, always had. It was too busy for him. He marvelled at how some of his nephews and nieces had managed to live in a city while at college or university, or even how Tamar found living in New Zealand to be such a breeze. He'd likely never leave Shetland. Here he was safe, and nothing could harm him, especially if he stayed home. His house was his castle, and the surrounding lands his kingdom.

But finally, Rasmie looked ahead and saw the familiar sight of the Bressay fish factory come into view, and then came the dip in the hill leading to Lerwick. Shortly after this, Bertha parked up at the Toll Clock, and the two made their way inside, Rasmie trotting after her meekly like a dog in disgrace.

Even before getting to the shop, Rasmie felt anxious. The Toll Clock had changed hugely since the last time he'd been inside it. He barely recognised any of the shop names. The menswear shop was still in the same place, though. Bertha ushered him inside and told the two sales assistants that he needed a suit for her daughter's wedding. Rasmie stood rigid and sweating as one of them took his measurements. Thankfully it didn't take long, and the gentlemen told them that they would get that sorted and let them know when it would be ready.

The place they went for lunch was a small café a couple of units along from the menswear shop, so Bertha and Rasmie went there for their lunch. Although they managed to get a table, the place was busy and loud, and Rasmie could feel the anxiety come creeping over him. Bertha sensed this and went to the counter to order his food for him. As Rasmie sat alone he tried not to make eye contact with anyone. Finally, Bertha came back with their coffees, and a little while later their food arrived. Rasmie ate in silence, letting Bertha do all the talking as usual while he concentrated on his lunch.

'Weel noo,' said Bertha after they had left the premises, 'yun wisna sae bad noo, wis it?'

'I dinna keen,' Rasmie replied, 'I widna do it ageen ony time shune.'

'Dinna be sae silly,' Bertha laughed. 'Du'll come tae da weddeen in a couple o weeks' time, an du'll be juist fine. Dey'll aa be blyde tae see de. I hae plenty o fokk axin eftir de, winderin' how du is an' when du plans tae laeve da hoose. Noo I kin tell dem at du's been ootside. Will'n dat be fine?'

Rasmie grunted and shrugged, and he and Bertha got in the car and drove home.

Some weeks later, Tamar helped Rasmie straighten his suit.

'Du looks handsome,' she smiled at him. 'I'm so blyde du's comin tae dis, an Sheila's juist delighted at du's giein her awa'.'

Rasmie couldn't help but smile at that. Then they heard the bridal car pull up in the driveway.

'Come du, den,' Tamar went on, 'let's get goin'.'

She set off in the car she'd hired, and Rasmie got in the back of the car with Sheila. She looked a vision, and he felt tears prick his eyes looking at her. As they drove away, Rasmie looked out the back at his little castle. Today he would be fine with leaving its safety as he walked Sheila down the aisle to her husband.

White Bricks

Karen Ashe

Jade and Stephanie burst in the front door, beads of rain clinging to their blazers, dripping from the ends of their hair. Brown envelopes on the doormat swirl in the wind like litter. Stephanie bends to scoop them up as the door slams shut behind her.

Fuck sake, great start tae the holidays!

Jade flops onto the couch, puts her feet on the coffee table, picks up the TV remote and presses the 'on' button. Stephanie flicks through the mail, pausing when she sees a brown envelope with her name on it, 'University of Edinburgh' stamped in blue ink in the corner. She shoves it into her blazer pocket, hangs the blazer over the back of a chair. She's taking a towel to the ends of her hair when the TV bursts into life.

Feet. That's no even paid for yet.

Jade gives Stephanie the finger, sliding one foot, then the other, onto the floor with a sullen thump. The rain on the window sounds like a pot boiling. In the cul-de-sac a wee boy in a blue cagoule rides his bike round and round, weaving expertly around the swirling carrier bags and crops of broken glass. He stops to pick a crisp packet out of the spokes of the front wheel, then carries on.

Stephanie picks up a framed photograph from the window sill. It's her and Jade, first day at Primary school.

Check us out.

She hands it to Jade, who hoots with laughter. *State ay us! Look at your hair!*

Ma hair? Your teeth!

Ah mind yer maw was ragin cos you got sat beside me. Though ah'd be a 'bad influence.'

Stephanie draws back to give her a look. *Ye were a 'bad influence!'*

Jade grins. *Mebbe.* She nods at the TV. *Whit is this shite?*

A lion prowls across the Serengeti Plain, shoulders rolling, whiskers taut. The camera travels to a young gazelle grazing oblivious at the rear of the herd. Back to the lion gaining ground. A head tilts to the side, ear cocked. A shiny black nose tests the air. Then wild-eyed alarm sweeps through the herd, and they scatter in a cloud of dust. All except the youngster, who gets the signal a fraction too late and on frantic bambi legs scrambles to catch up to the rest. The lion adjusts course, and in three bounds is grazing the gazelle's back hooves with his claws.

Nope. Jade changes channel, shaking her head. *They gazelles. They never fuckin learn; keep up, cos there is always, always, some cunt lion behind ye.*

Jade presses the button. The channels flick and blur.

Chrissake, Jade, gonnae just pick one?

Awright, calm doon. Ahm just lookin for sumthin we both like.

The channel changes and they cry out in unison; *The Cube!*

The audience is applauding as an overweight man in Converse and jeans waves and takes his leave. Philip Schofield, in a grey three-piece with no tie, smiles to camera, welcomes the next contestant.

Jade nudges Stephanie. *Would ye?*

Who, Phillip? Stephanie tucks her feet under herself on the couch and considers. *Maybe. Could I get a trial run?*

That's your right as a contestant, but remember, once you're committed, you can't come out til you've had a go!

They collapse against each other, giggling. *I dunno, Jade. The face disnae match the hair if you know what I mean, and he's a bit too...something. Would you?*

Oh, aye. And I'd film it and threaten to send it tae his wife if he didn't set me up in a wee penthouse and buy me stuff.

Stephanie stares. *Harsh. Better than doin nails for a living, though, gie ye that.*

Just wait til we've got our own salon. Me on the nails and make-up, you running the place. We'll be minted. Stephanie, focussed on the screen, doesn't answer.

The next contestant, Kate, is wearing tight black leggings and a long pink top. More Converse trainers. She stands before the first game; a tower of red bricks inside a clear plastic tube. About two thirds of the way up the tower is a single white brick. The aim is to get the white brick to the top of the tower by sliding the red brick on the bottom out of a gap and placing it on top, and so on until the white brick is on the top. She has eighteen seconds.

She fumbles a brick at 12 seconds, loses a life. Philip bites his lip. Her family look concerned.

She's nae chance. Jade nibbles on a thumbnail.

5 lives, first go, betcha.

But she gets through on the second attempt and stands beside Phillip making a phew! swipe across her forehead. They are about to find out what her next challenge is when a succession of loud raps on the window makes them jump. *Fuck sake!* Jade clutches her hands to her chest. *What the fuck...?*

Stephanie goes to the window, peers out, and two faces pop up like jacks in the box; Sneakyboy and Ding-Dong. Sneakyboy holds up a blue carrier bag and gives her a thumbs and a let-us-in nod towards the door. Jade lumbers off the couch. *Who is it? Sneaky? Yes! Fuck, where's my lip-gloss?*

Stephanie stays by the window as the boys bang on the door.

Whit ye waitin fur? Let them in. When she moves towards the door, Stephanie grabs her arm. *Just leave it, eh?*

Whit? How come?

Stephanie lifts one shoulder. *No in the mood.*

The boys are yelling through the letterbox. *Fuck sake, it's pishin down oot here! Shift! We cannae let them in, ma ma's still ragin about Baz's party.*

But Jade is already heading for the door. *We'll just see whit they want.*

On the doorstep, Jade is twirling her hair round her finger. Sneakyboy sucks on a cigarette. He gives Stephanie a quick wink only she can see.

Yez cannae come in.

Aw, c'mon Steph. They'll be good, won't yez? Jade nudges Sneaky Boy, who flicks his cigarette onto the grass. He runs his eyes over Stephanie, looks away.

C'mon, Steph, Jade pleads. *It's the last day! I don't want to spend it sittin on your shitty couch watchin The Cube.*

Dingdong sniggers. *Fuckin Cube.* Snotters shoot out his nose and land on his upper lip. Sneaky Boy laughs like he's the only one who gets the joke.

She wonders now how she could have let him, but on his own, without all his eejit pals around he was different. Better. She remembers him kissing her in Baz's bedroom, the taste of cider on his tongue, the feel of his hand under her skirt. She remembers kissing him back, liking it, liking him, too much.

Stephanie folds her arms. *Ahm no letting them in.*

Cool. He looks down at his feet, and when he lifts his gaze his face is hard. He focuses his attention on Jade, leaning in close, turning his back on Stephanie. He makes his voice soft. *You could come wi us. Unless ye huv tae dae everythin she tells ye...*

Jade flushes. She sends Stephanie a pleading look. Stephanie mouth-shrugs. *Do what you want.*

She leaves the door open as she walks back down the hall.

Cmon, we're boostin. Ye comin, Jade, or are ye staying here wi yer lezzie pal?

Stephanie curls up on the couch. On TV a woman with shiny hair is in an agony of indecision over which type of fabric softener to choose from a supermarket aisle full of fabric softeners, while two toddlers whine about scratchy clothes.

The front door slams shut. Then Jade is standing in front of her.

Whit the fuck's the matter wi you? Everybody else is away getting aff their faces, and you want tae sit here watching this shite?

Kate is back inside the cube, reviewing her options with Phillip.

Stephanie takes a deep breath. *Jade. I'm no stopping ye. If ye want tae go wi them, it's fine. I'm stayin here.*

Cmon! It'll be a laugh. It'll no be the same without you. Ah think Ding-Dong fancies ye. Me and Sneaky, you and ding-dong. Be brilliant.

Kate's is ready for her next challenge. £50,000 is at stake. In this game, she must throw a red ball through a diamond-shaped piece of glass near the top of a frameless door.

If ye want to go, go! I'm no goin...

But how? You used tae like running aboot wi them.

I know, but...a carry out in the park? In the rain?

Have ye had any better offers?

Rain throws itself against the window. They glare at each other. Jade looks away first, flops back down onto the couch.

Fuckin weather. I'm stayin till the rain goes aff.

Stephanie curls up on the other end of the couch. *Suit yerself.*

They sit in silence. The contestant discusses her next move with her family. They think she can't do it, think her to quit while she's ahead.

Think how you'll feel, Kate, if you go home with nothing, says a balding man with a doughy-looking belly. *Take the twenty grand, love.*

Jade leans forward. *Fuck. Is she on fifty grand?*

Aye.

The red light flashes. She throws the ball at the door. It hits the glass but bounces off without breaking it. Philip arranges his face in a sympathetic frown, and the game recommences. The contestant bites her lip in concentration. This time when she throws the ball, she misses the glass entirely and the ball shoots over the top of the frame.

Use your simplify, ya daft cow, Jade yells at the TV.

She's awready used it, Stephanie tells her.

Hus she? Trial run as well?

Aye.

How many lives has she got left?

Three, I think

She is so fucked.

Stephanie sniggers. *Ah know. 50 grand as well.*

Jeez. Should have taken the 20 grand, right enough. She's no as clever as she thought she was.

Stephanie shrugs. *Worth a try though...*

Kate is committed. Last life, last chance.

God. Stephanie picks up a cushion. *I can hardly watch.*

Kate picks up the ball. Sweat blooms on her upper lip. *Check oot her moustache,* Jade whispers.

Shh!

Kate picks up the ball and hurls it at the pane of glass. In high-definition slow-motion it arcs through the air.

Jade grips Stephanie's arm.

The ball peaks and starts to drop, dropping, dropping, dropping and then it hits the glass dead centre and goes straight through, sending a shower of splinters into the air.

Yeeeessss!! Jade and Stephanie are off the couch, jumping. *She did it, she did it!*

Well done hen! Now ye can get yer moustache waxed!

And new teeth!

Kate is hugging Phillip, in tears. Her family are shaking their heads in happy disbelief. Stephanie sighs. *I knew she could do it. She was right not tae listen to them.*

Jade mutes the adverts. She glances at the window as Sneaky boy and Ding-Dong pass by on the way to the swing park, a posse of three trailing behind.

Rain's aff.

Aye. So it is.

They watch the silent mouthing of the actors on the TV. Outside, birds chirp and fuss.

In't it funny how the rain keeps them quiet?

Eh?

The birds...Never mind.

Jade exaggerates a shiver. *Listen, I'm freezin sittin here. This skirt's soakin. I'll go up the road and change, and I'll come back down after, awright?*

Then she's out the door, calling *See ya!* over her shoulder.

Stephanie goes to the window. A line of sparrows on the telephone wire takes flight, sending silver drops into the air. She sees Jade cross the street at a run, heading for the swing park. Ding-dong, head back as he drains a bottle in a blue plastic bag, sees her watching and gives the finger, grabbing his crotch. Sneaky-boy screeches with too-loud laughter but doesn't look at her.

She turns away from the window, reaches into her blazer pocket for the brown envelope with her name on it.

Bite

Graeme Smith

He asks me to open wider please. I do and he attacks my tooth with the drill. It batters my brain it feels like my life will just end when he does this. Electric drills should not be near a head or scalp or brain or skull or kopfe who talks German these days. The Germans. He replaces the drill with the more powerful one do not forget about those Austrians either or the Swiss imagine what it was like before anaesthetic this must have been a nightmare. Probably Liechtenstein as well that is something I should find out later why am I thinking about German-speaking countries is this what my life has been reduced to I mean really life should be full of wonder and all I can think about is countries and their native tongues. Tongue? Tongues.

Drill. The word doesn't sound real. Drill.

Dust the window-drill please.

Drill the gap with concrete.

Yes, of course you use adrillic paint for this.

You have a drill voice.

I can't come into work today I'm too drill.

I'll have a can of Drillt please.

Just do it, I'm on the drill, I promise.

What do you want for tea oh I don't know how about a duck-drilled platypus oh for hang sake stop your yapping.

He removes the drill and says numbers to his assistant. She is pretty but her mind is vacant; hoy enough of that talk how can I tell she is dumb she hasn't even spoken! Poor girl is just doing her job for whoknows how much pay and people like me judge her for what, for what!

For nothing, that's what. Us men what are we like.

He leaves his fingers in my mouth, hanging, touching the lip. His touch is gentle, his rubbery gloves feel pleasant on my half-numb lips because this is obviously the result of being touched by something with a texture so tangible what do I even mean by that I really don't know. If I dribble these gloves will catch it. These gloves will only touch one set of lips and then will be discarded along with other things deemed bin-worthy. They have one task in their life and that is to protect his fingers from my germs. Or my mouth from his germs? Both. No the former. That's it isn't it. How presumptuous of him to suggest my mouth is dirty though! But no I suppose things will be much easier for him if he wears gloves unconditionally rather than choose whose mouth to protect himself from on the spot. Imagine if he just looked at people when they came in the room then reached for the gloves or not! Snap decisions would be made and probably regretted regularly. You couldn't exactly stop halfway through a mouth-probing and put gloves on what an insult! And people would soon know that he makes these choices and how offended would you be if he put the gloves on for you! He has no idea who I am or where I've been, of course he's going to wear gloves! And of course, people aren't exactly going to want glove-less fingers in their mouth anyway are they? I don't know.

Who do I think I am.

He is in discussion with his assistant I bet he fancies her. No wedding ring unless he takes it off for surgery. He must do, save it clanking into patients' teeth. Against fillings. Should I ask him? I'll just ask him, that is a normal thing to ask people...don't be ridiculous I'm not going to ask him if he's married imagine asking your dentist that he'll think I'm off my head and call up men in surgical dress and tell them what I did. But would they respond and come all the way out here to get someone because they enquire about marital status all the way out here what am I even talking about we're in the middle of the city for hang sake they're probably stationed round the corner. First-name terms.

But his discussion with her is taking longer than expected and his fingers are just lingering there, pulling at my lip just a teensy-weensy little bit. Perhaps they are pulling harder than I know but the anaesthetic has numbed my senses haha haha numbed them! Numbed them! These little moments of hilarity are what makes life so precious.

What would happen if I just bite them. Bite his fingers. Just crunch into them. He'll think it's a mistake at first and look at me and expect my grip to loosen. But when it doesn't loosen, when I just stare back at him he will know it's on purpose! Imagine if I just do it. I feel sick with the excitement. What a thing to happen. Incisors into flesh. Why don't I just do it just crunch down hard on those lingering fingers and see what happens. Do it!

But then for hang's sake imagine Nora getting the call from me at the police station saying I won't be home for tea. Why not she would ask and I'd just have to tell her I couldn't lie. I bit the dentist and didn't let go. I bit his fingers to see what would happen and I got arrested. I'm sorry Nora, I'm sorry.

On our blinking anniversary as well. Happy anniversary darling, buy yourself a present because I'm oh actually that's a serious point the shops will be closed by the time I'm done here bite or no bite. What a way to escape the repercussions. Imprisoned, shredding an immaculate criminal record. Suburban lives, safety on these streets.

Maybe she'll be impressed with this new man I'll be a wise-cracker, a new fun man a changed gentleman of stature with wit and guts and, and... a joker, yes, I will be a joker. Biting him will be one big joke and she will smile at me again like she used to. She hasn't laughed at my jokes in years could this brighten her up... Oh for God sake a fifty year- old woman will not be impressed if I bite our dentist what a ridiculous idea!

Criminal charges. The shame of telling my work hang sake they'll kick me out the door. Word will get round the community and the kids at school... other kids will make biting motions with their mouths in their direction. How will they explain to their kids, my grandkids, why they were ostracised at school? Because Grandad was a biter. Yes, he was. A biter.

Maybe they'll be proud that their father was unique, yes that man is my dad, yes my dad did bite the dentist's fingers for an experiment I bet your dad wouldn't be so adventurous at the dentist now would he? They will be proud, so proud of me.

What a load of codswallop of course they're not going to be proud of me they'd probably disown me. Practically childless I'll become and shunned and broken and Nora would chuck me onto the street. Well there's always internet dating.

Internet dating!

Be realistic man who's going to internet-date the man who bites dentists, the man who bites people who are trying to help him, albeit for substantial remuneration these dentists make a fortune!

Biting the dentist's fingers. Just biting them as hard as I can then standing up and walking out without looking back. Would he even call the police? It is assault. It is biting someone else. It is probably a crime. They have my address. Would he bother though? He is a busy man and a finger bite is not life-threatening. Perhaps I could clamp down gently, enough to make sure he knows it is intentional but not quite enough to draw blood or cause significant pain... And if the police are involved I could say it was an accident! Play the dumb old codger who can't control his teeth movements!

What is life if we don't take these moments to explore new possibilities. This may be the greatest thing I ever do who knows what opportunities this may lead to what are we doing here if we don't take risks? As a wise man once said, a man who bites is a man... No that is the wrong phrase there are no wise proverbs about biting for hang sake! Biting! A child's act! Not an act from a professional gentleman in a place of work just clamping and biting down for no reason other than curiosity!

His hand still lingers there, touching, probing around. It is now or never. To bite or not to bite. Will I take the coward's route or seize the moment. He is still talking to her. I close my eyes and make my decision.

I love you Nora, I'm sorry.

Kanoom

Marjorie Lotfi Gill

—for my great-great grandmother Kanoom, who was separated from her daughter during the closing of the Iran–Azerbaijan border in 1917

I am not interested in Bolsheviks.
Instead, it's the way light fell
across my daughter's sleeping face,
how she ate pomegranate, mouth brimming
with tiny jewels, the way her nostrils
would flare at the sight of mulberries,
but when offered, *taarofing,* she'd eat.
Like swallows, we migrate,
but there's no spring and no autumn
in this place. Along with the *samovar*
and the *janamaz,* I was walked
from Baku across the border;
one hundred and fifty miles,
a distance I measured in the steps
it would take to return. Now in Tabriz,
my grandson skips into the courtyard
where I spend daylight wearing
a path around the lilting fountain,
speaking to the birds. He sits
next to me under the mulberry tree
and listens before asking
if he can send a message
back home, too.

Elogium

Loll Jungeburth

Then, war again Then again—war War again, then! Then war, again. War then, again. War—then again:

Four Corners: A World

Loll Junggeburth

I.

four angels hold four corners of the world, four winds roll the globe round, white and crisp like sheets

II.

Persephone goes downstairs for winter: the sun went in the fire went out the future went out, flickered. She peels her first orange of the year

she says: i peel you like the man used to peel a woman with his eyes and hands, before he found manners and was told that women are humans too.

she tastes: a closed-eyed explosion, sweet blind light reaching and bursting for tongue, for mind, a warm fast dance

III.

an avocado, just born of hard skin, drops to the floor in Glasgow as someone stamps their foot in the flat upstairs, just

as a man drops feet-first into a pit, dangling like strange fruit from rope made for more wholesome things.

IV.

Break! Break— the dry bone of time cracks in black dark where calm wrestles with chaos, that divine maker, makar, breaker white on waves' crest falls in to blue.

364 BC

Hugh McMillan

Let us remember the fallen
of the 3rd Sacred War:
these hundred thousand men
with their set jaws,

the blazing sun
on their breastplates.
They died to make the Phocians
keep their cows off temple land.

Their blood will never congeal.
In autumn we will put on
the wild crocus, each petal
hot from a Greek vein.

Let us remember
in the millennia of peace
to come, their rare
and selfless sacrifice.

An Eala Bhan

Hugh McMillan

The pipe band
from Peronne is playing,
each one wearing
the badge of a soldier
of the Somme.

The evening is wet,
the flags droop,
this Thursday in July is
collapsing to an end
and the sky will darken.

No matter the weather,
the waste, the sadness,
 it will darken,
the last piercing
note fading like a bullet,

and the moon will return
to pieces in puddles,
where for those still here,
in the fields, the streets,
it will shine like a swan.

The Carob Tree

Rached Khalifa

The branches entwined and shot,
a perfect canopy for our truant noons.
Like sparrows we'd hide into their
dark green foliage and send out songs
we learned at school on work and diligence.

Each one of us had his own charted nest.
The first dared to climb the studded trunk
won the panoramic nook on the crest
that swayed most to the gentlest wind,
while the rest were happy with their lot
executing the commander's orders from the top.

We would invade the leafage like magnified locusts
cracking and bending branches that obstructed
our way to our ensconced cockpits,
flattening twigs that prodded our rumps
turning them into cushioned seats
and others into buttons, gears, and wheels.

We hissed, screeched, thundered, and bombed
in unison enemy areas in Baghdad and Palestine.
Our squadron cruised and soared up and down
imaginary skies, as we shook the tree branches
and swayed, enacting images we saw on TV screens
and stories we heard from our fathers
of usurped territories in distant homelands.

Craiglockhart
(War Hospital for Neurasthenic Officers)

Jackie Kay

At night, my walls close in on men
Who have closed in aroon their selves
Young men – auld souls – whose een
Replay the shocking things they've seen and been.

Men, who'd prefer an all-nighter,
A chain of cigarettes, a book,
Than to see the look of those up closer
Wandering forever lost in the in-between

At night, when the moon has slipped
Over the Salisbury Crags,
Men within my cracked walls
Meet ghouls o' themselves coming back.

I feel the weight of them,
Whose hearts are in lock-down,
Whose deaths are in their mouths,
Who stammer through to dawn.

What would you do if you were me
Listening night after night to broken men?
Would you put them under lock and key?
Or would you unlock their hearts again.

I would give them my art, my poetry
I'd give them my land and the grief of my sea.
I'd give them the spill of my Pentland Hills
I'd give them my will and my word

So I would, so I will -here's my hand,
here's my heart- to put an end to war

Sassoon

Jackie Kay

The night I met him the moon
Sailed in the sky, a big eye,
Looking down on the Hydro, at Sassoon and I,
Young men who refused to tell the old lie -
Dulce et decorum est pro patria mori

The night I met him, my heart flew, I won't lie.
For an hour after breakfast I'm a poet.
By night I'm a sick man ruined by dreams.
The thing that keeps me going is him, Sassoon,
The way he makes me look up at the moon.

I felt myself spinning around, but you fixed me,
And I know, dear man, I'll swing out soon
I'll be that dark star when you blaze,
I'll be that word in the sky; for all our days,
Sassoon, it'll be me when you look up at the moon.

Outlook Tower

Jackie Kay

Stars in the night sky, ants in the earth
Birds on their winter way
Trees in the forest
Babies in a womb
Cells in a bloodstream
X or Y in the chromosome, in the alphabet,
Rivers running into the sea
You Sassoon, you, Wilfred Owen
You flute, you cymbal, you bassoon,
You Pluto, you Mars, you moon,
You love, my dear, my darling,
You world, you precious earth
You beloved field, you forever Scotland,
You foreign face, you looking glass,
You microcosm, you black hole, you star,
You lad, you lass, you water, you fire.
You you you you you you, just as you are.

Letter Home

Jackie Kay

I feel a sort of reserve and suspense about everything I do.
I have seen things beyond your understanding.
I can't think what room to put them in except here
Where men have shared the same nightmare.

Here where we are brave enough to relive the horror
Where we stretch our arms out to nature
Where we learn, everything is part of the whole
Where we think of who we are to the world

And Dr Brock teaches us to talk, to open- up
We're not taught the stiff upper lip here, to shut up
But to break the ground, break it up, to hurl
Ourselves to the ground, to hear the shells burst again

I know I am in a very shaky condition
I know I am nervy, highly strung
I know I might be suffering from depression
I know I stammer, words stick on my tongue.

At night, I dream of dug outs and faces of men
A soldier choking to death on sudden gas

I know I am self-effacing, withdrawn.
Edinburgh castle looks like a hallucination.
And this hospital a decayed Hydro
In a great sweep of moor and mountain.

I am the man whose mind the dead have ravished.
I have witnessed murders before my eyes.
I am one of the weary who don't want to rest
One of the ones who call out at night in bed.

Return

Jackie Kay

And for the rest of my life it was Edinburgh,
The place I'd most like to return to
Where love was thrown at me not grenades
Where I stood, and watched the stars from the tower
Where I loved, and felt his gaze.

And if I ever come back to mend my broken heart
It would be to Craiglockhart
Where I was the happiest of my days on earth.

If I could live a night again
It would be the one where Sassoon and I
Went to the Observatory, late summer,
And we shared the same night air, the same skin,
And we watched the moon rise and disappear
And we knew we had made a little crater;
Together we'd created a bit of forever.

National Day

Stephen Keeler

The politburo huddled
under hats of satire,
like pigeons on a ledge.

There'd be snow
on their circus epaulets
before the last polished weapon

rolled past on painted tyres:
another kind of spruced-up corpse,
in an open coffin.

And anyone who could be bothered
envied them only their greatcoats
and imagined layers of wool and fleece.

They stood motionless
as ancient chessmen
carved out of something better.

Once a year, on an immemorial day,
it was the nearest we ever got
to sharing their shame.

I hear the cries of the dead: those whose lives
Are cut short call out louder
There is no way being remembered dead
Is better than being forgotten when we lived.

Phoebus Apollo

i.m. Julian Grenfell

Martin Malone

Warm with late spring, in a field near Ypres,
you were never so happy than on this big picnic,
chatting with the General when that shell struck.

For you it was a job you'd a flair for and loved,
and, when the Great War finally came,
a permit to go hunt the biggest game.

If your Dad twice swims Niagara and shoots
everything that moves, what else is a well-bred boy
to do but stick pigs in India and dream of Troy?

Long, long before a love of Homer and boxing gloves,
habitual peril was the deal cut for privilege:
yours, then, but the tribal code witnessed in blood.

As with all sport, you took to it well, bagged a laurel;
found increase in battle, love in the taking of life
and gilded your game book with three Pomeranians.

O Sarpedon! O Hotspur! Your burning moment broke
upon the grubby *kudos* of shrapnel, its splinter driven
an inch-and-a-half into classically educated brain.

And 13 days later, the languid death in a curtained room
stricken with sunbeams, holding Mummy's hand, serene
enough to trim a *Krupp*-made end with Phoebus' gold.

*'Phoebus Apollo' were Grenfell's last words as a shaft of sunlight shone through a gap in the
curtains of his room.*

the fallen and the missing

Jim Ferguson

life has fallen into such a giant shape of weird
friends die in the night without disturbing me to say:
good bye
cheers
adieu
or toodle ooh

sleep is easily odd and upside down
sometimes
i need
a lot
but can get by
on almost none,
every chest pain is a heart attack that never gets begun

life is such a giant shape of weird
gets more fucked-up and crazy
every passing day,
in future stars will die and I'm afeared
of a cold and coal-black cosmos
ever dimming, though this won't happen
for 35 billion years,
it's something
                I will never know or see
so why the fuck's
                    it bothering daft auld me?

and it seems it's even worse than Donald Trump
who bothers me a lot and makes me think
life is so totally, massively, black-hole weird
and most of the universe isn't really there,
apparently, as far as physics sees,
which isn't too much wood but lots of trees

then again,

      that's another story aw the gether,
      an episode of *Missing* not yet made

rhythm of political heart-break

Jim Ferguson

do i know what words are worth
all set in place and bound in books
who dares to delve into the archives
sneak a surreptitious look

through bertolt brecht's mistrustful eyes
i glimpsed europe

look there goes macheath
from then to there, across
two hundred years to sing
the words of poor b.b. unmasked

through maria rilke's angelic eyes
i glimpsed europe

unmasked the lives of worthy souls
forgotten in the mass and drudge
of stagnant rivers crying foul
at nazi sailors tugging sculls

through bohomil hrabal's inky eyes
i glimpsed europe

sculls with break-heart rhythm
what cruel gods we did invent
to circumvent the brittle wonder
once flourished liberty and went

through simone de beauvoir's forensic eyes
i glimpsed europe

went out into a sea more skilled in killing
than ought was ever thought could be,
bright hope dull with age and time
sunk, and sang, the *song of the end of the republic*

through theresa may's vampire eyes,
i glimpsed, deluded England

The corvid liberator

Fiona Rintoul

A wild throaty call. A crazed battering of wings. He hears the bird before he sees it. Drawn towards the terrible noise, he steps off the path and pushes through a clump of pine trees, emerging in a small, verdant clearing fringed with reeds. The ground squelches underfoot. The mossy tang of sodden earth nips his nostrils. It's been raining most of the day, a penetrating drizzle that turned the mountains to a smudge. As he steps forward, his left foot sinks into the ground. Freezing black water seeps under his gaiter and into his walking boot. Cursing, he yanks his foot free. He scans the treetops, looking for the source of the frantic cry. Nothing.

Then he looks down. The bird's ebony eyes flash behind the wires of the Larsen trap, terrified and defiant. He sees a gleaming hooked beak, a frenzy of iridescent feathers.

The bird is almost two feet long. A beautiful hooded crow the colour of pitch and ash.

Shit. He kicks the trunk of one of the pines. He kicks it hard, wanting to feel pain.

Then he reads the notice fastened to the top of the cage. This is a legal trap...

Back in the south country, he once released a score of crows from a funnel trap on the hillside. Before deciding to let them go, he stood for a moment, sunk in shame, watching them flinging themselves against the cage walls, their eyes wild with terror and hate. So this was what men did with their mastery of nature. The trap was ingenious. Shot rabbits were laid out on the floor as bait. The narrowing funnel let the birds fly in but not back out. The carrion had scarcely been touched. Once the birds realised they were trapped, they lost interest in it. The gamekeeper would be able to use the rabbits again, he thought, as he opened the trap door and watched the birds rise into the sky. It was a Sunday in early May. He hoped the gamekeeper might be in his garden, weeding his flower beds, that he might look up, see a murder of crows crossing the hillside and know he'd been foiled.

The funnel trap was large, like an infernal aviary. This trap is much smaller. He kneels beside it, watched by the shrieking, flapping bird.

He has hesitated longer than he should have, perhaps weighing up the plea on the notice not to interfere with an important conservation measure, perhaps feeling the power he has over this wild creature's fate. Don't worry, pal, he tells it. I'm going to set you free. Then he flips open the lid in the cage roof and steps back.

But the bird doesn't fly out.

This way, he says, tapping the opening. Look. Here.

He shoots a look behind him. He hasn't seen anyone all day but he's getting closer to civilisation now. And he knows what people round these parts think of bleeding-heart incomers who don't understand the ways of the countryside.

But the bird can't get out. The opening is too high for it to reach, and there isn't enough room for it to open its wings and fly.

Bastards, he spits. He thinks he's been outwitted. He thinks the person who built this cage foresaw the possibility of someone such as him coming by and wanting to release the bird, wanting to release it despite all the stories he's been told of crows pecking out the eyes of new-born lambs and attacking ewes when they're giving birth. But that's nature, he whispers to the bird. That. Is. Nature. This – he pings his middle finger against the side of the cage – is not.

Then he sees how to fix the problem. He tips the cage over on to its side with his foot. For a moment, the crow stands motionless, gazing at the aperture in front of it, unable to believe what it sees. Then it hops out, takes off and soars into the grey-white sky, where a fuzzy silver sun is now dissipating the rain clouds. It circles the clearing once, performs a shallow dive and then salutes him with what he imagines to be a kraa of joy.

Ha! He laughs, face raised to the heavens. He grins as he watches the liberated corvid rise higher and higher in the brightening sky and turn in the direction of the mountains, where creases of grey rock now glisten against the rich amber of the early spring turf. Not until the crow has become a speck does he turn away.

He pushes back through the trees and regains the path. He knows there's a house up ahead. A big one with a turret and other castellations. He saw it from the other side of the loch when he set out on his walk that morning. But the house is much closer than he expected. From the path, he glimpses the stonework through the pine trees ahead. He walks towards it, boots crunching on stones. He should have righted the trap before leaving the clearing. It's obvious that someone kicked it over, and there's no one here but him. Too late now. If he turns back, it'll look suspicious. Hopefully, there won't be anyone at the house. If there is, they'll hear him. The smash of his boots sounds louder now than the crow's one glorious shriek of freedom.

He emerges into a large gravelled clearing. There are two houses. The old estate house, which has a grand stone entranceway flanked by Greek urns, stands at distance of some 100 yards. Across from it, nearer to him, is a converted barn with large modern windows. Through the patio doors he sees overstuffed armchairs and a four-seater sofa draped in dust sheets. The estate house looks empty too. The windows on the ground floor are shuttered, though those on the upper floors are not. It's the kind of place a rich absentee landlord might visit for a fortnight in summer, having first had the midges exterminated with an anti-midge machine. He strides past the converted barn, swinging his walking poles, confident he has the place to himself. But as he nears the estate house he sees he's mistaken: two Range Rovers, their navy blue paintwork shining in the emergent sun's final rays before dusk, are parked side by side in front of a garage to the side of the house. Do they belong to the estate owner or the gamekeepers? Of the two, he'd prefer the owner. The locals have soft, gentle accents, but it's a mistake to conclude that they're gentle folk. He's seen puppies drowned in buckets, sheep left to starve on the hillside in freezing winter, majestic ravens plucked illegally from the skies.

He thinks about what he'll say if someone appears. I didn't come along the path from the loch, no. I came straight down off the hill. Very boggy up on the hill today. Look at the state of my boots. (Laughs.) It was worth it, though. Even in this light, you could see all the way to... Aye, no need to go on. He'll just say that he came straight down off the hill.

But no one does appear. The house is silent. The place feels empty, spooky almost. He walks towards the Range Rovers, which are protected by a canopy that extends out from the garage. They have matching tan leather upholstery and sequential number plates. And look at that: there's mud on their tyres and splattered up their wheel arches. But it's dry. Those cars haven't been driven today. Or for some time.

His shoulders drop. He hadn't realised how tense he was until now. There's no one here. Hasn't been for days. He walks past the garage towards the gate, which is chained shut. He goes through the kissing gate at the side and heads out on to the Land Rover track, which follows the river back to the single-track road where his small red Corsa is wedged into a passing place. He's in the clear. Still, he quickens his pace.

The mile to the car seems to go on forever. The peat-darkened river tumbling at the side of the road creates a fiendish racket. Twice he swings round, thinking he hears tyres crunching gravel behind him, only to realise it's river water crashing on rocks.

The light is fading when he reaches the car. He throws his walking poles and rucksack on to the back seat. He hangs his damp waterproof jacket from the passenger seat headrest and lays his wet woolly hat on the dashboard to dry. He tears off his muddy gaiters and lobs them into the boot. He sits down sideways on the driver's seat to pull off his walking boots and socks. His bleached feet look dead, and he savours the warm caress of clean cotton socks, the cushioning pressure of his trainers. He throws his wet boots and socks in the boot and bangs it shut.

Before getting back into the car, he looks up the track one last time. Nothing. In a final salute to the freed corvid, he raises his fist towards the mountains, which have turned blue-black in the gathering gloom.

In the car, he pulls on a warm fleece. He starts the engine, switches on the lights and turns on the fan heater. He takes a thermal cup of tea from the glove compartment, opens it and places it in the cup holder next to the steering wheel. He's adjusting the rear-view mirror and getting ready to go, when he sees twin lights behind him.

The lights are approaching fast. A car is speeding along the Land Rover track from the house, bouncing on the stones.

Steady on, he mutters. He shoves the Corsa into gear. The handbrake needs adjusting. He pulls it high to release it. He turns the steering wheel sharply to the right and bumps out on to the single-track road. Tea slops out of the thermal cup on to his thigh. He draws the seatbelt across his chest as he pulls away from the passing place. Rounding a bend, he clips the fastener in the holder.

The Range Rover is on his tail in moments. Its headlights are on full beam. His small vehicle is flooded with light. Almost blinded, he accelerates. The Range Rover stays with him.

The Search for Survivors Continues

Vicki Jarrett

That's her away then. Her girl gone. Two red ribbons of light hang in the damply echoing bus station air and ripple in the backwashed noise of receding gears. That's fine. Her bus leaving. That's good. She'll be safe in her new place before morning, her smart new clothes unfolded and ready. That's all you want for them. To have a chance. The blurred egg of her daughter's face through the steamed up window. Her own hand reaching out and her unable to stop it, the arm lifting of its own accord, levitating, fucking possessed. Put it down woman.

She should go now, get herself home, but she stands just a few minutes more, breathes the spent exhaust fumes, the residue of combustion collecting on the roof of her mouth. Each part of this is a stone dropping inside her. If she moves, that'll be another stone to add to the cairn in her guts, maybe a big one, maybe the biggest yet. Maybe she won't be able to move at all. She'll be too heavy if she so much as tries to lift a foot.

She blinks. The glowing after-image of taillights plays like the flapping scrag end of an old film reel on the underside of her eyelids. The rain has stopped but the weight of it is all around, the air full of water like a not wrung out properly dishcloth. You could just reach out and squeeze. Her eyes are wet with it. Or, perhaps, tears. Which would at least be appropriate, understandable, standard issue normal. Tears here, now, in this particular situation or one like it, could be explained and folk would sympathise, even try to cheer her up by saying something well-meant. She blinks again. God no. She doesn't want that. Red worms under her lids.

That's her away then? His words tight and high, pretending lightness. Him not looking directly at her, holding himself in.

She makes an uh-huh sound good enough to pass for yes and everything's fine and let's not talk about it right now because if we do then we'll both burst wide open all over the carpet so let's just have our tea and watch the telly and not look at each other properly until maybe tomorrow or the day after or the day after that okay.

And they have vegetable soup from a can. She stirs her bowl and watches pieces of she can't tell what rise and submerge. Vegetable should not be a flavour. An onion and, say a beetroot for the sake of argument, have nothing whatsoever in common apart from both being vegetables. They are not the same flavour. Same goes for fruit flavoured things. Apples. Bananas. Christ. Do they think folk are stupid? Well. Here she is eating it. Chewing unidentified bits of vegetable that all taste exactly the same so who's stupid now? She puts the spoon down too hard on her tray and his eyes flick in her direction then back to the TV. Her throat hurts and there are red hot pins at her eyes. Jesus wept. It's only fucking soup.

Any time you want it, there's always news now, straight out the can, day or night, it's there. Grey-blue images flicker across his glasses, the back of her spoon, the framed photos on the sideboard, reflections chasing each other, children pulled from under rubble, dead and alive, mothers howling on their dusty torn knees, heads back as the sound comes barrelling up through them, vibrating through every knuckle of spine and out, climbing into the sky, forming the towers of an invisible city in the air where their real one should be but isn't anymore. Cut to a panelled room where men in suits sit importantly in upholstered chairs and nod their agreement.

He swears. Not at them, not at the mothers and their broken children. He's not that way. He calls Assad a cunt and changes TV channel to the football. What can you do? What the fuck can you do? Thousands roar full-throated at the back and forth of the ball, the sound of the crowd rising up and rolling back down.

She's still thinking about the dictator's hair. The way he keeps it so neat. He must take care of it, look in the mirror and spend time considering its shape, combing it into place. He must do other ordinary things. Wash his face, brush his teeth, shower, he too is entirely naked under his clothes, has a certain pattern of body hair, has nipples, think of that, soft belly skin, ticklish places. Does he curl up at night with another warm human, their sleep breath innocently falling into a single rhythm? Can he also be that kind of animal?

There are real things happening, terrible things, wonderful things too, we must believe that despite the lack of evidence, and here she is stuck not being able to eat her soup and thinking about bloody Assad's nipples. Are they small and hard or big and soft like undercooked drop scones? She needs her head examined. She pictures the inside of it like an old black and white picture from when telephones were not long invented, operators with those masses of wires and huge boards to plug them into. Hold please, we're connecting you now, they'd say. Please hold. The operator in charge of her board has lost the plot, maybe doesn't sleep so well or is having other troubles of her own, puts the wrong connectors in the wrong holes and now her head's stuffed to bursting with a tangle of crossed wires.

Leaking out of one of the loose wires a voice dribbles on about how she should think herself lucky her girl is whole and well and has only grown up and moved away for work. Not that she wanted to but she must take her chance and go to where the work is. The machinery of the world will turn whether she likes it or not and her daughter is safe and she herself should be thankful she is not on her knees in the rubble. The voice has the slither and broad reek of vegetable soup about it. She doesn't want it, pushes it away. A wrong number. She takes her bowl to the kitchen and pours the stuff down the sink, pokes the slimy bits through the holes in the grill and runs the tap longer than is needed.

In the shower she turns the heat up until it stings her skin, and shivers. She washes her hair and thousands of other people are also washing their hair at this precise moment, and then there are the thousands, probably millions for whom hot water and soap are not ordinary at all. She closes her eyes and lets the froth run over her face.

With a sigh she reaches between her legs, holding no great hopes but all the same, from time to time she feels she should check whether the fault has corrected itself. There's been a wrong connection there, right there, for a while now. A misfire. It comes as a low punch of grief that doubles her over, leaves her trembling, small and locked outside of herself. She thinks of circuit boards and sees the short distance a fork of voltage has to travel between the system of delight and the system of loss. Love and torment, hope and fear, gratitude and guilt. All stacked together far too close, sparks stuttering back and forth. Accidents waiting to happen.

He stifles a yawn, reaches over and puts the remote on the arm of her chair. I'm going up, he says.

She loosens the towel wrapped around her head. My hair's still wet.

He pauses in the doorway. She'll be fine, he says.

She presses the damp material into her hair, leans forward and lets it cover her face.

Night then, he says.

Night.

His slow footsteps creak up the stairs.

She flicks through the channels. Nothing connects. Her hair curls and dries in unplanned shapes. She flicks all the way and back again, quick, quicker: sofas, celebrity quiz shows, loan company adverts, war planes, fast cars, burgers, movie shoot outs, burning buildings, lipstick, insurance, sofascelebrityquizshowsloancompanyadvertswarplanesfastcars— stops, on a patch of blue amid the noise.

It is an undersea scene, camera panning slowly over coral all the same pale bone colour. Nothing alive. A diver drifts over it, gloved hands gesturing mournfully. She turns the sound down low and rummages in the pocket of her dressing gown for her mobile. Checks the display. Nothing. She'll still be on the bus of course and said she'd text when she got to the flat. She won't pester her. Could be sleeping on the bus. She'll wait a while. There seems to be no end to the desiccated coral.

Her hand jerks and the phone falls to the floor. Did she fall asleep? How can she sleep at a time like this at any time it's outrageous how can she sit and sleep and do any of it when she can't do anything to stop anything to make anything alright to help how can she be—

Hold please.

Maybe her phone isn't working. There are any number of ways technology could be to blame. Withholding messages, diverting them. Someone else hundreds of miles away even now could be reading a text that says something along the lines of I am here I am safe. How could she grudge anyone that? Perhaps that's exactly what they need to hear too.

The coral has gone and in its place something has collapsed into more rubble. Bombs or storms or earthquake or did it just crumble under the weight of its own bricks? The search for survivors continues.

Near dawn, she slips into her side of the bed next to the shape of him under the covers and lies still. His breath catches then resumes its regular steady rhythm. Her body is buffeted by currents, her hair ripples around her head, she raises an arm into the soupy dissolving dark, fingers dabbling in the tide of messages, the air thick with intangible reassurances I am here I am safe See you soon Love you. You could just reach out and—

Hold please. We are connecting you now.

The Gutter Interview:
Do we just need poems? A Franco-Scottish poetry conversation.

Benjamin Guérin, Calum Rodger & Andrew Rubens

The Gutter Interview: Benjamin Guérin, Calum Rodger & Andrew Rubens

Based in the Cévennes, **Benjamin Guérin** is a poet whose career has blossomed in the past couple of years. His first book *Metropole Oubliée* [*Forgotten Metropolis*] was published last year by Lucie Éditions. A translation by **Andrew Rubens** was published in Issue 16 of *Gutter*. He has recently been featured in the prestigious French poetry magazine *ARPA*. He is also a contributing editor for the review *NUNC*. In collaboration with his partner, Florence Pichot, he is also a sculptor working in ceramics, incorporating his texts into his sculptures.

Calum Rodger is a poet, researcher and events organiser based in Glasgow, working in performance, print, and digital media. He performs regularly throughout Scotland, co-runs the occasional Verse Hearse reading series, and has written a PhD on the work of Ian Hamilton Finlay. More recently, he has been working on the Cinepoems project across Scotland and Quebec. His chapbooks, *Know Yr Stuff: Poems on Hedonism* and *Glasgow Flourishes*, are published by Tapsalteerie. He is also one of the Reviews Editors for *Gutter*. Some of his work can be found online at www.calumrodger.co.uk.

*

Andrew Rubens: Today we're simply hoping to establish a connection between two poets from different countries, namely Scotland and France, and get an informal conversation going around the context of your creative processes. Hopefully you will get along as well as Mary Stuart and Francis II, but we'll settle for anything better than David Hume and Jean-Jacques Rousseau. To get us started: what are you working on at the moment?

Calum Rodger: I'm working on a cinepoems project, for which I was in Montreal for a week with a Northern Irish poet and two Québecois poets. We made four poetic short films, one for each of us. We were at a poetry night last night and my colleague Rachel McCrum read the poem she used for her film. It was great and I love her film but actually watching her read it was the best performance of the poem I've seen. That's the second time I've seen her read it, with the film that's three times in total. Much as I love the film I got more out of it with the intensity and directness of the performance. So I suspect the same may be the case with my film. A couple of friends of mine have said it's a great poem but it doesn't need the film...

AR: And you do quite a bit of performance poetry yourself.

CR: Yes, I tend to focus more on performance than the page, generally speaking. So I'm feeling a bit of a devil's advocate about the whole thing. When I see Rachel later today I'm going to ask her, 'Did we need all this? Did we need the films after all? Do we just need poems?' So anyway the project began with a 48 hour filmpoem challenge in December where a dozen teams went away and made little films – great fun. The next stage is to build an online magazine. We've given it the name 'All these new relations' after a Margaret Tait film, Margaret Tait was a Scottish filmmaker/poet who worked in the 1960s – 1980s. We want to create this online hub to try and get more people to make film poems. Although there's a very lively performance scene in Scotland and a lot of people make videos, it tends to be basically just performing at the camera.

AR: So you're making these films but the project's almost as much about bringing poets together? We'll come back to that. What are you working on Benjamin?

Benjamin Guérin: Just to respond to Calum, I find your cinepoems very interesting and they evoke the work of Benjamin Fondane, during the inter-war period in France. An avant-garde project from a hundred years ago and now you're doing it today. Your work is avant-garde too, performances, innovations, continuing to explore the same themes somewhat. I think it is great that you are taking up the torch.

As for myself, just in the past few days, I have been writing a text for a magazine based in Kinshasa in the Democratic Republic of Congo. There is a wonderful journal called *La Plume Vivante* which is bringing poetry alive there. They are publishing one of my poems and also a sort of testament because the issue is a special number on Benjamin Fondane, whom I've already mentioned. I'm asking myself the question 'what part has Benjamin Fondane played in my own work as a poet'? In fact this is the first time I have stopped and asked myself this…

CR: Can you tell us, Ben, how does your poem respond to Fondane's work?

BG: I'll read it later, once I get my computer started… A question for you, Calum – do you write on paper or on a computer? I've always been interested in the rhythm of the means of writing.

CR: I was talking about this with a friend yesterday – almost always computer. Almost always. Because it's faster. If I have a goal in mind, then always the computer. I only like writing on paper, on a notebook, when I want a more receptive way of writing – I write there for the pleasure of the writing itself and without any end or goal in mind. It's slower, isn't it, more tactile. I've done quite a lot of archive research, and you'll see great dead poets have three or four drafts of a poem, all in a folder in an archive. Poets of our generation won't have that in the same way because of the nature of word processing software – you cut, you delete, you lose what you've previously written in the act of writing the new thing. I'm not trying to put in any value judgement there at all but it's worth noting. How about yourself?

BG: I really like your idea of speed. That's the key – what speed does it go at, in our heart and in our head? At what speed do the words come out? I have three methods – the pen, typing, I type quite fast, but also the microphone, voice recognition. I've noticed that this creates three very different kinds of writing. Poetry is very irregular in terms of speed. Sometimes I need something very rapid, in which case either

I type or I write little notes, in the middle of the night or whenever. With poetry it's mostly on the computer, like yourself Calum. But I think at some level we remain attached to paper, for its romantic side and because of the transmission of the poets we ourselves have loved, and so I also want to publish in paper form. Although digital is something that speaks to me, I would struggle to be as engaged with the internet as you are.

I have the poem for *La Plume Vivante* - I am going to read it just so you can have an idea of the sound.

> *J'ai traduit*
> *et j'ai converti*
> *j'ai changé et me suis maintenu*
> *dans une commune*
> *communauté*
> *de sens et puis de*
> *VIE*
>
> *Où est donc la langue intraduisible*
> *celle des secrets et des merveilles*
> *celle de la belle*
> *la belle qui est.*
>
>   - « Il faut être amoureux pour
> traduire la langue de l'aimée »,
>   *me souffle mon ange*
>
> *En mon sommeil,*
> *j'anesthésie*
> *adieu logique, adieu raison*
> *je choisis l'impossible et puis l'amont*
> *j'affirme la vie comme la déraison.*
>
> *Le poète ne pense pas*

> *pas comme on pense*
> *le poète ne panse pas non plus*
> *il affirme :*
> *OUI*
>
> *comme un cri primordial*

CR: Sounds lovely!

AR: I think that turns around some of the themes we're talking about today and it made me think of yourself picking up from Fondane, Benjamin, and Calum picking up from some of the forms that these avant-gardes were approaching a hundred years ago, and this process of translation which can also be a translation of something from the past into the present.

On the theme of the Auld Alliance, I want to ask: Calum, what French-language writers influence or excite you, and Benjamin, what Scottish writers influence or excite you?

CR: Georges Perec and the Oulipo writers, Breton and the Surrealists, Tzara, all the great isms: Dada, Surrealism, Oulipo. The Surrealists and the Oulipos are great because they're like two sides of the same coin, the coin being poetry. The French led the way with the avant-garde, didn't they, and we followed.

BG: A difficult question, I will show the full extent of my ignorance... I have primarily read Scottish philosophers, the Enlightenment writers, and I must admit that I have seldom concurred with them. However I have a great passion, which I share with my son, for the Scottish rugby team. There is a true passion and poetry in the team which easily surpasses the philosophers. So of course Flower of Scotland makes my spine tingle! More seriously, there are two Scottish writers who have been essential for me: Robert Louis Stevenson and Kenneth White. These two travellers each took a special geopoetic look at my native land, my Cévennes. As a child I met White when he was retracing Stevenson's journey across the Cévennes.

CR: The team is a tragedy though, right…

AR: What do you think people know of Scottish poetry in France in general?

BG: I'll focus on the theme of translation. I think there is a great difficulty in getting Anglophone poetry into France. There is something very paradoxical. On one hand we are completely immersed in the rhythm of the English language, through songs, American culture etc., but on the other hand there are classic poets who are, I find, difficult to get hold of in translation. I am trying to decipher my great-grandmother's dusty copy of Keats in the original English, a little bit at a time. I find it very beautiful in English, whereas none of the French translations I have speak to me. With everything that is at stake in translation, it is something that requires an *interprète*. In French the word *interprète* is something we use in music, we don't say simply a 'player' or 'musician' but an interpreter.

I find that you, Andrew, were genuinely an *interprète* in translating my text for *Gutter*, there are parts of my poem which I prefer in English, in the rhythm, in the words, also in the manner in which the sounds pulsate.

And it's important because the *interprète,* as a transmitter, is someone who leaves his or her mark, a sort of co-author. There is not the idea of the neutrality of the machine, for example just pressing the 'play' button on a hifi or a computer. No, an interpreter is someone who transmits, but there is a mediation, he or she transforms things, modulates them, brings them alive, gives them breath, and that is a beautiful idea.

AR: What is it about France or French culture in particular that makes this process more difficult, do you think? What creates this barrier?

BG: I don't know… perhaps I would say the same thing to you if I were English and we were talking about French texts. I think on each occasion an excellent translator is required, and often in France we have lauded translators, we know the names of major translators. For example, with a text as important as Homer's *Odyssey*, I can't really read it in the original. I love it, but only Philippe Jacottet's translation. So when I talk of Homer's *Odyssey* I always add Jacottet's name, who was himself a great poet and who played a phenomenal role in the text for me. Also, the idea of the connection between music and language is very important for me. A tic I have is to try and understand the workings of many different instruments: the accordion, the piano, the trumpet, and each time I come back to the guitar, the instrument I learned first, and I play in a completely different way. And for years I have tried to learn new languages – Hindi, Persian, Arabic, Spanish – and when you come back to your own language, it does exactly the same thing. After exploring another language, I come back to French and I succeed in contorting it, in a really interesting way. Which means that today I understand many languages very badly, and I play many instruments very badly.

CR: There's a sort of unfortunate mirror of that. For example, I'm a great fan of Japanese haiku. There's a real kind of Orientalism in the way that they're translated as free verse, unrhymed, because there's a whole tradition, a convention, in metrics and so on, to the original haiku, which is actually completely ignored in modern translations of the haiku. To the point that there is a haiku tradition in the west, certainly in America and the UK, which is barely a haiku compared to the traditional Japanese way of recognising a haiku. It's almost a completely separate form, which may have virtue for its own sake, it definitely does in some cases, but arguably it could be seen as a dissimulation of the original convention and tradition. Probably haiku writing in the West would benefit from more close reading and understanding of the original Japanese tenets of making a haiku.

AR: Calum, just while you're on some of your international interests, what's your impression of what people in Scotland, in general, know of French poetry today?

CR: Rimbaud, all the big ones… but I want to pick up on the Mallarmé connection. Mallarmé is notoriously difficult to translate, all that wordplay, the syntax… there's a great Glasgow poet called Peter Manson who recently translated Mallarmé's verse poems. Going back to what you said about every translation being an interpretation, that's very much the case with Peter Manson's reworkings of Mallarmé. But the one I'm interested in is 'A roll of the dice', which of course had a big influence on concrete poetry, which is a very strong tradition in Scotland. 'A roll of the dice' is very wordy, it probably presents some of the same difficulties of translation as the rest of his work, but the way it influences concrete poetry, it's almost a drive towards a poetry which doesn't need translating. You have the Swiss poet Gomringer wanting a pan-national poetry, and this idea in the sixties that concrete poetry was an international movement. There are so few words in the concrete poem that it almost makes no sense to translate it, although poets like Edwin Morgan did translate concrete poetry, ostensibly, with some success. But it's interesting to see how that linguistic energy, that kind of singularity, in a way that is ultimately untranslatable, comes to influence a different kind of linguistic singularity, which is also untranslatable but for completely different reasons.

AR: I think maybe that's a good juncture to ask: where do you yourselves look for meeting points between your own work and what might be called the international poetry diaspora, other poets from other countries? How aware are you in general of poetry in other countries today?

BG: That's what we're doing today…

CR: For me it's mostly American poetry, the trends and so on. Both in the scholarly work that I read, and the blogs I follow. To some extent, the UK avant-garde follows the American avant-garde.

AR: You were recently at a Russian literary conference, weren't you?

CR: That's right, yeah, it was amazing, they had a Russian literature conference in Moffat. It was the strangest thing, maybe thirty or forty Russian academics and poets arrived in this small, sleepy Scottish town. What was interesting was that in literary studies in Scotland, in the UK and so on, we're very critical about our own practice, why are we doing this? Why is this poem great? and so on. Refreshingly this was less obvious among the Russians, they revered the poems. They had a much more philological approach, they treated the poems like these artefacts, held in such high esteem. Somebody said that thing about, was it Mayakovsky said [*editor's note: it was Osip Mandelstam*], they really love their poets in Russia because they'll kill them. You know they must love their poets if they'll send their poets to the gulag or whatever. There's a real passion for verse, for the word, which was fascinating to see. I don't think we have that in the UK at all, in fact I think there's a deep scepticism born of ignorance really, towards poetry. It threatens people, I don't know why.

AR: I'm not sure it's quite the same in France.

BG: In France too we come back to that question of language and its limits, which also opens onto *la francophonie*, other French-speaking parts of the world, notably in Africa. French therefore gains wonderful contemporary poets like Nimrod, Abdelatif Laâbi, or Gabriel Mwènè Okoundji, or Linda Maria Baros. And for a number of years now there have been poetry festivals in France which are very international, notably the festival in Sète, a town with links to Paul Valéry and Georges Brassens, and most importantly a port which opens onto the Mediterranean. Every year there is a truly international gathering of poets there. But it also depends on people's preferences. I am quite affected by English-language poetry, particularly American poets, in their phrasing, in their rhythms, I must admit I am a great fan of Patti Smith, who gives me great pleasure and who I think has played a role in the way I write poetry in French, in terms of both structure and sound.

CR: At these festivals, is most or all of the work performed in French?

BG: No.

CR: So you get a whole different range of languages too.

BG: Often with translators who follow the poet, but the reading of the original always comes first. It is Arabic and Persian which touch me the most. There are things in these languages which have greatly directed my poetic inspiration and shown ways of contorting language. My partner and I have travelled a lot, we spent some time in Syria, we saw Palmyra and Aleppo before the revolution, and the experience left a great impression. We even went across the border through Turkey and Kurdistan, and we wanted so much to return to the area around Aleppo that we went to a place no one went to, to Kilis. Now it is known around the world because it is the closest border town to Aleppo and it is a place that is poetry made flesh, with the heat, the sun, the stones, the green colour of the pistachio trees which stand out against the red of the earth. I found a language and a culture of poetry which has had an enormous effect upon me.

Iran too is a place which has left its mark. My son is named after an Iranian town. I feel nourished by Iran, by ancient poets like Hafiz and Omar Khayyam, but also by contemporary poets, especially Sorab Sepehri. His way of expressing himself has had a great bearing on the way I think about poetry. The place of poetry in Iranian society is also important. Poetry is very influential in Iranian and Arabic societies, there are poetry competitions, things that don't really exist in the West. I would play a game in Iran, I carried around a pocket edition of Hafiz, translated into French, a beautiful little book with illustrations… you can find magnificent books there. I would take it out of my pocket in very normal, public places, on a bus or in a taxi, and I would start to recite Hafiz in French, and the people on the bus would spontaneously take the book, start to recite themselves, someone would begin to say a poem in Iranian and someone else would finish it… I made friends in Iran, I have connections there which are perhaps slight but are very important for me. It's important not to be naïve here, because there are many terrible things which happen there. I know there is horror there but you cannot simply define Iran, it is also

a country of poetry, of culture. There is the Iran of the mullahs, but there is also the Iran of the poets. When you visit the tombs of Iranian poets, there are always a lot of people there. They are busy all day, especially with young people, lovers will meet at the tomb of Hafiz to kiss.

CR: Possibly changing the subject a bit, I understand you put your poems in ceramics…

AR: Exactly what I wanted to come onto next – you were also very affected by visual forms you saw in Iran, in the architecture and in stones and geological formations, and the poem *Forgotten Metropolis* is in part a reaction to that geology and architecture. You are both concerned with the literal forms of words in many aspects. Benjamin, as Calum has just brought up, you work with one of the most ancient media in the world, pottery, as a way of creating a place for your words, and Calum you work in the most modern, digital and internet poetry. Why is the form of your words so important?

CR: Well let me ask you that Benjamin, especially in terms of the word made flesh and the place for poetry in cultures such as Iran. In your use of ceramics are you in some way trying to find a place, a locus, for the word? What is your inspiration there?

BG: I think there could be a very interesting link between your work and mine. What I have seen of your work interests me very much, stretching poetic forms. I really like some of the poems, that desire to carry poetry into other places, it comes from the same starting point, except that you are a lot more gifted than I am, and you do things I would like to do – for example, you have created what might be called simulators on your site, which would delight Perec and the members of OULIPO, and automatic poetry creators, these are things which I get a lot of enjoyment from. Your public performances also.

As I don't know how to use such modern approaches, I set to an archaic way of working. My instinct was to write my poems onto clay. I saw something very beautiful in a museum, I can't remember if it was in Iran or somewhere else, something which tickled me. Clay tablets with cuneiform inscriptions of one of the oldest texts in the world, from around six thousand years ago, and what is it? A love poem. So I tell myself what could be more natural than wanting to write my poems onto clay? What I enjoy about it is that as well as being somewhat eccentric there is also a rebellious side to it. As a young poet you have trouble getting published, you find that publishers drag their heels…

CR: And sometimes you have to compromise in terms of what the editors want to read…

BG: It takes them some time to understand what you're doing. A little bit of the impulse was also to stick my tongue out at French editors who were slow in publishing my work, by publishing myself on sculptures. I really liked that.

CR: I also couldn't help but notice, with some affection, the Keats book you mentioned earlier, and of course you've got the Ode on a Grecian Urn, which seems

very much to signpost what you're doing with the ceramics. Do you know the work of Ian Hamilton Finlay, the Scottish poet? He was my PhD project so I've spent a long time thinking about his work. At the Little Sparta garden he takes poetry out of the page and makes it an object in the world. The idea that poetry can be an object that can be encountered, like the clay tablets, from concrete poetry to experiments with digital media, even performance I guess, is a very powerful one and I think has quite a redeeming power for poetry in general.

BG: When it comes to looking for new places for poetry, I think it could seem as though we're at opposite ends of the spectrum. But with what you say about Finlay, we see that there is no difference between wanting to inscribe poetry on stones, in a garden, in situ, or as I do with exhibitions of ceramics in galleries or showcases, and finding new directions, new spaces, on the internet or elsewhere. In the end it's the same thing, it's the question the poet asks themselves, how do I make poetry live? How do I find new spaces for poetry in a changing world?

CR: I absolutely agree and it's also a question of the role poetry plays in culture. In Scotland it's not like Iran, where poetry has a significant role in cultural life. Nowadays it's quite a niche thing. But there's still the idea of poetry. Even if people don't read poems, the idea of poetry, of the 'poetic', still has a hold on people. That's why people still get so angry about poetry and modern art, 'oh it doesn't mean anything'. But why should they? They don't have an investment in it.

Why do they care? It seems that this idea of poetry and the poetic goes deeper than any actual poem. Maybe getting beyond the page and breaking free of those kind of cultures, trying to find new spaces, new places for poetry is a way of trying to think through that.

AR: A new context for poetry, getting people to see it, to approach it in a different way.

BG: I don't know if in English the word has the same meaning, but in French the word *intérêt*, it means being in the middle of things, bringing people into the middle of things. With this etymology in mind, Calum, how do you interest people in poetry with the events you participate in, with your performances? Is there a link there with the work of Finlay, who I believe has been an influence for you? You each follow a different path, but you are both concerned by the ways people are interested in poetry…

CR: Yeah, I think in Finlay's case… he's cleverer than I am, for one thing. And also I think he's more ambitious. Finlay invents this word, the non-secular. For him, poetry, and especially the idea of finding a place for poetry… it's an almost religious place, an almost sacred space. For him poetry is an effort, or a means, to think about what religious experience might be after Nietzsche's death of god, after the 20th century and the failures of the great meta-narratives of the 20th century. The problem with the contemporary age for Finlay is not just that god is dead, it's that we don't even mourn his death, we don't even long for god. Finlay's work is a kind of longing for a spiritual wholeness. That's a hugely influential way of thinking about poetry for me personally, but it's almost too great an ambition for me to even consider. Most of my work, especially in performance, tends towards the humorous, the personal and perhaps more than anything, I wouldn't even say the political, but the self-consciously Scottish cultural. I think I'm in a good position to play with the myths and traditions of Scotland in quite a frivolous and irreverent manner. Not nearly as ambitious as Finlay but still using a shared cultural framework and, I suppose, at best, trying to adjust it a little bit.

BG: We've talked a bit about opening out internationally, which is easier in the 21st century. In France there are a lot of poets on Facebook, which I find a bit strange… There is real activity on Facebook, ways of meeting people, people are constantly looking outwards. But at the same time there is a need for anchoring. I quite recently had an encounter which has changed my life. I met one of the greatest living French contemporary poets, Frédéric Jacques Temple, who is very elderly, he is almost one hundred years old, but who is, well, he is pretty impressive, I wouldn't fight him in the boxing ring, he would scare me too much. Something he has said is that he is a travelling tree. His branches seek to voyage outwards, he spends his time travelling but he keeps his roots. He has travelled all his life, opened himself towards others, but at the same time stays deeply anchored in his country, in his land. As for myself, the more I speak of the poetry of Iran and elsewhere in my poems, the more I end up following my local, my very localised culture. The Cévennes, l'Aubrac, lands where I have my anchors. I think that's what you are saying too, making the link between Scottish tradition and looking outwards.

CR: I suppose that's one of the great paradoxes that poetry can accommodate. Being both rooted and somehow, I don't know, disorientated? Maybe that's too strong a word. But it's a fascinating idea. I suppose I would add that there are two facets of my work. To think about it in terms of form, there's the performance, which is absolutely singular in terms of time and place, and I almost always perform in Scotland, so it's got that rootedness to it. Then on the other hand there are some of the machines I make for twitter, for different websites and so on, they kind of exist without an author as such, there's no sense of place in any conventional sense. It's funny you should mention Facebook, because what we might call those two polarities come up against each other with the absolutely exhausting activity of trying to maintain an 'online presence'. And a lot of poets, indeed a lot of people in general, get caught up in that constant performance, which potentially compromises some of the anchoring, the rootedness we've been talking about.

BG: That is very important. If it's performance all the time, not only is that exhausting but it loses its meaning. Performance should remain exceptional. I am less brave than you and I can't make myself give performances. I make my sculptures in collaboration with my partner,

working together, which is partly because that makes it easier but also because I am a shy poet. However I have met other people who have given performances of my poems. And in some surprising ways. I'm thinking of two examples in particular. There is a singer named Roula Safar, who has appeared at the festival in Sète and worked a lot with the Musée de l'Homme in Paris, and who can sing in several languages, notably Babylonian. I had the fortune to have her accompany a reading of my poem by Simon Eine from the Comédie Française, singing in Babylonian. I had showed them my poems, and not only did they like them but they spontaneously came up with the idea of an event, and it was wonderful. The other example was with a town crier, who came across my poems at a ceramics festival, took them up and set about calling them out in public, walking everywhere around the town crying them out. These are little gems, things that erupt into time, and I think that's great. I don't know if you've had that, people spontaneously taking up your texts, it's a beautiful experience.

CR: Again it's that idea of putting it into a different space.

BG: Actually I was really embarrassed with the town crier, I was hiding behind my sculptures!

AR: Another question: you've spoken about this a bit in terms of performance, but I'm also thinking of your machines, Calum, and your sculptures, Benjamin – how do the words and form emerge? How do they find each other? How does the physical form of sculptures, or the 'concrete' or digital forms of poems come together with the words?

CR: Good question. I'll go first – I think it comes back to syntax. Trying to find a syntax. Especially with the generative works, which just combine elements. So the form is really the syntax that holds those elements in place. It follows concrete poetry. That was the struggle of the early concrete poets, to find a spatial syntax, a non-linear syntax. I see it in that tradition. Likewise with GIF poems and the like, finding a syntax and with that a tempo, or what you might tentatively call a metre. To fit.

BG: I think that is brilliant because there is a play element. On your site there is a section called 'Toys'. Poetry needs to remain something which can be mischievous. In jazz, I like it when players are mischievous. It's something that you bring out that we're familiar in France with through OULIPO, around Georges Perec and others, and it's something I find very exciting. I haven't succeeded in doing it with my sculptures, they're too cumbersome to work with for me to make games, but I would like to, I love that whole aspect.

AR: Although you do work with many different forms, your sculptures aren't just the same form repeated. On the Noùs Atelier website you have very interesting headings for each grouping of sculptures, there's a lot of variety, it's not simply working the same form again and again.

BG: I was saying anchoring is important. One of the reasons I am less connected with any scene than you is because of where I am based. I have chosen to live in a place which is pretty cut off from the rest of the world. We're on a mountain, on a large plateau, the nearest house is two hundred metres away. After that neighbour, the nearest village is three kilometres away. This isolation has allowed us to work on our ceramics as it suits us. We make contemporary art, but we use the same techniques as the Romans and the Greeks. We turn the pieces with a basic pottery wheel, we have a wood-burning kiln which takes ten hours to fire a piece. That simplicity, putting your hands into the clay, brings a humility and an anchoring. I think that's important to my work. That's where the variation comes from. We make pieces, we also work with fracture, because fracture is important. We all carry cracks, fissures, so Florence and I use that a lot. But it's also the fire, the flames create a lot of variety, we work with the elements.

AR: Perhaps for both of you, Calum with what you were saying about a new syntax, and Benjamin with working with a form that is at once very contemporary and very ancient, there is something of a parallel with the end of the 19th century and beginning of the 20th, with free verse and the search for a new syntax that still required an immersion in the old syntax. It's not that what was trying to be expressed previously was necessarily misdirected but that certain forms had become stale. What do you think about this parallel between physical and digital form and the words themselves? It's quite a thing to invent a new syntax, it can't come out of nowhere.

BG: I'll just reply quickly, I'm sure Calum has a lot to say on this. I have written poems my whole life, but I started writing in a very different way after returning from a long period of travel. We have travelled a lot, in the Amazon, through India… we came back from a three-month journey through India and I was writing but I didn't know what genre I was writing. I didn't know if it was a travel account, a letter, a novel… I had no idea. I gave it to a few people to read and they said it was poetry. At that point I began to voraciously read contemporary poetry and I said to myself, well, actually, it's true, the syntax I have here is modern poetry. And I began to be interested in free verse, especially by way of contemporary Iranian poets, who are fascinating in their move from very tight, traditional verses into free verse. I think about it the way I think about jazz. The classic metre, the alexandrine, can be as uninteresting to me as a nursery rhyme. It's always the same thing, la la la, la la la, la la la, la la la, it's boring. Whereas jazz permits variation and complexity. I work on it as though I were playing jazz.

CR: I guess it all goes back to finding new ways to say things. To go back to the great Gertrude Stein… of course she has the famous line 'a rose is a rose is a rose'. And she's not a fool, she knows people don't go around saying 'a cup is a cup is a cup' or whatever, but she says of that line it's the first time that a rose has been red in English poetry in over a hundred years. All we're trying to do is to say what we want to say with a freshness. Without falling back into those same tralala rhythms. That's what experiment with form, pushing things, whether into sculpture or into digital media, is driving towards.

AR: In response to that, I want to put a question to you that's perhaps a bit provocative, considering that words are your daily bread… what about the limits of language? The actual expressive limit of words, the fact that there is always something that words fail to say. How do you think, consciously or unconsciously, that the limitations of language have pushed you towards combining it with other forms and going beyond the words themselves?

CR: Again I'd go back to Finlay here. Very early on in his career he said, 'how can one write tree and mean tree?' That's the great dilemma all poets face. The dream of the poet is to be like Adam in the garden of Eden, to name a thing and for it to be the thing, the perfect correspondence between word and thing. Which is of course a myth, an impossibility. Yet that very impossibility is the dream that motivates poets. The reason we'll never get to that point is because language is inherently ambiguous, but the irony is without ambiguity the poetry couldn't happen at all. So in that purist reading, poetry is the articulation of a failure. A constant kind of 'failing better'. It's based on a dream.

BG: I think all poetry leads to the poet. Which means we carry an inheritance. Writing in the 21st century we come after the experience of Arthur Rimbaud. Which is complicated. The life of the poet is at stake . His happiness. At twenty, like Rimbaud, I was ready to die if I could not find the poetic word which was able to say the world. But in the end I found the most poetic thing there is, which is not words but life. I had the chance to have what Rimbaud never had, love and happiness. Which has involved hard times, wounds, many things – life – but I am a 'happy consciousness'. I think this is very important. Despite misfortunes, despite tragedy – I lost my daughter last year – it is important to feel happiness and to go beyond Rimbaud's experience. The poet also counts in the poetry. And poetry does not only exist as words.

CR: That's a beautiful thing. It's that idea of anchoring we've been talking about. For all the play, the syntax and all the rest of it, it all comes back to consciousness, and us beings trying to communicate and express ourselves. It's a beautiful and important thing to remember, in all these games we play.

BG: To finish on a lighter note, and to continue the idea of poetry being more than words... I think that there is something very poetic in pottery. It's a favourite theme of Iranian poets, you can also find it in the Bible and many classical sources. But there's something else which is very important, especially as I am French, and that's cooking. The publication of my book *Forgotten Metropolis* was aided by an incredible act of support from a three-Michelin-starred restaurant, Bras, which helped the printing to extend to a thousand copies and bought a good number of them. That was a great opportunity, of course, but it was also an opportunity for me to meet the people who run the restaurant, and when I see how they cook... they're the really poetic artists.

AR: This leads in well to one final question: what opportunities should poets in the 21st century look for if they want to collaborate and present their work internationally?

BG: As I've been saying, encounters with people who are not necessarily poets are important. I went on a toucan hunt with the Boni people, deep in the Amazon. It was a poetic experience which greatly affected me. So travel is definitely important. But in terms of other experiences, it's also important to connect with other disciplines. Collaboration with actors or with musicians, with great chefs...

CR: Filmmakers...

BG: ...even in ceramics it's possible to break disciplinary boundaries. Take yourself among ceramicists, actors, musicians, chefs... even simply among toucan hunters in the Amazon.

CR: I absolutely agree... it's fascinating that you have the patronage of this restaurant. In the live events that I run, the poetry readings and so on, so much of it is just about community. Good food and good wine makes the poetry better. Again it goes back to the consciousnesses behind the poems, that community and that connection. And... we've been talking about form, and form is political. Different forms have their own cultural associations and so on. It's too easy for poets to shut themselves within one trend, whether that's performance poetry, avant-garde poetry, lyric poetry... it becomes stratified very easily. Certainly for me it's important to remember that it's all poetry and it all has the potential to be good. To not fall into the patterns of a particular milieu. To create community but not to be stratified by that.

AR: By the doctrine of genre.

CR: Exactly.

AR: Thank you so much for joining us today.

CR: It's been a pleasure to meet you, I've enjoyed our chat very much.

BG: I think we've been able to have a real dialogue, it's a pleasure to meet you. I think the idea of a French-Scottish connection has definitely been brought to life... I see that the context and the vision of a poet in France and a poet in Scotland, in the 21st century, are not so different.

*Benjamin's words were translated by
Andrew Rubens.*

Grasping at

Lars Horn

The seat was that kind you often get in waiting rooms: overly square, as if it had been made out of Lego and then scaled-up for human size. It was one big 'L' shape. Two blocks of foam had been screwed into squares of MDF to form a seat and a backrest. These, in turn, had been screwed into a metal frame. The foam was upholstered in a synthetic material designed to look like cotton but which looked like acrylic trying to look like cotton. It was a browny-orange colour. All the other seats were blue – same shape and size – but blue. Newer. The browny-orange one had holes where people had pulled out bits of foam. And it had polished hard little black discs on it; some were a sort of coffee colour. They looked like plastic studs except where a couple had been smeared or picked at – then you could see it was gum.

You hadn't wanted to sit on the chair but all the others were taken; and it's not done – you can't just stand when there's a seat free. Or, if you did, you'd have to make a show of being disgusted by the seat so that the other people knew you weren't odd: you were like them; you knew how to pick your seats. But then, if you did that, you'd risk looking a right stuck-up bastard, a 'too-good-for-this-seat' kind of bastard. And especially if they missed the bit where you made as if to sit down and then stopped. If they missed that, and then they looked up and saw you standing next to a chair, right next to it but not sitting on it, that's an odd thing to do. You don't do that in a waiting room. Problem is, all this has been going through your head as you look down at the chair. If you had just stopped at the doorway, then you could have got away with leaning on the wall. You would have passed for the doesn't-give-a-damn type. You would have been the one no-one will look at.

But you didn't do that.

You came in, right up to the chair; and then you saw the gum and the stains and the hairs clinging to it; and you thought for too long about not sitting down, so now everyone knows that you are of the nice gives-a-damn variety. You are the one everyone looks at. You breathe in. You sit down and don't look up. You position yourself halfway on the seat and clench your thighs so that they are half off the fabric. The dust from the chair you're sitting on is catching in the sunlight. It reminds you of the images on cigarette packets, the ones of tar-coated organs. The chair is like that: filthy-sick lungs giving up the fight.

You think. You list types of waiting rooms: the doctor's, the dentist's, Accident and Emergency. You rank them. You've never liked the doctor's. All your doctors' clinics have been in converted Edwardian or Regency houses. Normally you like period buildings, but in this context everything feels unclean. The rooms are carpeted and strangely warm. The bay window frames are always flaking; and the putty is always thick with mould. The damp makes you feel uneasy. It makes you think of spores. The other sick people make you feel uneasy. You don't want to exchange air. Whereas the dentist – that's better. You aren't necessarily ill if you're at the dentist. And anyway, you can't catch what people go to the dentist for. At least you don't think so. You don't want to know if you can. You like the smell of dentists' waiting rooms; it's somewhere between mouthwash and disinfectant. You put the dentist's above the doctor's. You think about the Accident and Emergency waiting room.

It's a difficult one. As far as infections go, it's not too bad. You might see a lot of blood or limping but that doesn't bother you. It's the people who look okay that make you uneasy. They remind you of the Outpatient Department – of how everyone looks fine but that's because whatever is wrong with them is on the inside. They're here for blood samples and test results and morning verruca clinics. You also don't like how the seats have wipe-clean covers. You know it's better that they do but it makes you think of what has to get wiped-clean. You stop thinking about the Outpatient Department. You don't want to walk those corridors. You think about Accident and Emergency again.

The strange thing about A&E is the time element. You never know how long you'll be waiting. Not even roughly. The shortest you have waited was fifteen minutes. You had sprained your hand, and required a routine X-ray to check for breaks and fractures. The longest you have waited is four and a half hours. A ten-foot workbench had fallen on your left leg. You were wearing shoes and trousers but it had degloved your shin and taken off your toenails. You remember sitting with a towel under your leg and it turning red, then brown. You remember watching a television. The television was suspended from the ceiling by a metal bracket. It was in the far corner of the waiting room. There was no sound. A hospital drama was playing. A man was rushed into the operating theatre. The editing cut rapidly between shots of scalpels and heart monitors and pumps. Then the camera locked still on an angle shot of the heart monitor and the surgeon's face. The man died. You remember laughing. You knew it wasn't funny. You couldn't stop. You remember your mother telling you to be quiet. People were staring.

You try to think of other waiting rooms where time is as elastic as in A&E. Instead though, you see the room stretch and blur like when you pull a rubber band between your fingers. Then it snaps back how it was before – the blue chairs are solid and in-focus again. You realise that, actually, the quickest you ever went through A&E was when you were hit by a car. The paramedics wheeled you in on a stretcher. You wonder if there are other waiting rooms like that: ones that aren't only stretchy but can disappear altogether. You look around you. The dole office. You wonder how this waiting room compares with the other ones.

It doesn't feel like a proper waiting room. But then, it isn't: it's waiting room and destination combined. It is an open-plan office with chairs in the middle. The desks run along the walls of the room. They are separated into booths by plastic partitions. The windows in the building have been tinted. It's part of the personal privacy policy. You'd read a sign telling you so on the way in. The desks face into the room towards the blue chairs. There's a distance of about three yards between the chairs and the desks. If you concentrate, you can pick out what people are saying across the desks. Occasionally someone behind a desk calls out a name. They don't look up as they do this. At any given time, there are several unoccupied booths. It is difficult to discern which one the call came from. Already, several people have had their names shouted two or three times. Your name is not pronounced how it's spelled. You often don't recognise it when it's called out. You try not to hear the people in the booths; you listen for the names.

You re-focus your eyes and look at the twenty-page form you were given at the door. It's on recycled paper. It's a muddy yellow colour. The first page explains administrative procedure: *from the date of his / her claim, the applicant enters a two-week waiting period. During this period, the eligibility and value of a claim will be assessed. The claimant will not be allocated any form of unemployment benefit for this period regardless of his / her subsequent eligibility status.* You skip a paragraph. *If found eligible, the claimant must comply with the terms and conditions of the Jobseeker's Allowance scheme; failure to do so will result in the claim being nullified. By signing this document, the claimant agrees to be monitored for the duration of his / her claim. In the event of non-compliance, the claimant will find his / her allocation cancelled. In the event of any fraudulent information or activity the claimant will face prosecution.* You un-focus your eyes again. You turn the page. At the front desk they gave you a pen – one of the branded ones where you twist the top. The pen is advertising life insurance.

 title
 name
 age
 income – current, previous, estimated
 claims
 no claims
 risk of prosecution
 your rights
 more about you

This doesn't seem much about you to your mind. You want to yawn but you don't because you don't want people to be looking at you again. You start to fill out the form. You write neatly, use the oxford comma, a semi-colon. You pause. You look up. You wonder how far this form has travelled to get to you. You imagine the room radiating outwards: at the centre there's you and the other people on the foam seats, then there are the people behind the desks with the computers and the forms and the pens; but then, who is behind them? You would like to know if that's someone's job – thinking up the boxes and ticks and crosses of this form. You think what it would be like to do that job. Then you think what it would be like to decide who-gets-what-benefit. You're not sure you would apply for that job.

The pen starts to run out. You sigh. People look. You sit on the seat, properly this time: sink into the gum and the crust, press harder on the pen, and carry on.

How would you rate your grasp of English?

Below average

Proficient

Good

Excellent

You look at it. You look again. You don't know how to answer. You don't know whether they mean written, oral or aural. And you're unsure of the criteria. You suppose "Good" refers to Standard English but if so, you're unsure where that leaves "Excellent".

The question reminds you of a table you had once used. The table was designed to measure foreign language proficiency according to a standardised and transferable scale. The table was divided into three rows. The rows were respectively assigned the letters A, B, C. Each letter was subdivided into numbers. "Beginner" was classed as A1 and "Mastery" as C2. You think about the "C2" band and remember another table, this one from secondary school. There were graduated bands in this table too. But these bands were subdivided into age groups. There were three columns: reading, writing, speaking and listening. Everyone in the class was sixteen. The age groups in the table ranged from "9-11 years" to "25+ years". When you were studying Samuel Beckett, you remember someone saying: how do you think that mad bastard would fair on the literacy table?

You think this and you stop.

You leave the question blank.

You sign and date the back, click the pen down and let the form flop in your lap. You think what it would feel like to grasp a language. You pick at the foam. You imagine rolling words between your fingers like that. You shift on the chair and watch the dust spiral out.

*

It's wet. You are in a field. The ground is waterlogged. Everything flattens into monochrome. The grass isn't blades or green anymore; it's a measure of wetness – the water it leaves over your hand, the soak of it into your shoes. And the trees and the fences – those wood textures – they've become degrees of damp, leaving your coat and trousers clammy and clinging. The edges of you are dissolving. You are having trouble thinking you had once been something separate. Instead, you wonder which degree of damp are you in this landscape. Have you become the same shade as the trees yet? Or the brambles? Or are you given-in enough to join the ground? Would your limbs let themselves be ploughed into the mud, decompose into elements and break down? Calcium, magnesium, oxygen, carbon, the lot. Off you go now, yes that's it, metal-mineral smells and bits of fat tickling through the mud. Carbon. Yes, off you go. If you bury the eyes now, and fill the ears, yes, fill those up – yes, wet enough now. Carbon, that's the one, the founding stone, but what does it matter now? Why do you keep wondering how wet you are? What an odd thing to wonder. Bed further down; it's warm here, down here in the ground. The earth takes you through itself. You swallow it. Things rearrange themselves – move in and out. You grasp at where grass and air should be; you feel for the edge of yourself. But in this geography, none of that makes sense.

One of the desks calls your turn.

Now, if I could just check the forms we requested you to complete. Right, that's all in order, except here – you appear to have skipped a question; you'll need to tick a box before we can move on.

Blame

Lily Greenall

Ellie sat in a booth in the corner of the pub, picking at crisps and sipping a vodka and coke. From this angle, she had a clear side view of the stage. The boys strutted between the amps, fenced in by mic stands and skipping over the wires that snaked about their feet. The music was loud and the booth vibrated slightly. She thought Jake's vocals sounded flat. Ellie would be singing with them after the break. No one was out yet on the sticky dancefloor. Most of the people in the pub were gathered at the bar. Ellie drained her glass, washing down a wave of crumbs. People always danced when she went on. She made the band sound more like music. She glanced at the door, that swung inwards every now and then on a gust of the strong island wind, looking out for Melanie. She chewed the inside of her mouth and picked at a hole in the seat cushion, wondering if she could risk going to the bar by herself. She was underage by a few months but Donny, the manager, turned a blind eye because he liked her singing. She was the only reason people came to see the band, he said. He let her drink as long as one of the boys bought it for her, and as long as she didn't get drunk enough to attract attention. Jake had bought her the double vodka but she felt bored and awkward sitting alone and wished that she could have another. It helped her on stage if she was tipsy. Not drunk, she wouldn't be able to control her voice then, but if she was woozy and merry then the crowd seemed to respond. Donny said he liked it when she swung her hips in time with the music. It got the customers excited. Ellie didn't think it went with the music though. It was rock. It was meant to be angry and dangerous. She always wore lots of eyeliner for her shows and sprayed her hair with dry shampoo so that if she scrubbed her hands through it it would stand up.

Donny was behind the bar. She could see him towering head and shoulders above the men slumped at the counter. He had a big square head and a pot belly that somehow made him look strong rather than fat. He was leaning back against the side with his arms folded and watching the band with a sceptical frown. She got the feeling that he didn't like the boys much but tolerated them because they brought in custom on a wet Saturday night. He'd never serve her if she went up. The other woman, Donna, might, or she might serve Melanie if Melanie was dressed up properly. If Melanie ever arrived. She rifled through her hand bag and pulled out her phone but there were no missed calls and it was only quarter to ten. Across the room, in the opposite booth, a bunch of young men were watching her.

She didn't recognize them which meant that they had probably come in off the trawlers. They sat in a semi-circle in the booth, hunched over and nursing pints. Every few minutes they glanced at Ellie. The man in the centre of the booth, the only one facing her directly, was wearing an Iron Maiden t-shirt and she thought he looked vaguely familiar.

She wondered if he had come up from Harris. He had long hair that had been dyed with streaks of purple. It hadn't taken properly with the colour of his hair though and made it look dirty and grey. She didn't like his face. It was gaunt and long in the jaw.

He was staring at her constantly and whenever she caught his eye he gave her a crocodile grin. When he spoke a ripple of laughter ran through the group. Ellie glanced at the door hoping again to see Melanie. She pulled her sleeve over her fist and swiped her hand down either side of her mouth, rubbing for stains. It was beginning to creep into her mind that the men might have noticed something wrong with how she looked. She was wearing dark lipstick for the first time outside of her bedroom. She and Melanie had gone to Superdrug at lunchtime and Melanie had come out with the two bullet shaped containers hidden up her sleeve. Cherry Red for Melanie, Aubergine Midnight for Ellie. Ellie thought that Aubergine Midnight sounded like a horror movie about a night when vegetables attacked. Melanie said it sounded like a porno and the two had giggled helplessly, clinging to each other's arms as they traipsed back to the school. They tried the colours on in the girl's bathrooms, kicking all the stall doors first to make sure they were alone. Melanie was better at putting hers on than Ellie was. When Melanie did it she sculpted two perfect little waves on her top lip. She turned her face from side to side, admiring herself in the gum flecked glass. Ellie's lipstick was a lovely, shady purple but she applied it too thickly and it ended up making her mouth look sloppy, like a clown's. Melanie then decided she wanted to trade as she said that Cherry Red sounded like lipstick that a slut would wear. Ellie refused. She was in a band, she said; she needed to look hard.

She dabbed at her mouth again and looked at her sleeve for marks but her top was black and she couldn't tell. She could go to the bathroom but she might miss Mel, and besides, getting up would mean walking across the empty dancefloor alone, in full view of the men. Although Ellie was not shy, the thought of this put her on edge. Even sitting huddled in the booth, she felt strangely exposed now that she had noticed them. The band were playing a song that she liked and she sat up slightly and nodded along. Jake was messing up the vocals. She watched him lean up to the mic and close his eyes, straining to catch a high note. He thought that he was very cool and good looking, she could tell. He cast a smug glance around the bar and did something clever with his strings, turning to grin at the bassist.

'Ellie!' Melanie was tottering across the bar towards her.

She was wearing huge platforms that made her bare legs look spindly, sticking out beneath a winter coat. Her hair was mussed with the wind and she wasn't wearing her lipstick. Her eyelids were heavy with a pair of thick, fake lashes. Ellie thought enviously that her older sister must have helped her put them on.

'Why are you sitting by yourself?' Melanie yelled over the music, scrambling into the booth, 'I want a drink.'

'Me too,' Ellie cried.

Melanie shuffled further along the bench and turned sideways, leaning over her bag.

She unzipped it and revealed the red cap of a vodka bottle. Grinning at Ellie, she slid the empty glass down from the table and onto the seat between them. She poured a shot into the glass and handed it to Ellie under the table. Ellie ducked behind her and swallowed it. She came back up wincing and Melanie waved at her to pass the glass back. They performed the ritual once more, Ellie leaning forwards this time, peeking furtively around. Donny was leaning on the bar talking to a woman with glossy red hair. In the opposite booth, the young men laughed. The noise almost rose above the music.

Ellie sat back and Melanie reappeared, patting down her hair.

'Let's get some cokes to mix it with,' she said.

'We won't get served,' Ellie shook her head, 'Donny says I'm to stay away from the bar.'

Melanie curled her top lip, 'Even for softies?'

'Yeah. You might get served but if they ID you you'll get kicked out.'

Melanie pursed her lips and looked thoughtful.

'There's Dan Hearadh over there,' she said, 'He's staring at me.'

He's staring at me Ellie wanted to say, but she stayed quiet and nodded.

'I bet he'd buy me a drink,' Melanie said.

Now that she knew she was being watched there was a showy exaggeration to her movements. Her smile was wider than before and she arched her back, sitting up straight.

'I'll see if he can get you one too. Let's go sit with them.'

Melanie darted out from the booth and began to teeter across the dancefloor. She stood in front of Dan, blocking him from view. Ellie could see the surrounding men looking her up and down. Melanie giggled a lot as she talked. It seemed as if everything she said was hilarious from the way her shoulders shook. She flipped her hair as she pointed back at Ellie. Ellie watched as Melanie wriggled out of her coat and felt a combination of envy and embarrassment as she revealed a tight, thigh high dress underneath.

Dan didn't move but one of the guys on the end of the circle rose and lumbered away towards the bar. Melanie hovered for a moment. She turned and, seeing that Ellie was still sitting down, rolled her eyes. Ellie rose reluctantly and made her way across the floor, horribly conscious that she was walking in time with the song that was playing. She could feel her face starting to burn and hoped that this would not show up under the pub's dim lights.

'This is Ellie,' Melanie squealed, snatching Ellie by the elbow and dragging her forwards to stand in front of the group, 'She's singing with the band.'

Dan was looking at Ellie across the table top. There was something mismatched about his face, she thought, like the two sides had been fitted together wrong. His nose was long and unforgivingly crooked, as though it had been broken. One of his eyes seemed to stare out while the other sunk back into shadow.

He said something to the man sitting beside him and the man shuffled to one side, making room on the bench.

Dan patted the space and nodded to Ellie.

She blinked and glanced at Melanie, who had now dropped Ellie's arm and was leaning back, giggling at something the man on the end of the bench had said. Dan waved at her, shuffling over himself this time so that there was a large space in the centre of the booth. Clutching the ends of her sleeves, Ellie picked her way over the other men's legs, bending awkwardly to squeeze around the table, and slotted herself in beside Dan. Melanie, who had now perched on the very end of the bench, shot her an offended glance. The band were coming to the end of their set. Two or three more songs and they would be off for the break.

There was a smell of smoke coming from Dan's clothes and Ellie felt a squeamish twinge as his knee brushed against hers. He didn't look at her now that she was there. Instead, he turned his eyes to the stage and sipped his pint. The man who had gone up to the bar came back and a drink was handed round to her. Ellie watched as Melanie downed hers in one, screwed up her face and shook her head with a laugh. The men let up a murmur of approval. Ellie tasted her own drink. It was too strong and she lowered it quickly from her mouth. Dan, who was watching her now, smirked. She noticed suddenly that his eyes were different colours. The one that seemed to push forwards was a ghostly pale blue, the other was beady and dark.

'You're singing for us, tonight are you?'

Ellie nodded.

'How about after?' he said, 'You going to come back to mine?'

Head spinning slightly from the drinks, Ellie said, 'Where's yours?'

'Not far,' he said, grinning at the others.

Ellie shrugged, 'Maybe.'

She wanted to seem cool and non-committal. She tried to take another sip from her drink but it had a burning, chemical taste. She noticed that the other men were watching her and she began to regret sitting down, feeling suddenly penned in. Melanie had wandered off and was talking to some girls clustered on the dance floor. They made their way in a pack to the bar, Melanie weaving slightly and taking clumpy steps in her high heeled shoes.

Ellie took a deep breath into her diaphragm; the type she would take before singing a high note. She was just drunk enough to go on stage. Her head was light and her face was hot but her movements were still clean and alert. She felt very calm, as though she was looking down at herself, floating above the scene.

The band were striking up the first bars of the last song. Ellie pushed herself up and made to clamber out of the booth.

'Hey, hey!'

She whipped round as Dan's hand closed about her wrist, tugging her back down. She dropped onto the bench, startled. All the men around the table were suddenly looking off in different directions or had their eyes glued to their phones.

'Where are you going? Stay till the end of the set.'

'I've got to get ready...' she protested.

'Drink your drink,' he said.

'I don't want it.'

The band were careering through the final song.

'It's Saturday night! Come on, drink up!'

He sidled closer to her and she found herself recoiling, bumping against the man on the other side. He glanced round and looked right through her – as if she was air, as if she was nothing. Ellie felt almost like laughing. Dan was lurching towards her, the smoke smell pouring from between his squint yellow teeth, his blue eye flashing.

'Come on,' Dan cajoled, 'Drink up. Just a waste otherwise.'

Ellie looked at the glass and half expected to see it steaming, the traces of some unctuous poison evaporating on the surface like a scene from one of the vampire novels she liked.

The music ended abruptly, three swift crashes on the cymbal. Jake muttered 'thank you' into the mic and began to unsling his guitar. Ellie watched him hopefully as he hopped off stage. He didn't look over and was immediately surrounded by the small group of girls, Melanie among them.

Dan slid his arm around her now. A sour stench of sweat reached her from his armpit.

'She's staying with me tonight boys,' he teased, dragging her close.

She squirmed, feeling her hair mussed as she slipped down on the seat, trying to slide out of his grip. He wrapped both arms around her and pulled her back against his chest. Ellie was half laughing now, little spurts of indignation escaping as she tried to free herself. His t-shirt felt slightly damp as she felt herself pressed against it. He loosened his hold enough so that she was able to break away and she sat for a second smoothing her hair and, quickly, mentally, putting herself back together. She cast a look round the table. To her surprise, the other men were considering their pints or looking off towards the bar. Near the stage she saw Melanie and Jake laughing together.

Dan was slithering towards her on the seat once more, a sardonic smile on his lips.

'No,' Ellie spoke firmly, as though she were addressing a dog, 'Stop it.'

'Oh come on, what are you worried about?'

She felt an irresistible pressure on the back of her head as her face was forced forwards. She realised with a jolt that her face was being pushed into the crotch of Dan's jeans. She breathed in an acrid scent that she associated suddenly and overwhelmingly with 'maleness.' A low cheer rose up from the surrounding men. Dan's hands were over her ears and, though he was no longer pushing very hard, her nose brushed against denim.

'Oh hey, hey, hey! What's this?' a jovial male voice cut through the jeers.

Ellie jerked herself upright and saw that Donny was leaning over the table, red faced and chuckling. She looked at him and made a noise that felt like a laugh but sounded more like a bark. It was shrill and utterly mirthless.

'None of that in here,' Donny sang teasingly, eyes dancing between Ellie and Dan with a wary look, 'This is not an after-hour's club. This one's got to get onstage.'

The men on the benches moved aside now and Donny caught Ellie's upper arm and pulled her out of the booth and onto her feet.

'What are you doing bothering these lads?' Donny teased, swiping a clump of hair from her face and tugging her sweater by the shoulders, tweaking it where it had rumpled, 'You're trouble you are. I've got my eye on you. Better get over to the stage. Don't forget, wiggle your hips.'

He held his hands up at chest height in two loose fists and gave his own thick hips a little shake, raising an eyebrow at her. Ellie floated back across the room feeling as though she was in a dream. Part of her was still laughing, in fact she was making little sounds, and another part of her was looking around the room in stunned disbelief. She couldn't believe that all these people had seen what had happened and that none of them had thought it even remotely strange. Perhaps it wasn't, she thought. With another little laugh, she thought, how utterly ridiculous!

She reached the stage where Jake and Melanie were standing. Jake was drinking a beer, Melanie a greenish drink in a tall glass. Jake raised his eyebrows at her and said, 'Ready?'

She nodded and Jake loped away towards the stage.

Melanie was giving her a cool, suspicious look down the end of her nose.

'What were you doing to Dan?' she asked.

'Nothing,' Ellie shook her head, 'Can I have some?'

She held out her hand. Melanie shrugged and handed over the glass, lip curled as though she was looking at something faintly repellent. Ellie ignored her and took a long slurp through Melanie's straw. The drink tasted of lime and Ellie felt bubbles crowd her nose. She gasped, handing it back to Melanie, then hurried up the steps onto the stage. Jake had moved back a few paces to clear a space at the front for her. Craig jogged back across the pub from the bathrooms and hopped up behind the drum kit. Ellie shuffled forwards and switched her mic on. She craned up slightly to murmur 'one, two; one two' into it. Her lips brushed the plastic mesh. Behind her the boys were tuning up with a series of discordant strokes. She glanced down at the room and felt a little, muted thrill as she saw that more women had arrived and were gathering on the dancefloor, grinning up at her with drinks in hand. She smiled shyly and wiped her sleeve over her mouth, trying to get rid of her lipstick which she was sure must have smudged by now. She didn't care now though. A numb yet strangely buoyant feeling was coming over her. She felt light and disconnected from the room, from her body, and the people spreading out below her. In the side booth, she saw Dan smirking into the crowd. Donny, back behind the bar, gave her a nod and wiggled his hips. Ellie was glad that she was about to sing. When she sang she didn't have to think about anything. She glanced over her shoulder at Jake. He nodded at her, to the bassist, and then back at Craig. They struck up the first chord in unison. A shrill whoop went up from the crowd and, soaring now, Ellie began to sing.

Baudelopark, Ghent

Richie McCaffery

The days pass now and rarely
even make eye contact with me.

Old buildings are being knocked down
and faceless flats rise in their place.

If I sit on this bench long enough
someone might make a project of me.

Pigeons peck at a hunk of stale bread
like they're sculpting with hunger.

It's raining, always raining. I'm wet.
I stick out my tongue, it stays dry.

Everyone around me is speaking Flemish
as if my life's a TV that was switched off

suddenly and switched back on again
with a different language setting.

There's a tree branch in the wind knocking
against someone's window, like one

of those tedious people you get at parties
who flick glasses to see if they're crystal.

I'm waiting for the tree's verdict:
is this all for real?

Jellyfish

Nathan Breakenridge

Wasn't much to see
after the fact;
a thing like a burst blister
left to dry on the pebbles.

But that's where it happened.
No trace now but that dead thing
to mark where she waded out.

As if they'd swapped places.

Polymer

Rebecca Parker

Don't the new five pound notes always look clean?
Resisting sweat stains from hands that part with them,
swap them for a four pack of Tesco Finest beans:
tomato acid stripping off the tin insides to give your lunch
that desirable metallic toxicity.

Spring-loaded strong paper substitute,
won't sit still in my purse like compliant cotton paper,
uncreasable, untearable, plastic bags in a toilet bowl,
circulating, in and out of vaults,
reproducing clones that leave empty fly larvae shells
wherever they land
until all we hold
are crumbling exoskeletons
of things that ate through our pockets.

All those hundreds of fine etched lines,
iridescent fibres,
bright hue of delicate blue:
such refinement in this currency
we can wear it as costume jewellery
like Bill and Josella in their finery
as the very streets disintegrate.

Containerization

Samuel Tongue

A ship earns money only when she's at sea.
— Malcom Purcell McLean

everything is here   iPhones and drones   a
thousand dud dolls
rolls of AstroTurf   smurf calendars coloured pencils   penicillin
silicone muffin trays   ways of clearing up spots   dry rot [in the
flat-pack cabinet]   nets – *phishing and inter* –   winter boots for the
huntsmen in the bananas sultanas dramas made for tv a
refugee curled around the tight toasters warming on her
own breath death masks for museums reams of blank
paper   draper's dummies gummy bears in a million
colours and flavours favours for rich CEOs everything
pitching in the ocean's swell like a fat ark hive of
everything we value and don't   the globe shrunk to a
plastic glob of efficient intermodal

Justin Bieber slowed down by 800 percent sounds like a celestial being

Colin McGuire

Just one, of Adonis, of Ganymede
carved from maple wood, dipped in sun-honey,
a chiselled, Michelangelo glory.
Oiled Greek torso, anointed one, our seed.
Sculptural, hard to deny, to concede
your body, your bright tones, your effigy
praised by all holy, scaling heavenly
high melismas, blessed with a strength we need.
But the Gods graced the world wise with your youth,
YouTubed it, captured every flippant gaze,
lost soon in the mirror like Narcissus.
A young boy warped by his own hard-earned proof,
feuds of ego and immaturity,
poor twenty-first century Juvenis.

Porty-Belly, Portobello

Max Scratchmann

Valentine's Vista-rama seaside village
Trying so hard not to acknowledge
Its hunchbacked twin,
Amputated at birth
Along your bloodless and leafy streets,
A Tuck's True-Colour postcard collage of
Strident voices along your sweltering prom,
Timothy, I won't tell you again, do we need to take a little time out?
Whit? Five pounds fura pint? C'moan, we'll get cans...
As the somersaulting circus parade
Tumbles by your melange of grand houses
Rubbing reluctant shoulders with cheap-brick council flats,
Pram-pushing yummy mummies with
Hessian carrier bags chinking with Sainsbury's ready-chilled whites
Talking fasting and fad-diets over marshmallow treats,
No Waitrose yet, but we're working on it,
While the new Aldi, like a sinister shadow, creeps up silently in the background
Cheek-by-jowl with cinnamon-scented artisan bakeries and white-walled cappuccino houses,
Bucket-and-spade shops and discount chemists smiling down on
Laughing lines of silver-eyed Polish girls striking out along the prom,
Plastic bags bulging with tin foil barbecue stoves and own-brand larger,
Timothy, stop that, I won't tell you again...
Art walks and guided talks,
Whole food stores and spit-and-sawdust bars entangled with
Methodist churches fund-raising for refugees
Here in Edinburgh's non-partisan seaside,
Her welcoming arms open to all and sundry,
The tired, the poor,
The huddled masses yearning to breathe free,
The wretched refuse of the teeming shore.
Timothy, I think we need to talk...

Fish Counter

Samuel Tongue

Fish that have a pebble in their heads; Fish that hide in winter;
Fish that feel the influence of stars; Extraordinary prices paid for certain fish.
      — Pliny. *The Natural History*

Cod that have been skinned. Cod that have a pebble
of sage butter in their heads. Cod breaded. Cod battered;
tempura or traditional. Breaded haddock. Battered haddock.
Wise lumps of raw tuna. Scaled, pin-boned pollock, de-scented.
There *are* olfactory limits. Bake in the bag; no mess.
'This piece of halibut...' etc. Fishsticks pink as lads' mags.
Fish fingers mashed from fragments of once-fish. Hake
three-ways. *Extraordinary prices paid for certain fish.*
Monkfish defrocked, gurnards gurning, fish so ugly
you must eat them blindfold. It's Friday; get 'em frying.

Walls

Stewart Sanderson

*'We're going to build a wall. And
it's going to be a real wall. And it's
going to get built fast. And it's
going to be beautiful.'*
                    — Donald Trump

This world of ours contains so many walls
and some, not all of them, are beautiful.
Though new walls rise, sometimes an old wall falls.
No wall is ever insurmountable.

Think of those walls the Romans built, to keep
a race of painted horrors out of sight
and mind, so their imperium could sleep
safe from the howling in the northern night.

Those walls protected no one, at the end.
Today they run, reduced, from hill to hill
through central Scotland and Northumberland.
They have a certain broken beauty still.

Imagine looking down from outer space
towards the Great Wall, which kept back the horde
till it was time for Peking to replace
the old regime with some new overlord.

These days a wall of fire invisibly
encircles China, keeping Google out.
The worst walls aren't always the ones you see.
The highest walls of all are walls of thought.

Waking in Grez

Stewart Sanderson

I wake in France, an hour ahead
and seven hundred miles from where
you sleep on in your Scottish bed:
the far recipient of my care.

For you it isn't quite today
as I check headlines on my phone.
Swaddled in smirr and woodsmoke, Grez
brightens: a blear of old, wet stone.

A whole year since *les attentats*
shook Paris, says *Le Figaro*.
Breakfast is *pain-au-chocolat*
and Trump is on the radio.

Across the Loing, November woods
disclose denuded, leafless bowers.
It seems that nothing very good
has happened in the last eight hours.

For you there's still some time to dream
as Glasgow floods with light: a low
glimmering wave, which ebbs like cream
through black coffee; a wintry glow.

For me it's time to take a shower
then try to write reality:
the vast vulgarity of power;
the falling short of poetry.

Taste and See

Elizabeth Rimmer

A tomato should be warm,
the skin loose as on a granny's hands,
fine as satin, but electric bright
with hoarded sun, a blaze.
The scent of that twiggy stalk
will cling to your hands all day

Your knife must be sharp.
When the edge is only a little blunt
the silky skin puckers and the cut
is ragged, the flesh bruised,
and all the sweet fluid lost.
You pierce the skin, and slice.

Red circles fall under your hands.
Seeds cling to the core, suspended
in a jelly carapace, a swim of juice.
Salt grains, fragments of crushed
black pepper, sweet balsamic sting
of dressing – summer on a plate.

The pigeon's eyes had been pecked out, and a crow sat two or three feet away, seeming to think about how to eat the pigeon or perhaps wondering what else could be pecked from the body or the small world around it. We watched all this from the office window and agreed on our moral disgust before turning back to the spreadsheets and deciding to intervene at lunchtime. By the time we got around to it the pigeon had developed a fairly terrible neck wound that whistled as it laboured its breathing.

The Pigeon

Chris Kohler

The Pigeon

Chris Kohler

The pigeon's eyes had been pecked out, and a crow sat two or three feet away, seeming to think about how to eat the pigeon or perhaps wondering what else could be pecked from the body or the small world around it. We watched all this from the office window and agreed on our moral disgust before turning back to the spreadsheets and deciding to intervene at lunchtime. By the time we got around to it the pigeon had developed a fairly terrible neck wound that whistled as it laboured its breathing. We dropped a large book, a dictionary I think, on the crow and as I ran to the corner shop to buy a couple of pints of milk for the coffees and teas I could hear the sound of my workmates repeating a few truisms and proverbs about the strong defending the weak.

I took the dust jacket off the dictionary and ran it under the tap before drying it off and running back to my desk.

'The pigeon is disgusting,' the boss said.

'No no, the pigeon is not,' we said.

'Why is it wheezing?' he asked.

'It is weary,' we said.

We sellotaped a biro to the pigeon's wing and set it to work. It was very lazy which could have been to do with the neck wound. We sellotaped the neck wound and it seemed to perk up a little.

When we returned in the morning, it looked like the pigeon had tried to turn itself inside out. All the sellotape was lying loose on the desk with a few feathers stuck to it. The pigeon was trembling and burrowing its head along the top line of a computer keyboard. QWERTY, it said on the screen.

'We didn't realise you were qualified!' the boss said, and he set up a spreadsheet for the pigeon to work on. After an hour a joke occurred to me, I took out the notebook which I keep for these occasions and drafted a few versions of it. It took an afternoon of hard work, in which I had to put on my glasses, before I stood and said, 'We might need to change the name of the *human resources* department.' Everyone began to laugh and I noticed that the joke was being repeated by several of my colleagues. I was concerned that my work would go unnoticed, so I walked through to the boss's office to claim ownership. On hearing my joke the boss congratulated me and said, 'I didn't realise you were qualified!' In my surprise I was quick to correct the boss, while joking is something I commit a good amount of time to, I would confine it to the private sphere of my life, for fear of committing some error which those qualified could view as an embarrassing and amateurish misunderstanding of their work. My boss agreed with me and commended me for my honesty, which I counted as being a sign of his favour. I marked it up as such in the page of my notebook I keep for such occasions.

By lunchtime, the pigeon had done some very disappointing work. His ceaseless typing had ruined the spreadsheet. 'You are an energetic sort, but you must use all the different keys,' I said. 'Ideas cannot be expressed with only one letter, or they would all come out the same. What else separates a friendly *chat* from a friendly *cat*?' A look of horror crossed the face of my colleagues as I had forgotten the pigeon's natural enmity with the cat. However, I did not apologise. Although history weighs upon our actions at every turn, I believe (naively perhaps) in the possibility of individual agency. I decided to illustrate my position with a visual cue and began to search through the drawers of my desk for the birthday balloons that I am in possession of. As I searched, a curious group of my co-workers formed around me.

'A history of oppression cannot be merely shrugged off,' said one. 'And if violence begets violence, does the pigeon not have a right to its fury? The cat can expect nothing else.'

'Assuming the pigeon is furious...'

My colleagues turned to the pigeon, which kept its own counsel.

I blew some air into the balloon until it was half-inflated, I tied the end and began to squeeze alternating sides of it.

'If we imagine the repetitions of 'violence begetting violence' as the to and fro of my hands on this balloon. Are we not able to imagine the occurrence of a new event which breaks this cycle?'

On cue, the balloon blurted between my fingers, pushing a grotesque polyp between either deflated end. My illustration was perfectly timed. I held it up for my co-workers to see and the conversation stopped as they accepted my premise. I could no longer remember why I had been talking, so I propped the pigeon's chest on a stapler, to allow his wings some access to the keys. I closed the spreadsheet which he had ruined and opened a fresh one for him. 'Try to expand your ideas into the space which language allows,' I said. 'Your monotone is pleasant enough, but in the field of music this is considered irritating.' This allusion to music will mark me out as a man of culture to my fellows.

Although I had given the pigeon a full two days to come to some kind of understanding with our working methods, he had proved himself to be an unsuitable candidate. At home time, I waited at the exit for my co-workers to leave and fell into step with the designated 'prankster' of our office. This man is a complex and anarchistic sort, with whom I would normally have little dealings save laughing along with his various jokes and attacks. I proposed a prank on the pigeon for tomorrow morning and invited the prankster to my home to work through the particulars. We went to the stationary shop and bought a large notebook and a few marker pens, then to the takeaway restaurant for some boxes of that kind of food. We worked into the night and I believed we had become friends, ensuring some safety for myself against his incessant pranks.

Early the next morning, we tore the pigeon to pieces in the staff room and began to attach them to a discarded plant pot we had found in the strip of flowers and weeds which the council had recently created. We sellotaped the pigeon's head to the top of the upturned plant pot and punched holes in the side for the wings to fit into. We were giggling quietly as we attached the legs and ran a length of twine over the light fittings. 'What are you rascals up to?' the secretary asked and we laughed. We showed her the pigeon and the pulley system we had devised to allow it to fly again. She didn't find it very funny, but agreed that it may be a difference in the culture of our generations. She explained that people of her age preferred word play and the sight of others in misfortune to the shock tactics and surrealism of those under forty.

We were to wait until the end of the staff meeting that morning before letting the pigeon loose, to swing over the heads of our baffled colleagues. I worked in a distracted way that morning, owing to the smell of blood on my fingers and the sickness I felt in my stomach, possibly from having laughed too much the previous night.

When our boss called the staff meeting together, he began to talk about how we had forgotten all about the pigeon's historical function as a communicative device. An afternoon of searching on the Internet had returned some very interesting ideas, he said. Our phone system was notoriously unreliable, and recourse to some other method could be useful. In the eyes of our clients, our combination of tradition and innovation could mark us apart from our rivals. The boss then asked to see the pigeon. I tried to shake my head as widely as possible, but the prankster was so anarchistic!

'We will let you see him!' he said and ran towards the doorframe where we had tied the end of the twine. When the pigeon was released, it followed the prescribed arc perfectly, but as it swung towards us the knots seemed to loosen and the various parts of its body scattered into the boardroom where we were meeting. The manic laughter of the anarchist was broken only by his chants of my name. He pointed and directed all credit for the jape in my direction.

Thankfully my contract stated nothing about violence and cruelty towards co-workers, so the boss was restricted in his powers. As I wept, he began to strip me of certain duties and merits I had accumulated over my time there, naming each of them in turn. He then stepped towards me and tugged at my clothing. 'You will have to button your shirt to the top from now on,' he said. 'Causing discomfort to your Adams apple.'

I hung my head in shame and pulled the knot of my tie to the very top of my shirt. That afternoon, my co-workers were let out into the fields behind the office to scatter bread and attract a phalanx of new pigeons. There were many seagulls attracted to the bread, but no pigeons. I took it upon myself to travel into the city that night and capture a few pigeons. I tied them up in the plastic bag I had with me and took them back to the office. A few had died during the long bus journey. After travelling to the office and storing the remaining pigeons in my desk drawer, I stopped by the prankster's house and gave him the dead pigeons, knowing that he would find a use for them. I wouldn't have stopped at any other employee's house, seeing as it was past midnight, but the prankster was still awake, drinking alcohol and watching television as I had expected. He invited me in and we watched a few cartoons together and I laughed so much that he said 'You're drunk, I never thought you had it in you.'

I emphatically denied it, but due to the lateness of the hour I was slurring my speech and this only encouraged him in his accusations. As it apparently raised me in his esteem, I admitted (falsely) that I was drunk and asked him not to mention this to anyone else at the office. After a half hour of teasing, he agreed not to tell anyone. I joined him for 'one last drink', although it was the first drink I had ever had. After a short argument, I agreed to stay at his house, 'in your condition you won't make it back' he said. I agreed and lay down on the couch. As I was falling to sleep, the prankster nudged my foot and said, 'You can sleep in my bed.' As I opened my eyes, I saw a young woman standing in front of me with a blanket draped around her. It appeared he had woken his girlfriend and persuaded her to switch places with me. I thanked her for her hospitality and the prankster and I slept head to toe in his bed.

If only I had not agreed to it! His girlfriend woke in the morning and left early for her work. But the prankster and I slept long past working hours started. We woke and panicked, the prankster laughing the whole time. He was used to sneaking into the office at eleven or twelve o'clock. But he had been rendered immune to criticism by assuming the role of the jester, I explained. For me, this was a terrible occurrence!

And sure enough, when I arrived at the office I was promptly dismissed as the prankster shouted my name, over and over. But not before I had collected my pigeons from the eves of the building using a lasso made of sellotape. Now I can wear a tie if I want to or not. I can even decide not to wear a shirt or any trousers. I take my cues from the pigeons I have grown to admire. I live communally. I hobble on one foot. And as I pass beneath bridges and underpasses, I clamp my hands over my face for fear of crows that might peck out my eyes. My monotone is pleasant enough, but in the field of music, they consider it irritating.

Vardø's Daughters

Noëlle Harrison

Vardø is a small island in Finnmark in the extreme north-eastern part of Norway. During the seventeenth century, this Norwegian island, along with parts of Scotland, and Germany, was the centre of the some of the most intense and brutal witchcraft trials in the whole of Europe. Nearly 100 persons, Norwegian, and Sami, most of them women, were convicted and burnt at the stake. In 1662, six girls, between the ages of six and thirteen, were accused of being in league with the Devil. One of them was Maren Olufsdatter, daughter of a notorious witch.

island rock

sharp dark

wearing

the air

as

a

way

down

white sky

begins to flatten

eyes awaiting

night loneliness

lies the way

traced back

I

There are no trees on Vardø. The island is as barren as a mountain summit, as sheer as the frozen fjord. Yet my dreams of Vardø are full of forests. I run through birch trees, sliding down mossy banks, pulling on roots as I clamber up the other side. I chase the spears of midnight sun that pierce the dark foliage. The undergrowth rustles and crackles beneath my bare feet. I spy an arctic fox in its summer brown running alongside me. I pick up my skirts; laugh as I run. My heart is light for I know he is here, deep inside the wood. I have been hunting for him ever since I was a girl. Joy swells within me at the promise of his love. I am as certain as my very own living breath that he is there in the darksome forest, waiting for me, his molten eyes seeking me.

Out of the murky forest one day we will slide into the glowing dawn of a northern spring, skiing across the snow-laden fjord beneath a sky touched graceful by pink. He will take me by the hand and he will spin me. We will dance so wild that not a soul can break us.

II

The Dark Lord has been shadowing Maren her whole life. On the island of Vardø, he lurks between the clusters of turf cottages, emerging in the hostile stares of her neighbours. He is lapping against the sides of the fishing boats, hissing from the lips of the fishermen as they stare her down. None forgives her, and none forgets.

The Devil is a trickster, but Maren does not fear him. She never has. This very day she feels His presence as the wind builds, and a storm begins to blow upon the island. She does not dread the wild gales of the North as others do. When the wind cries out, she can hear those witches calling, returning from the nether regions. As the storm begins to build, the power of it courses through her body. She imagines herself facing all the people of the island of Vardø, her black hair streaming behind her, her stance as solid as a warrior's. She would speak the whole truth. That it was their very repentance that damned the women of Vardø.

Some nights Maren wakes to find herself back in the big trial chamber in front of Governor Orning, Deputy Bailiff Lockhert, and the Vardø jury of important men. She is but girl of twelve, and yet every single man is held rapt by her. Two rows of the most important bodies, and as many of the populace of Vardø that can squeeze into the chamber are breathless, waiting for her words. It is so quiet that they can hear the snow falling upon snow outside, stacking up all around them in white oblivion. These judging men are beacons of light, gleaming in front of Maren, all so clean, and neat in their white shirts, black justacorps and hats. Some of the older ones wear ruffs; others wear starched neckbands, and most have beards as pointed as spearheads. They are echelons of all that is proper and holy. They are order, their power derived directly from that of the King and from the King straight to God. They are The Good.

Mistress Anna Rhodius is beside her, holding her hand. She laces her fingers within hers. She can smell her refined scent, an impossible aroma of wild roses.

'Tell them Maren,' she whispers into her ear. 'Tell them everything you told me.'

She licks her lips, preparing to speak. There is the taste of lemons upon them.

Upon other nights, Maren might fall from her marriage bed onto the cold cracked floor. It is the Day of Judgement. Bailiff Sørensen Fiil stands to attention in Merchant Bras' house before the jury of Vadsø and he declares that these evil girls should burn. Maren is the worst one of all. She is named the ringleader. The girl with no hope for her soul.

The wooden floor splits wide, mud bubbles forth, and her legs are sticking as if in thick boggy mire. She must speak or else she will sink to her doom. Only the truth can save her. Eyes fixed upon her sleeping husband, she clasps her hands as if in prayer. She opens her mouth, yet what emerge are black words, and dark deeds. It is her essence to be bad.

One time Joseph woke and asked her what she was whispering, but she did not tell him the truth.

'Prayers,' she lied.

'We have already said them,' her husband murmured, before drifting back to sleep.

Anna Rhodius may still be a King's prisoner but Maren was once her captive. She had been entranced by her, for Mistress Rhodius knew everything about science, and healing. The Danish lady had read so many books written by the most learned men in the whole of Europe. Mistress Anna's God was a crusader against chaos, but she also knew about the Devil and his upside down world. The power He could give to the powerless. This is what drew Maren to her.

In 1652, when Maren was two years old, her mother was accused of causing a huge storm that wrecked a ship belonging to the Bergen merchant Jon Jonsen. Maren's mother and nine other witches had held the wind in a bag, and undid the knot so that it spilled forth again. It was said that her mother had great power to create whirlpools within the sea. All knew this because she was an outsider in Vardø, raised on the western island of Rødøy, so close to the legendary mælstrom of Røst.

Maren's mother had created a wave the height of a mountain. She had been inside that wave, conducting the ruinous power of the sea, forcing Jon Jonson's ship down. She was burnt at the stake for her crime.

Everyone believed that Maren followed in her mother's footsteps. When she, and the other girls on trial, Ingeborg and her sister Karen, Sibylle and Kirsten, were sent down from Vardø fortress to collect seaweed for the cows, Maren would sometime sight her mother inside a big wave of water far out to sea. Tossed and turned by the violence of nature.

'Do you see my mother?' she would ask little Karen, pointing at the sea. 'She is there, inside a big wave, do you see her?'

Karen shook her head.

'All I can see are the stakes on Stegelsnes,' she whispered, clutching at Maren's skirts, her eyes filled with tears.

'Do not look to that place,' Maren said, pulling the little girl closer.

'But will they burn us Maren, will they?'

Maren had been as fearful of a fiery end as the other girls, but she did not show it. Deep down she had been proud of her mother's power. Maybe she too could harness nature, not to destroy but to save them?

'Do not be afraid Karen,' she said to the small girl. 'If they try to put us to the fire, we shall turn to birds, and fly away.'

Even so, by that time, she had not felt the full conviction of her words. Anna Rhodius had made her doubt. She chained the girls to the yoke of repentance. Maren had wished so much to be free again, to roam the fields of her home village of Vadsø with the Dark Lord at her side, and her mother's fearsome destiny leading the way.

The past nine years have not been easy. Not even Karen speaks to her any more for she is afraid to be seen with her. Maren knows that the women of Vardø are still watching her, waiting for another chance to bring her down. How it is that in a place where she is loathed, she has found love. The devotion of her husband, Joseph Abrahamson. A man who refuses to damn her.

When she was a girl, she would challenge the Devil to come for her. If folk thought her bad than she would not disappoint them. It nearly got her burnt. She remembers Ingeborg counselling her to stay silent, and yet she could not. She would have her vengeance on all those women who had kicked her and called her witch's child since before she could remember. Sølve Nilsdatter, Widow Krog, Guri from Ekkerøy, Kari, Willardtz's wife, and Barbra Olsdatter. All of them together spitting out insults at her. Had Anna Rhodius read this dark intent inside of her and used it to her own ends?

Now for the first time, an agonising fear has entered Maren's life. It has consumed her since the day she bore her child. A girl, Synnøve, three years of age, with Maren's dark hair, and Joseph's blue eyes. The idea that her daughter might be treated as she was, branded the daughter of a witch, called a witch herself, sears Maren with anguish. Worse than any pain she has ever felt. She would gladly take a hundred lashes for her daughter's good name and reputation.

It has been impossible to forget the dark portent of Governor Orning's last words to her before he left Vardø. Three years after the trials, and the last night she served him.

'You can never be returned to God, Maren Olufsdatter,' he said, his finger trailing from the tip of her chin, down her neck to finger the edge of her collar. 'The Devil will never give you up. He will keep you and all your daughters in his grasp for all eternity.'

The old bastard gave her a look of triumph, as he forced her upon her knees. 'You are a creature born to tempt men to break their vows.'

She had wanted to curse Governor Orning and hurt him just as he hurt her. Yet she did not. For it was the Governor's protection that saved her from the workhouse, worse yet the stake. Furthermore, it was Governor Orning who had stopped the whipping that time. Hauled Anna Rhodius' maid Helwig away, the birch branch still in her hand, as all the Governor's men looked upon Maren in condemnation.

'Whore,' they hissed behind her back. 'Witch.'

Maren had let Governor Orning do as he wished to her, for he allowed her Joseph. And now the old Governor is long gone from Vardø, the memories of his touch fade, and she has her husband and her girl as rewards.

*

Maren knows the Evil One is close by when Joseph gives her news from the fortress. 'Anna Rhodius is dying,' he tells her, his eyes shining with relief.

Her husband thinks that the threat against her will soon end. But Maren knows that these hours, these moments, until the last breath is grasped from Mistress' Rhodius body are the most dangerous for her, and their child.

'They found her wandering in the snow, half demented, half froze, still wearing her mules,' he says as he takes off his wolf skins. 'It will be the end of her Maren.'

'Where is she now?'

'Why back in her prison longhouse, attended by her maid Helwig. The Reverend looked to her earlier. He said she will not last the night.'

'Does she speak?'

Her husband does not reply. He shuffles over to the cooking fire, warms his hands.

'Joseph, what does she say?'

'She raves, Maren, says that witches have cursed her.'

She feels the blood drain from her, her mouth dry and empty.

'The Reverend does not think it so,' Joseph reassures her. 'It is clear that she is bitter, long due for death.'

'Does she name the witches?' she whispers to her husband.

'Do not shake so wife,' Joseph takes her in his arms. 'Anna Rhodius is harmless. She can wreck no more damage in Vardø.'

His words do not comfort her. Maren presses her lips to her husband's bare skin at the base of his neck. She tastes the salt upon him. She knows he does not like her to be so forward but she cannot help it. She wants to feel him inside her. Her family is only safe when she is part of Joseph.

'I would wish to give you a son,' she whispers to him, as she kisses his neck.

Joseph glances to where their little girl sleeps. He blows out the candle, so that the only light in their tiny cottage is from the cooking fire, and leads her by the hand to their bed of birch branches and reindeer skins. She lies down for him, and he lifts her skirt. She has an urge to pull his garments off. She wants to feel his nakedness against hers. The thought of it brings heat to her belly, makes her breathless. She can feel his hardness brushing against her bare leg. How she wants to touch it.

She is completely his. She always has been. Her love for Joseph covered her back in whipping scars and once put her on trial again. He could have abandoned her for the stories of her wantonness, the gossip about her and Governor Orning, but he did not. He married her. He made her respectable. If Joseph were to put a blade into her heart at this very moment, she would let him do so.

Maren pulls him deep within her, wrapping her arms around his back, as she lifts herself towards him, and he touches her so far inside. She must make no sound, yet it is so hard not to sigh with the rapture that fills her. Is the creation of a perfect soul meant to fill his parents' with such mutual ecstasy?

They are awash upon each other. Her husband gently pushes the damp hair from her face.

'Maren, my love,' he whispers. 'How glad I am to have found you.'

She is close to tears. She imagines his seed within her, the child she hopes taking root.

The brother that will protect her daughter.

A boom of thunder crashes outside and she trembles as she feels the fury of it from the roots of her hair to her fingertips.

'Hush my sweet, it is but the storm beginning,' Joseph says, believing she is frightened. The thunder continues and she hears pellets of hail striking the roof. A storm in Vardø can only mean one thing. The black hound is back. Her body is tight with anticipation. Though her husband faces her, it is as if the vision of his gentle eyes, his flushed cheeks, and yielding mouth recedes.

Joseph holds her tight. Maybe he senses it too, that Maren's soul is running away from him like grains of dry snow through his hands. He fears the morning she may be taken from him. And he is left, their marriage bed full of ashes.

Centre Ville

Claire MacLeary

The clock on the village church chimes midnight. Phil lifts his head from the desk. Looks at his watch. Yawns. Annie will be sound asleep. Keeps different hours from him these days: up at six, in bed by nine. No argument, not now she's been elevated to the Examination Board. Phil sighs. Pushes aside the lesson plan he's been trying to polish off for the past hour. By the time he got home from his coaching session, walked the dog and had his supper, his brain had atrophied.

Best turn in. The autumn term is going to be full-on, what with the new syllabus and the planned field trip to France with his Fifth Form lads, not to mention rehearsals for the school play. Fuck, he'd forgotten about that. There's a mountain of stuff still to be done, and the date he's set for the performance is only weeks away.

Before he heads for bed, he'd better make a start on that shopping list. Start with the underpinnings. Phil chews on the end of his pen. There's nothing he can filch from home, Annie's underwear too flimsy to re-mould a male torso: T-shirt bras: too yielding by far; little Lycra briefs that leave nothing to the imagination. No, it will have to be more solid: an old-fashioned corset, something like that. But where to source such a thing? The local Ladies' Outfitter? He banishes the thought. A vintage store? He's spotted one in town, near the university, the window crammed with retro stuff: wide-lapelled jackets; flared trousers; A-line frocks. But a corset? He thinks not.

He powers up his computer. Logs onto eBay. Throws up innumerable results: Boned Corsets and Basques; Bustiers; Waspies. In the crotch of his work trousers Phil's penis stirs. They're there in profusion: gold; black; scarlet; purple. Fashioned from satin, lace, faux leather. And here's the very thing. His cock jumps to attention. 'Ladies Garter Corset £12.99. Free P&P.' In one illustration its suspenders dangle tantalisingly. In another they're attached to sheer black stockings. He unzips his flies. Fumbles in his boxers till he makes himself comfortable. Saves the link.

The stockings won't present a problem. He's already done a quick recce in Marks & Spencer's lingerie department. Left Annie in the Food Hall. Pretended he was off to buy a book. She didn't suspect a thing. Not that she'd care. She doesn't take much interest in anything these days, not unless it's to do with the Exam Board. Ever since her appointment was confirmed she's talked about little else: the overnight hotel stays, the room-service suppers, the big squishy bed all to herself. But, back to the job in hand. Phil eyes his flaccid crotch. He hadn't expected to find stockings, not in Marks, but they had a surprising selection. He'll have to check out the sizing. Goes by hip measurement. That figures. He'll need to take measurements anyhow for the outfit.

Phil hasn't quite decided on the outfit. A pencil skirt, maybe, to accentuate those slim male hips. With a split up the back. Yes, definitely a split. And best if the stockings are seamed. Then a pretty top: a soft silk shirt, something like that. Open at the neck, enough to show some skin. No, that won't do. No cleavage. A pussy bow, then. He stifles a titter at the pun. Seriously, though, the ensemble needs to be stunning - the very apogee of femininity. He dismisses the shirt and skirt idea in favour of a frock.

Over the past few weeks, he has appropriated various items of make-up, something else his wife has been oblivious to. He found it hard at first, the fiddly brushes unwieldy in his awkward fingers, had some difficulty working out what went where. But he's improving. By the due date - assuming a hairless chin - he should be able to produce a maquillage like a pro.

Shoes will be a nightmare. I mean, size 9? How many women does he know with feet that size? His lip curls. How many women does he know? Men neither, not unless you count his colleagues and, since he fell out with his Department Head, Phil doesn't get much change out of them. Anyhow, shoes, not trainers. He could find those in a 9, easy, but they'd ruin the look. And no sandals. He shudders as he recalls the Birkenstocks Chippy Hicks in Physics adopted during the summer term, crusty toenails and all. Yes, proper shoes, with heels. None of those ballet flats the younger teachers scuff around in. Court shoes, then. The look he's going for is feminine, but not overtly sexy. Understated, yet oozing sophistication and class.

The clock on the village clock strikes two. Phil runs tired hands through his hair. The shoes will have to wait.

He pushes back his chair. Rises stiffly to his feet. Before he hits the sack best double check the back door. Annie has been so absent-minded of late. He shuffles through to the conservatory. Sure enough, the thing's on the latch. Darkly, he mutters under his breath. Still, he appraises the new bi-fold doors, the retractable blinds with their remote-controlled mechanism. They couldn't have afforded these on two teachers' salaries.

A solitary brown leaf scratches against the glass. That's early, surely. Phil checks the date on his watch. Can't believe he's into autumn already. Where did the summer go? He pulls a face. Remembers that's the Exam Board's busy time. Annie had been so elated to land the job she hadn't factored in the downside: the trek up to London, the sacrifice of their annual motoring holiday in France. France? The very thought elicits a smile. They'd had such fun, the pair of them: puttering along rural roads, picnic-ing by poplar-lined rivers. Landed in such quirky overnight stays: the hilltop auberge run by three ancient sisters where they'd snuggled on a prickly feather-filled mattress, then that other place - Burgundy it must have been – where the toilet sat, un-curtained, in one corner of the room and the drapes behind the bed concealed decades of mould.

His gaze lights on the wall of the wooden garage. The arrow-shaped blue enamel sign reads *Centre Ville*. He rolls his eyes. Annie never has entirely segued with Phil's particular brand of humour. That and the other things. In fact, he lets out a long breath, she accused him only the other day of being secretive. Said he'd clammed up about school. Had stopped asking people round. Not that they were party animals, she allowed, but wasn't it agreeable to have friends for drinks now and then? *Like when?* he demanded. *When you're not up in London? Too right,* she shot back. *And you're not mired in those bloody coaching sessions of yours. Or the field trips. Or that damned play.*

Drink, that was another sore point. According to her, Phil's intake had been climbing steadily, their bills with it, so much so she'd the cheek to suggest he take up wine-making. He assumed it was said in jest, but took her on out of devilment. The garage was ideal, and she couldn't then complain if he spent time there, nor if it was so crammed she had to leave her car in the drive.

In the garden, an east wind whips fallen leaves into eddies. They flutter and swirl, delicate as moths, before landing in damp heaps on the lawn.

In the garage, Phil's spare frame is bolstered by a sumptuous velvet sheath.

His face is subtly made up, his fingernails manicured.

Sheer silk stockings encase a pair of muscled legs.

Beneath the length of tow-rope, mascara-ed eyes bulge, carp-like.

From scarlet lips protrudes a bloated tongue.

Across the concrete floor a stain creeps silently.

Within it lies one high-heeled size 9 shoe.

Billy the Kid and the KO at the Coral

G Armstrong

It's Guy Fawkes night n it's a Friday. There's fireworks burstin aw over the place. The six ae us ir standin outside the newsagents, waitin on somebody tae jump in fur our drink. We're aw on a bottle ae Tonic each the night. We see an eld alky stoatin down the lane in boggin jeans n ripped trainers. A walk across the road n whistle him over tae us. The boys slowly walk over anaw tae join us. These kinda cunts wur mostly harmless… but if they had been takin ten Diazepam as a side order tae their daily cider dosage then they could be a harmless cunt taking their pet *Kitchen Devil* a walk. A stoat up tae him but ma swagger makes the eld cunt a wee bitty nervous. A disarm him wae a friendly bit ae chat, 'Happnin, eld son! Fancy jumpin in the shop fur is n we'll gee yi a pound each fur a few cans, mate eh?' a say actin pure sound wae the eld boy. He counts the heads, there's six ae us. Six quid, jackpot. That's his full weekend sortit. These cunts drank bottles ae pound nasty, pure gut rot dry cider that cost a quid each. He kin barely hold his excitement back. Oor part in the bargain is a quid each. Pure loose change. We aw rustle in oor pockets. Danny swaggers up n pulls a fiver oot his *Berghaus* jakit.

'Here yi go, ma man, don't spend it aw it the wan shop!'

A shake ma heed it ma pal n mouth, 'fuck sake man.' The old boy's eyes ir is wide is two pence pieces n is dark is them anaw. 'Cheers, wee man,' he says wae a pure crocodile smile.

'Right, eld yin, in the shop fur six bottles ae *Buckfast*.'

Nae bother boays, nae bother ataw,' he says as he negotiates the lines on the road.

'Fuckin auld cunt,' Broonie says.

'Fuck it, mate, that's our drink sortit, ye ha!'

It's always a nervous wait. Should wan ae yir maws ir das come round n huckle yi up the road, yir bottle wis gone. Should two Strathclyde police officers appear, yir fucked. Should the eld alky use a few of his remaining brain cells, steal the fiver and the six bottles ae wine, yir double fucked. Tense affair this n a kin see it on ma boys' faces. This time he comes stoating back wae the bag. There's that wee moment ae euphoria, like yir first bottle again every time. Yir night ae madness lies within the cheap blue plastic bag, between a dirty hand with long nails. He walks up n Danny snatches the bag right oot his hand.

'Haw! There's only four fuckin bottles in here.'

'Four bottles will be plenty fur yooz wee pricks.'

The other two bottles ir stuffed upside down in his ripped and paint covered jeans. We aw look it one another fur a wee moment. In the pecking order, yir still only a wee guy. Wan ae us hus tae say suhin but…

'Listen, mate, git the fuckin bottles oot right now.'

'OR WIT YA WEE CUNT?' he roars in Broonie's face.

'Or yir gittin shot wae this fuckin firework, ya eld dick.'

We aw turn round tae see Finnegan, hoddin a *Sonic FX* inside a long red shoot. They're single shot fireworks but the noise n the pop aff them is fuckin crazy. We aw stand back tae either side ae the lane. The eld alky disnae know wit tae say.

'You try it, ya wee cunt...n a'll ...rip yi fae ear tae arse.'

'Mate, you couldnae bend doon tae tie yir fuckin laces,' Danny says wae a laugh.

'WIT? Yi think yir mad ...coz yir tall, wee man?'

'Fuck it man, we've got a good swally here,' Addison says.

'Fuck that,' Kenzie hits back.

'You're right, mate,' Finnegan says wae a nod.

'HAW YOU, YA ELD ALKY BASTERT! LOOK AT YI WALKIN UP THERE WAE OOR BOTTLES LIKE BILLY THE FUCKIN KID,' a shout.

He stops n straightens up n sits his own bag down. He spins roon wae his hands hoverin over the bottles.

'AM BILLY THE KIDDD!' he says in a drunken slur.

'Aye, well guess wit, Billy Boy...' Finnegan says as he pulls his lighter oot.

'Gawn grab they bottles fuck sake, that cunt couldnae beat sleep,' Danny says.

A crouch doon wae them aw laughin at ma back n run up silently n grab the fat end oot wan ae his pockets. The cunt is concentratin on every step he makes, avoidin broken glass n dug shite. 'YA WEE PRICK,' he shouts as he spins roon tae stop me n faws on his arse. There's a bellow ae laugher n abuse fae ma pals up a bit. The other bottle rolls oot his pocket and by some miracle, disnae smash. It bounces on the rim ontae a big fuckin juicy weed that cushions its arse n breaks its faw. A see ma opportunity. A dash like Indiana Jones fur his hat. A reach the big weed n dandelion heed. Billy the Kid tries tae grab ma leg but a snatch the bottle fae his clutches n turn tae walk back. His white bag is lyin spilt aw over. Six plastic bottles ae pound nasty rollin oot. Next tae the lane is a big sub-station, the wans wae the transformer n the DANGER OF DEATH signs aw over it. A pick up his bag n fuck it right over the spikey fence. Ma pals ir aw gawn wild. Laughin like fuck. The eld boy looks through the fence n we see his heed lookin at the spikes. He's thinkin about it. The warnin signs mean nuhin tae him, compared tae the six bottles ae happy on the other side. Every cunt goes quiet n a wait tae see wit he dis.

He goes fur it. A ripped trainer tries tae find purchase on the brick wall, behind the spikey fence. A know, fur a fact, that the gate disnae lock. The big padlock is just decorative n wis fucked years ago. We used tae bounce in tae get baws that had been kicked err by a skied penalty. Keeps weans oot, but cravin alkies ir a different matter. They're aw pishin theirsels at the eld cunt. A walk up by him. He's now on the deck wae his foot caught in the fence, troosers fawin doon tae his ankles. A put a hand through n open the gate. A step through n grab the bag. He's cut aw his hands n back when he fell. Aw ma pals ir laughin like hyenas at ma back, hopin a kicked him while he wis down but a put ma hand out fur him tae grab. His eld paw comes up wae trepidation, a think he half expected me tae hit him. He takes hold ae it n pulls himself up. His hand slowly goes tae the bag n picks it up. He fishes in his jakit pocket producing ten *Club*. The eld boy hands them tae me wae his heed doon.

'Fur yir troubles.'

A walk back up wae a wee bit extra swagger. Everycunt's lookin at us.

'Fuckin furget that eld cunt, it's a sin fur him.'

The group ir momentarily enlightened n nod in agreement.

'Aye man, true.'

'Fuckin pish fur cunt's like that int it.'

'It's nae life, man.'

'He's lucky he didnae git that *Sonic FX* right up the arse,' Finnegan says wae a smile.

'Mon, fuck it, let's go n git these things drank,' a say wae a wee laugh, still thinkin about that eld boy's empty two penny eyes.

We go down the woods and tan our drink. It's about two hours later n we're walkin up fuckin steamin, singin, shoutin n smokin snout, there's nae doubt, cos the fuckin Young Team's about! IN YER AREA! OH OH, IN YER AREA! Just lettin loose n gawn crazy. It's dark n baltic, a right dry night wae a crispy scent, but fuckin frozen. The hot wine in our bellies is keepin us warm. The cauld nips at our fingers n toes through black magic gloves n trainers. We've aw git the hoods up now, n jackits oan. The trick is tae tuck yir taps inside yir joggie bottoms. Means aw the layers heat up. Ave seen maself oot in winter tuckin ma trackies intae ma fitbaw socks. No cause a liked that mad Nineties look either, just cos it wis fuckin roasty toasty. We're listenin tae music comin fae the tiny speaker in ma pal's Sony Ericsson *Walkman* phone. It's a DJ Rankin thing fae years ago but its still tunage n its keepin us gawn is we trek through the frozen field, aw crunchin underfoot as we walk. Every wan ae us is hyper. The caffeine in the wine has done its job. We're aw natterin away like fuck, talkin shite about this n that. Wit burds we fancy n who we've awready went wae. There's two solid joints gittin passed aboot between us. The dope is takin the edge aff the bottles, chillin every cunt out a bit afore we go fur a few mare cans n a bottle ae *Red Square* tae keep us buzzin oot our nuts until we huv tae head in.

We're walkin by the few shops n the wee *Coral* bookies, always full ae eld men n a few odd younger heads. A heard once that one ae the punters kept his own wee book inside. He took fiver bets on who the first alky in the village tae die wid be. There wur four ir five regular wans, they would hang about the shop fur drink sellin time, half eight every morning they would be there n half eleven on a Sunday. They wur aw harmless auld basterts, like Billy the Kid earlier oan. Fuckin cynical, if yi ask me. The bookies is on the corner. Runnin doon by it is the road intae town. It's also the way tae the Toi, the scheme our elder wans fight wae. They've git aboot fifty cunts out on a Friday, so we're told…so there wis nae chance yi would walk down tae the high street past there anymare like we used tae when we wur wee. It's quiet fur a Friday, part fae the fireworks which keep burstin here n there.

'Look! Who the fuck's that?' Finnegan shouts.

Me, Danny n Kenzie start tae walk down. Next is Broonie n Finnegan n last Addison, on the phone tae some lassie. It's Kenzie who speaks up.

'Here boys, that's fuckin Taz, ma brur's mate.'

We aw look round it wan another. This is wan ae Big Kenzie's mates. Wan ae the elder wans in the Young Team. He wis gittin chased by about five heads. There wis six ae us. Danny's still takin a last swig out his bottle but after he drinks it he stuffs it back inside the map pocket empty. Broonie's still got his anaw. Taz looks as if he's awready had a bit ae a dooin. His jakit is ripped n he's got blood on his face. He sees us standin n straightens up. 'Mon, boys,' a say walkin doon towards the noise. 'Fuckin intae them, boys,' Danny says louder. Broonie n that are aw gem fur it. Wan ae our elder wans n a squad ae theirs. Taz's almost at us now, pantin like an eld dug fae runnin. A kin feel Addison shitin himself fae behind me. A kin see him in ma peripheral vision, still on the phone, but quickly sayin his goodbyes n stickin it in his pocket n zippin it. Big Danny is makin sure his trainers ir tied. Kenzie's shoutin about Tam tellin Addison tae phone him. Taz's reached us aboot a hunner metres fae them doon the street.

'Fuckin hell …boays… cunts jumped is walkin… up that backroad there… backin' is up …boays?'

'Obviously, mate!' Danny says.

Kenzie struts in like the delegate in charge.

'Aye, *ma boys* will back yi up, mate, nae sweat,' he says lookin gem, but wae a wee nervous glance towards the cunts walkin up the hill.

Danny's fuckin buzzin. A kin see him crackin his knuckles n rollin his shoulders. Broonie's dancin about on his tip toes, swingin his arms in the air. Finnegan's standin smilin like fuck wae his hand in his pocket. Addison's shitin his fuckin self. They're fifty metres away now. Taz's caught his breath again.

'Ah must be gittin eld man, a dunno any yooz wee guys…'

Calm down, Taz, mate, yir only seventeen, ya cunt, a think n don't say. Am fuckin buzzin anaw now. The wine ae moments earlier is the drivin force. We've been buzzin aw night, cos ae the fireworks, the swally n the Friday Feelin which is a force wae almost supernatural powers. We kin see the cunts now. There's five ae them. A recognise a few fae school n a know two ae them. JP - Jamie Peters, who's sixteen n a mad cunt, n Si O'Connor wan ae their best fighters, sixteen anaw. His big brur, Matty, wis the tap man. Yi kin tell the two ae them ir the maddest. They're powerin ahead, awready wae their arms in the air, shoutin the fuckin odds. The three others ir walkin slightly behind. A dunno them, but at least wan ae them looks aboot eighteen, an elder wan. Taz's confidence hus grown. He's seen Wee Kenzie, n heard Addison phonin Big Kenzie. The rest ae the Young Team wid hear through the webs ae social networks, *MSN* n an army ae wee thumbs tappin madly it mobile phone buttons. 'Fuckin mone then, ya dafties, YOUNG TEAM!' he says walkin back down. We aw share a wee smile n they look chuffed as fuck. A probably look the same. That second we aw go fuckin mental. The adrenaline, that sickmaking, dancing feelin in yir stomach that yi come tae love n dread simultaneously.

    The five ae them ir walkin up the middle ae the road. A wine bottle comes flyin up the street n bursts in front ae us. We're aw walkin down now adjacent tae the bookies. A hear a fuckin hissin in ma ear. Finnegan sends the Sonic FX screaming doon the street at them. Taz looks like he's gonnae lay a fuckin egg, the cunt. Finnegan's laughin his heed aff, dancin about on the pavement. The rocket whines up the street towards them, hits a car windscreen and explodes mid-air, wae an almighty fuckin bang. The five ae them dive oot the way n pick themselves up fae the deck. There's nae hesitation. The six ae us sprint at them, still shoutin like fuck in the middle ae the road. Their two tap boys run up towards us wae their arms oot, geein it straight back, pure bold cunts. Taz grabs an empty wine bottle n swings it at that Si's heed. The two ae them start punchin fuck out ae wan another. Me n Danny run fir JP, he skuds Danny wae a beauty ae a right, but he's a big cunt n rides it. BANG. Danny hits him a fuckin haymaker n as he stumbles on the kerb, a jump up n hit him a triple combo, a big dirty right, a wee cheeky left n a finisher. The cunts eyes go funny as he hits the deck. He's sparkled but he's awright cos his sleeve is comin up tae wipe his splattered nose. Si n Taz ur still scrappin over next tae a parked motor. Broonie n Addison ir chasin the two other cunts back doon the road. Their other mate, the elder wan is pannelin fuck out ae Finnegan. Danny sprints towards them first, n a follow. HAW YOU, YA FUCKIN DAFTY! he screams it the boy, afore skuddin him wae a right. The elder boy seems dazed. Danny grabs his jakit n pulls him forward, while aimin his forehead at the boy's nose. He folds n lands next tae Finnegan, whose face is fucked. He laughs, showin a missin tooth, n kicks the boy in the face as he falls n lies back, wavin an invisible white flag. A turn round laughin tae git a swift punch in the mooth aff Si O'Conner's right hand. A barely feel it, just that dull thud that yi become accustomed tae.

    They aw start walkin back down the way they came. Their shouts n threats still sound up the street. A KNOW WHERE YOU STAY, YA WEE DICK. Taz is handin the boys fags out his packet n lightin them. WAIT N SEE IT SCHOOL, YOU'RE GETTIN IT! He gathers us all around him. 'Am fuckin proud ae yooz boys… that wis fuckin MAGIC, by the way!' A turn tae aw ma ain pals, our wee six man gang. Danny's git a big daft smile on his face, wae a *Mayfair* cigarette in the corner ae it. He's got a belter ae a black eye. A big purple doughnut round his socket, puffy n tender lookin, wae wee ring cuts in the corner. Finnegan's face is fucked. That elder boy had smashed him, he had a face yi kin only git wae a good few punches. A broke nose n a missin incisor. A set ae black eyes on the way fur him anaw. Addison n Broonie didnae huv a mark on them, cos wan ae the wee cunts who sprinted, had the misfortune ae losin a trainer n tripping on his arse. Broonie n Addison kicked fuck oot him on the deck. His wee pal ran down n skudded Broonie, but it wis just a token gesture. They knew they had been done n we ran them oot ae town. As the adrenaline faded, Wee Broonie spewed. Taz wis laughin, in a proud paternal way, like his wee boy had come off his bike wae stabilisers. 'That's the adrenaline, son, disnae mix wae wine,' he says patting Broonie's back as he heaves up a brown soup-like concoction. Ma face wis sair anaw but a didnae care. A didnae gee two flyin fucks.

We aw turn away fae him bein sick n there's a mighty uproar. Loads ae shoutin n bawlin. The rest ae the Young Team appeared fae up the lane. Big Kenzie is at the front wae an aluminium baseball bat n cap, n needless tae say, nae glove ir ball. A few others huv got chibs, bottles n poles n bats. They stop their stampede on the other side ae the road n survey the scene. Their mate Taz standin the middle ae his wee brur's pals battered fuck oot ae. We aw swagger across the road, faces stingin n rid n bloody, but proud, every fourteen n fifteen year old chest puffed oot fur our medals tae be pinned tae *Berghaus* jakits n tracky tops. Big Kenzie spots the Toi wans walkin doon the road. He waves an arm n a few heads start sprintin down after them, shoutin like fuck. The rest ae the troops stand round the wee group. Big Kenzie is first tae speak.

'Fuck happened here then, Taz?'

'A git fuckin jumped walkin up the road, mate.'

'Aye, they fuckin Toi wans?'

'Aye, man, there wis six ae them, n just me maself.'

'Well no just yirsel,' he says lookin it Wee Kenzie n the rest ae us.

'Fuckin too right, mate, your wee brur n his pals backed us right up.'

Big Kenzie n the tap men surveyed us, wan at a time. They looked at our clothes, builds n war wounds. Most ae them ir quiet, waitin fur Kenzie n Eck Green tae deliver their verdict. Eck wis Big Kenzie's best mate. Big bruiser ae a cunt, easy six fit two n aboot fourteen stone. Some ae the elder wans huv git jeans on n duffle coats n parkas. Big Kenzie isnae the oldest there. A few of the oldest stand it the back, swigin it cans ae *Tennent's* lager n rollin a joint. They wurnae interested in the troubles ae the young team. They had done that in another life n wur contented now tae sit n swig their beers n puff a wee joint. It wis fae about eighteen, nineteen downwards, finally tae us at the bottom ae the peckin order. 'Wit fuckin even happened then?' Eck says under his usual growl. Taz goes in tae great detail in the tellin ae the tale. He acts oot the sound effects ae the firework, n each punch, kick and flying bottle. The audience sways n oohs n ahs it the right points, playin their part in the retellin ae our tale. There wis nae need tae exaggerate this story. It wis enough on its own. It would live on in memory and legend.

'So who the fuck ir these wee guys?' another wan ae the elder wans says.

'They're the younger wans, fuck sake,' Big Kenzie says.

'Awright, nae bother.'

'Fuckin proud ae yees, wee man, yees done well,' Big Kenzie says as he grabs ma hand n shakes it hard. The two groups merge. Every wan ae us is buzzin. A few ae the elder Young Team wans stand tae a younger wan, aw givin us our due n listening respectfully tae our wee story. 'Wit's yir name, mate?' echoes throughout the group. Hands are shook n bottles and joints ir passed between them n us. No initiation here, just prove yirsel tae yir troops. No many ae the Young Team actually works, n no many ae them done good in school... here they kin rise tae the tap. Drink n take drugs like fuck n fight like fuck. Tae the elder wans, we wur the next generation. It made them feel important, like it wis now their duty tae show us the ropes n look after us. While some ir always goin tae be dicks, most ir sound as anyhin honestly. They tell us about the elder burds n other stunnin lassies which we had only heard n dreamt ae...

The Hen Night

Rachelle Atalla

The tearoom was crowded and Janice had to wait to use the microwave. She tried not to look at the coffee stains that covered the Formica worktop or the germ-riddled sponge that lay in the sink, once bright yellow but now stained brown.

'There you go, Jan,' Tara said, lifting a plate of congealed macaroni cheese out of the microwave. 'All yours.'

'Thanks dear,' Janice said, placing her soup bowl inside. She had cleaned the microwave only two days before but already there was evaporated spillage on its walls. She was aware of conversation taking place behind her but the tea towel hanging off the cutlery drawer was holding her attention. She touched its fabric and, as suspected, it was damp from endless days of use. She sighed. The tea towel would be going home with her for a boil wash.

The microwave beeped, startling her. She collected her soup, gripping the bowl, despite its temperature burning her hands.

'Well, Jan, you excited?' Tara said, watching as she took her seat.

'What's that, love?' Her voice was slow to respond, like having to speak was an inconvenience.

'Are you excited about Lori's work-hen?'

'Yes,' she replied. 'Of course.'

'I still can't believe you're coming,' Lori said. 'I'm *actually* honoured.'

'What are you talking about?' Tara asked.

'I'll let you tell her, Janie.'

Janice blew on her soup. 'There's nothing to tell.'

'Not true, Janie. Come on, tell Tara how many years you've been working here.'

Janice swallowed her mouthful of soup before responding. 'Come October, it'll be fifty-two years in this space. It hasn't always been a gift shop though.'

'And... In all these years Janice has never once come on a staff night out!'

'Shut up!' Tara said. 'Seriously, Janice? You've never ever been on a work night out, like ever?'

'Work nights out are a new invention,' Janice said.

'Isn't everything a new invention to you?' Lori smirked.

Janice stood up. She flicked the switch on the kettle and opened the fridge. There was a blob of butter smeared across one of the shelves. It had been there for over a week and it disgusted her each time she had to look at it. It was Lori's mess and she was adamant she wasn't going to clean it up, but the game was going on too long now. 'If you're to be married,

Lori, you'll need to start behaving in the manner of an adult,' she said.

'I do behave like an adult!' Lori replied, letting a chuckle escape her lips. 'David thinks I'm dead mature for twenty-one. And I took his daughter to soft-play the other day.'

'Okay, dear,' Janice said. She gripped the milk's handle with her index finger, the liquid sloshing backwards and forwards. 'If you say so.'

'To be fair,' Tara said. 'I actually thought you were twenty-four.'

'Ah-ha!' Lori said. 'Did you hear that, Janie? Twenty-fucking-four.'

'Love, I'm not here to argue with you,' Janice said, taking her seat again. 'I won't bother coming tonight if it's going to cause a fuss.'

Lori jumped to her feet and came to where Janice was sitting. She threw her arms around her. 'Oh, Janie-Panie, don't be silly. You have to be there.' She rested her cheek next to Janice's. 'You're my work granny.'

Janice spent the afternoon on her knees in the stock room, sorting through boxes with Alana. The cards were getting ridiculous now, she thought, as she flicked through a handful. One read: *Happy Birthday, You Bellend*, and another read: *Happy Birthday Tiny Tits*.

'Who buys these?' Janice said.

Alana glanced over to see what Janice held in her hand. 'Everyone,' she replied. 'The alternative birthday cards are our biggest sellers. No one wants those shitty little bears holding balloons anymore.'

'I still like those bears. And the cats – I still love the ginger cat cards.'

'Got to move with the times, Jan,' Alana said. 'Nothing else for it.' She paused. 'You are still coming tonight, aren't you?'

'Yes.'

'Great! Don't bother changing your mind now. And just wait until you see what I've bought. Some of it's amazing! I got the usual – tiaras, a veil, the sash, but I managed to track down these chocolate willies off the Internet. They're minty, like an *After Eight*.' Alana laughed, nudging Janice with her elbow. 'They better be tasty!'

Tracy, the manager, popped her head around the door. 'Janice, your husband's on the phone for you again. I told him you were busy but he said it was an emergency. I don't know if you're counting but that's the third phone call today.'

Janice slowly got onto her feet and rubbed her knees back to life. She followed Tracy out onto the shop floor and lifted the receiver to her ear. 'Hello darling, is everything okay?' She gripped the phone, not daring to look at Tracy who was standing behind her. 'No, when I left this morning I said I would be here all day. I'll be back after five.' She paused to listen. 'Okay, darling, I need to go. I'm not on my break. Love you.' She placed the receiver down on the cradle and looked at her hands. They were shaking.

Tracy looked away. 'Everything okay with Mr Black?'

'Yes,' Janice said. 'He thought I should have been home by now.'

Janice's neighbour dropped her off outside the restaurant just before eight. She checked her watch, and stepped under the canopy, out of the rain. The street was busy despite the cold weather and hardly any of the women passing wore coats. It made Janice shiver on their behalf, gripping the collar of her own coat.

Tracy was the first to arrive. 'Janice!' she shouted as she got out of the taxi, joining her under the canopy. 'Lori will be so chuffed you're here. I thought you might change your mind.'

'You look lovely, Tracy.'

Tracy inspected her for a moment. 'You too,' she said, smiling. 'Let's go inside.'

They sat at a table reserved for their party of eight. Little plastic love hearts were scattered across the tablecloth and everyone had a party-popper. Janice had never pulled a party-popper before, despite having sold many.

It didn't take long for the other girls to arrive and finally Alana led Lori in, where she was met with a round of applause. Other tables were starting to fill up too and it seemed like everyone there was on a hen night. Janice counted six girls wearing veils and L-plates.

'Will we start a kitty, then?' Tara asked, addressing the group.

'Yeah,' Alana said. 'Put your twenties in the glass, ladies, and we'll take it in turns up at the bar.'

Janice took out a crisp, twenty-pound note from her purse.

'Oh no, not you, Janice. You don't need to bother,' Alana said. 'It's just for us alkies who fancy getting smashed.'

'I wouldn't mind a little drink,' Janice said. 'Plus, I want you all to have a drink on me.'

Alana arched her eyebrows and shrugged. 'Okay then, granny, pop it in.'

The menus were laminated and Janice lifted hers to eye-level. 'How is it possible that you can get three courses for only £6.99?' she asked, addressing no one in particular.

Tara started blowing a penis-shaped whistle. 'Choo, choo,' she chimed.

'Take it easy tonight, Tara,' Tracy warned. 'Don't forget, you're doing overtime tomorrow.'

'Like I could forget – I don't even want the bloody overtime. My name just magically appeared on that rota,' she said. 'Actually Jan, here's an idea... Do you fancy doing my shift for me tomorrow?'

'No, darling, I'm afraid I can't.'

'Oh, go on...'

'My husband wouldn't like it. Sunday is our day together.'

Tara rolled her eyes, before getting to her feet. 'I'll get the round in. Jan, what you on then?'

'I'll have a small vodka and water, please. And a wedge of lemon.'

'Vodka and water... Are you for real?'

'I like it.'

'Suit yourself, Jan. Each to their own.'

As Tara passed, Janice saw Lori grabbing her by the elbow. She was whispering something into Tara's ear and Janice suspected it was about her. Tara saluted Lori, calling out: 'Aye, aye, captain.'

Janice drank her vodka and water, requesting another. They seemed stronger than usual, like medicine, and the burning sensation was oddly satisfying. She had a prawn cocktail to start but it was covered in Thousand Island sauce. The prawns were chewy and she worried about their source. She cut open each tail, searching for excrement. When her steak pie arrived she was suddenly ravenous, slurping her drink in between chunks of fatty steak. She looked around, noticing that she was first to finish, her empty plate pushed away from her.

'We got an all inclusive to Marmaris for £260,' Tara said, addressing Alana. She was sucking blue liquid through a penis-shaped straw. Its colour was luminous and Janice couldn't take her eyes off of it. 'That's everything including flights, transfers, hotel, all our meals and booze.'

'Yeah but is it decent booze or their own cheap unbranded shit?' Alana said.

'Well the picture in the brochure showed *Smirnoff* bottles.'

'Where is Marmaris?' Janice said, slurring slightly.

'Turkey,' Tara said.

'Oh, don't go there,' Janice said. 'I don't think it's safe there at the moment.' 'Jan, they wouldn't let you travel there if it wasn't safe,' Alana said, catching Tara's eye.

Tara reached over and rubbed Janice's arm. 'Don't worry, Jan. I'll look after myself. I won't be going with any of those Turks.'

'Are you alright down there, Janie-Panie?' Lori shouted from the opposite end of the table.

'Great, darling,' she said, raising her vodka.

Dinner was cleared away and more twenty-pound notes were added to the glass. The chocolate willies were distributed and Janice ate three. She bit the balls off first and thought this was hilarious.

'Oh man, I love you, Jan. You're a great laugh,' Tara shouted. 'I'd no idea you were such a bad-ass.'

'Thank you, sweetheart.'

Finally, the karaoke machine was brought out, a projection screen pulled down and microphones plugged in. 'You got a song in you, Janice?' Tracy asked.

Janice shook her head and a lazy smile spread across her face. 'I can't do karaoke.'

Tracy grabbed Janice's arm and pulled her up and onto the floor, forcing a microphone into her hand. 'Come on, Jan. Me and you are doing a duet.'

Janice continued to shake her head but she was happy to stand in front of the crowd. She started giggling into the microphone. Afterwards, when they'd finished singing a rendition of Dolly Parton's *Jolene*, everyone applauded and tears of laughter streamed from everyone's eyes.

'I never knew you had such a lovely voice,' Tracy said.

'I might go up again, by myself,' Janice said, moving her hands excitedly. She turned suddenly and walked towards the bar, stopping next to some of the girls who were drinking shots.

'You going to do a Jagerbomb with us, Janie?' Lori asked.

'Don't be ridiculous.' She was laughing as she addressed the barman. 'Can I have a glass of water, please?'

'You alright, Jan?' Lori asked.

'I'm fine, darling. Just a little light-headed.'

It was getting late but Janice had no real concept of time. The group swayed, hugging each other, standing locked in a circle. But looking at the sea of faces, she couldn't find Lori and untangled herself. She felt unsteady as she walked and took careful, deliberate steps towards the toilets.

'Lori,' she called. 'Are you in here?'

'Yeah,' Lori replied from the middle cubicle.

Janice pushed open the cubicle door. Lori was lying on the floor with her head resting against the toilet seat, vomit staining her dress.

Janice squeezed in beside her and closed the door.

'I've made a mess, Janie – look at my outfit.'

'I see that, my love.' Janice fumbled down onto her knees and wiped Lori's face with some toilet roll.

Lori closed her eyes, hiccupping. 'You're too nice, Janie-Panie. I wish you really were my granny. You'd make a lovely granny.'

'You can be my granddaughter, if you like?' Janice whispered.

Lori lifted her head up off the toilet seat. 'I keep having to remind myself that it's me getting married. Isn't that strange?'

'It isn't something you enter into lightly.'

'How many years have you and Mr Black been married?'

'Fifty-one.'

Lori shook her head. 'See, the thing is – I still can't imagine being with only one guy for fifty-one years...' She paused to cup her hands over her mouth but nothing came up. Her breathing was heavy, rising up and down, her nostrils flaring. 'Mr Black's older, isn't he? He sounds older than you. Every time he phones the shop, I always think that.'

'I was young when I met him.'

Lori smiled. 'I'm young and I'm getting married to David. My David.'

Janice swayed backwards on her knees before rebalancing. She gripped Lori and pulled her in for a hug.

'Give me some wisdom, Janie.'

'Don't do it,' Janice whispered.

'What?'

'Stay single. Live your life,' Janice said, her lips pressed against Lori's hair.

Lori remained motionless for a moment, locked in Janice's arms before pulling away. 'What are you talking about?' She stared at Janice, blinking. 'Did Mr Black do something to you?'

Janice's hands were now balled into fists and she wouldn't meet Lori's eye. 'I'm lucky he let me work.' She paused. 'Thank God I couldn't have kids. If I'd had a child, I doubt he'd ever have let me go anywhere.'

Lori wiped her mouth. 'But he let you come tonight...'

Janice reached out and held a strand of Lori's hair. 'It's not so bad anymore. He's got dementia.' She smiled. 'I tell him what I like now.'

'What do you tell him?'

'Well, tonight I didn't have to tell him anything.' Janice finally met Lori's eye. 'I gave him some sleeping tablets and wound the clocks forward. He thought it was bedtime.'

Lori opened her mouth but no words came out. Janice tried to stroke Lori's face but her hand was swiped away. Lori got to her feet and patted down her vomit-stained dress. 'I'm going to go back to the party,' she said, stepping around Janice. She managed to get the cubicle door open without touching her. 'You should go home. It's past your bedtime.'

When Janice arrived home she checked everything was switched off, before heading upstairs. The place was spotless, exactly as she'd left it. In the bathroom she splashed water onto her face and scrubbed with a facecloth. She was finding it harder and harder to buy facecloths that she liked. No one seemed to want them anymore. As she dabbed her face dry she was aware that the previous lightness in her head was now growing to a dull ache. She opened the medicine cabinet and ran a hand across all the amber bottles lined in a perfect row. She took two paracetamol tablets and closed the cabinet over. It felt nice to have everything just so.

In the bedroom, she took her clothes off and folded them like you would a new garment in a department store. She climbed into bed and realised the electric blanket was still on. Mr Black stirred slightly. She took his hand in hers and squeezed it. 'I'm right here, darling, I'm right here,' she said. 'I've always been here.'

Soup of the Day

Dan Brady

Prunella lay in bed that night and dreamt of only one thing, she didn't want to have breasts like Jordan, hers were small but friendly and they never once complained, no, nor did she want Carol Vorderman's amazing ability to get 671 from 10,25,75,8,9 and 3. Prunella knew how to count when she needed to, so whilst admiring Carols gift on Countdown, she never once craved her numerical jiggery-pokkery, she did however, wish she owned some of Carol's gorgeous outfits, and she did sometimes think that it would be nice if she could have her hair (and make-up) done the way Carol sometimes had hers done, and if maybe she had one? or say two pairs? of Carols fabby shoes that she would allow herself a little smile. But other than these tiny, but very desirable goodies, Prunella didn't particularly like Carol, too much exposure, everywhere you looked she seemed to be grinning back at you, only the other day when Prunella was making the tea she opened a tin of spaghetti hoops, she could have sworn that when the saucy circles had settled into the bottom of the pot, a perfect image of Carols face beamed up at her, Prunella quickly put the pot on the highest gas mark available (no.9) to free herself from that mathematical puzzle that stared up at her.

No, Prunella lay in bed, her husband Alcedo snoring like a weasel with a giraffe's tongue next to her and thought about the competition. She smiled and sighed, she clenched her fist and raised it above her head like a winning boxer, This time, this time it's mine!' she whispered before bringing down her fist and giving Alcedo a straight right to
the back of his head,

     'AHHH...!' cried Alcedo rubbing the back of his head, licking his lips with his giant giraffe's tongue, scratching his posterior then shouting out in his slumbering state,

     'Don't order the swordfish!'

Prunella roled onto her side and smiled,

     'This time.' she whispered and she too closed her eyes and began to snore.

Prunella owned a take-away shop, 'Bake it or Sleeve It' making sandwiches, soups etc, she also took in small sewing and needle- work alterations. Every year Prunella would enter 'The Soup of The Day Competition' run by The Edinburgh Evening News, a competition to find the best tasting soup made in Edinburgh's take-away shops, the winner not only getting a financial reward, but, and this was what Prunella really wanted, a chance to have the big shiny silver cup displayed in her window for the next year.

Prunellas special soup was, 'Lentil and Orange Rind Treat'. This was a recipe passed down from her mother, Certhia, who in turn had had it also passed down from her mother, Sylvia, who in turn had , well anyway, let's just say it was an old family favourite. Prunellas children, Fringilla and Corvus were both big fans of the soup and they would often go off to school on a lovely hot bowl of it. Prunella worked hard in her shop, she put her heart into every slice of buttered bread and her soul into every tray of carrot cake she made.

But Prunella had a problem, every year she entered the competition, and this would be her fourteenth attempt to win the prize, she had been pipped at the post by Lanius, who owned 'Rock'n'Rolls', a little sandwich bar that also sold geological samples or bits of stone as you or I would call them, (someone had once taken a cheese sandwich, taken a bite from it and carefully placed it on a little stand in the display cabinet, between some Amethyst dated 300B.C and a slice of Jade dated 500B.C and attached a sign saying, Sannie, 200B.C. Lanius made the famous 'Chicken X'.

His soup was much lauded, his shop was famous and Lanius was a wealthy man and the shiny silver trophy had its own special place in his shop window. Sometimes at night Prunella would walk by his shop and stand and gaze at the trophy, she was a happy woman and she was content with her lot, she was happy with her size, not too big, not too small, she was pretty and although she knew that Alcedo had his finger in quite a few pies, she no longer worried herself about the games he played, she had two beautiful children and a lovely house with a front and back garden, but Prunellas mouth would slowly open and her tongue would slip forward over her bottom teeth and she would produce buckets of saliva as she drooled over the cup, often having to wipe her chin with a towel to hide her eagerness to possess the silver ornament.

Lanius had won the cup since its introduction, thirteen years ago, but Lanius was a cheat.

The man who made the final choice on who would receive the cup was Robin Rubecula, a man who liked his food and it showed in his rather rotund appearance, but a man who, like most people liked his food even more if they got it for free, and he did, every year 'round about competition time Lanius would send Robin Rubecula a huge food parcel packed with all sorts of tasty delights for him to sink his big fat teeth into, Chicken X, short-bread, blancmange, fudge, cream cakes, buns and lots more sweet fancies, thus assuring that Lanius would retain the cup. Lanius felt confident that the prize was in the bag this year. Unfortunately for Lanius, but even more unfortunate for Robin Rubecula, all that rich and very fattening food that he had been receiving as a little sweetener, turned out to be just a little too sweet, resulting in Robin Rubecula collapsing and dying whilst trying to run and catch a No.32 bus which would have taken him down to the Ocean Terminal so that he could return a copy of Carol Vordermans latest keep fit/garden/house makeover/ antiques from under your sink d.v.d.

A new judge was called in, Larus Canus, a local fishmonger with over sixty years experience of all things briney. Lanius sent Larus Canus a big hamper a week before the competition day, but Larus Canus returned it with a note thanking him but thought it would be inappropriate for the judge to accept such a gift. Lanius read the note, slowly walked over to the display cabinet and carefully selected a good hand sized piece of 300B.C Chalcedony (agate: semi-pellucid gem) and proceeded to throw it through the shop window.

The day of the competition arrived, Prunella was nervous, Alcedo tried to comfort his wife,
        'Relax Pru, it's your year, the cup must be yours this year, do we have any Paracetamol? I have a splitting headache!' Larus Canus had tasted all the soups, he had thinned all the entries down to the last two,Prunellas Lentil and Orange Rind Treat and Lanius's Chicken X. The Usher Hall audience was hushed, Larus slipped the spoon into Prunellas offering, he raised it to his lips, sniffed,opened his mouth and let it run onto his tongue, he rolled the soup around in his mouth, slurping and licking and sucking his teeth before swallowing with closed eyes. He repeated this with Chicken X. Lanius looked over at Prunella, his top lip curled up and he snarled. Larus Canus looked down at the two bowls on the table before him, he looked out at the silent crowd, shielding his eyes from the glare of the spotlights, he reached down and picking up a bowl, he held it above his head like a priest saying mass and cshouted,
        'By God it's got to be the Lentil and Orange Rind Treat!'

Fanatics

Finola Scott

(for the Wigtown Martyrs)

'Abjure.
Niver, nae us, nae the day,
nae the morrow. Niver.'

Feet glaur-stuck, rough hauns roped
unner the Maybricht lift,
twa weemin staun thegithir stake-gruppen.
The toon's hairt beats .

Quick-watter handsels anither baptism.
The Almichty bides his time
til tide's rise.
Saut-watter pirls ower brackish marsh,
the meenister on his knees.

Yin heid's held up, the girl
- the bonny yin.
The ither, thon auld
heid's pushed doon tae tempt
twa chynges o hart.
'Abjure.'

'Niver, nae us, nae the day,
nae the morrow. Niver.
We'll bide til Hindmaist.'

A butterfly converses with a terrorist

Rizwan Akhtar

I cordially dislike allegory in all its manifestations...
      — JRR Tolkien

Tragedies you create are similar
to butterflies and fireflies

but we consume air silently
cleanse ears and finish

you squander ominous sounds
on us, squash words with noise

the necessity of becoming sad
now taints our wings too

but under a vague hubris
you colonize our shrubs

blemish our romance
of wandering pools

ravens and vultures attend
your screeching consequences

under masks made of fragments
isn't it embarrassing

trapped between so much,
and yet denied of any ending.

Thurso River

Lindsay Macgregor

You libertine! Don't make me
look at tender stems of holy
grass or fleshy parts of oyster plants.

For god's sake, not
seedheads of meadowsweet
in heat, not mires of quaking sphagnum moss.

It's all too much – those parted
lips, those glistening slits of bivalves
poking out of river silt.

And everywhere we turn,
soft bodies, limbs, freshwater
pearls undoing themselves.

Six Poems

Andrew Blair

I CAN'T HEAR THE SEX PISTOLS ON THE RADIO.

The machine,
Its spin cycle;
Too much.
I should look into buying
Something quieter

THE SUN DECIDES TO EXPAND.

The sun
Is a good listener.
The sun knows your dreams are violent.
The sun will make your dreams come true.

I USED TO BELIEVE ANYTHING WAS POSSIBLE.

The train passes through pitch black
Unlit countryside, and all I can see out there
Is the carriage, its tilted reflection.

When the void ceases to be comfortable,
You'll see me scrabbling at the glass,
Desperately trying to reach the other timeline.

THE SONG 'FOUR MINUTE WARNING' BY TAX EVADING SERIAL-ADULTERER MARK OWEN ACTUALLY LASTS FOUR MINUTES AND FIVE SECONDS.

Conversely, an actual four minute warning would only give people around three minutes of time in which to settle their affairs.

ITEM 4: STAFF FUN SUGGESTIONS

There were no Staff Fun Suggestions.

ON FEBRUARY 7TH, 2017

The sky was fucking
the earth again.
I saw the rain destroy
A fallen choc ice in the gutter,
And thought about optimism,
Greed,
And the transience of all things.

High Ormlie 2016

an extract

George Gunn

(for the people of Aleppo)

4

The sea is normal & green
the sky is normal & grey
the *US Airforce C-17* transport plane lands
& takes off from Wick John O'Groats airport
each secret month as normal
the *MV Parida* onloads radioactive waste
at Scrabster & sets sail for Belgium
& catches fire as normal
& even though this is all happening
& has no end anybody believes
it is not reported or broadcast
because decommissioning is not normal
as everything must go on
& be seen to be normal
'Spiritus precipitandus est'
the spirit must be hurried onward
because everything has to be moved out
past the assimilating energy of the imagination
& everything is failing because it is the way
it has always been so because it is real
because it is functioning even if it is not
because it is accepted because what else is there
except the fake world which is real

as normal which is the alternative
to the green sea & the grey sky
which goes on & on & on & on forever
so why doubt anything why ask about anything
or think about anything or aspire or dream
better to sit astride a lion
while your sometimes sister
draped in expensive robes
flaunts her endless legs
posing next to the seated smiling dictator
with golden taps & golden everything
& everybody & nobody is left behind
the perimeter fence as normal
with a throbbing soundtrack of almost music
signalling everyone into the safety channels
to a place beyond geography
raising a false flag in a phony world
which as usual is normal
as we all take to the air again
as we all get back into the sea
the realization dawns on everybody
that everybody has always lied to us
us who are everybody
& the result of this is not
that everybody believes the lies
it is that everybody believes nothing anymore
& because of this everybody
cannot make up their mind
so we cannot act or think or judge
& everybody can do with us
as they like which is what they have done

these past sixty rediffusion years
stuck inside the site perimeter fence
on the normal raised beach where everybody lives
& far out at sea the Stoor Worm rises again
its brown mane flowing down behind its head
longing to return to the ancient high hill
to the Great Orm of Dream
where there is no normal or anybody
except the old skald who slouches
down the overgrown planting paths
to the long yellow strand
& the red sandstone cliffs
he turns birch leaves into pennies
& spends them in the hungry forest of his life

Untitled

Dmitry Blizniuk

* * *

You are a cat,
and all your nine lives are wasted on trifles,
on washing and cooking and tidying up,
on war painting your face and body,
on taking cat naps beside the cradle.
I have so little of you left to hold -
shall I pour you some moon milk?
I'm reading you like teenage adventures of Sherlock,
like crib notes written on a girl's knees.
All that is left of you is *La Peau de chagrin*
that gets smaller and thinner with years,
but I never give up wishing, longing.
A small feather sticks out of the pillow
like a skiing track on a mountain slope;
the caramel moon shines through the window,
and I'm looking at you through the years
as if through a heavy snowfall:
you're smiling, and your lips
look yogurt-stained
in the flurry of the falling snowflakes.

Reviews

Lost in the Woods

The Gingerbread House
Kate Beaufoy

Black & White Publishing,
RRP £7.99, 204pp

Much like the gingerbread house in 'Hansel and Gretel', the titular house of Beaufoy's novel appears sweet on the outside but holds darkness in its heart. The witch of the story comes to us in the form of Granny Eleanor, whom daughter-in-law Tess and her own teenage daughter Katia have come to look after. Recently made redundant, Tess comes to The Gingerbread House – as they call Granny's home – believing that caring for Eleanor will give her money and time to write a novel. From the point of view of her teenage daughter Katia, we watch as the strain of caring for an eighty-nine-year-old woman suffering from dementia pushes Tess to her limit.

Through Katia's eyes, Beaufoy shows us the tragedy of age. Eleanor, her brain turned to "Swiss cheese", is a burden on her family. Meanwhile, Katia's mother, a Baby Boomer whose career has been usurped by "The Young Turks", must find a place for herself in a world that has left her behind, all while the infirmity and recalcitrance of her mother-in-law threaten to break her. Tess' journey as a carer is instantly recognisable, and in voicing her frustrations the novel is cathartic to anyone

who has ever had to care for an elderly family member. Given that *The Gingerbread House* is loosely biographical, in that Tess' struggle to care for her mother-in-law was also Beaufoy's, it is hardly surprising that the book's greatest success is in the sympathy the reader feels for Tess.

Yet as the novel tells us: "There's a big difference between empathy and sympathy." And while Beaufoy focuses on generating sympathy for Tess, empathy seems distinctly lacking for both Eleanor and Katia. The moments of reflection that come from Katia on Eleanor herself – the old photos, the life she once lived that no one thinks about – are too few, too outweighed by the shock of her body, whose horrors – scales, warts, and wrinkles – are detailed in one of Katia's many gratuitous apostrophes.

Katia's voice reads much younger than fourteen, despite her literary language, which is constantly explained away by her love of stories, for example when she takes the phrase "fragrant unguents" from *One Thousand and One Nights*. Though capable of discussing Anderson's 'The Little Mermaid', Wilde's 'The Selfish Giant' and, most importantly, E. B. White's *Charlotte's Web,* Katia still calls her mother "Mama". Beyond this, she talks about reading *Heat* magazine and getting "hamburgers" at Nando's, which, let us remember, doesn't even sell hamburgers. Her characterisation is unconvincing and her role ill-conceived; a palpable failing given that this character's trajectory sustains the novel's ending.

Beaufoy aims for sympathy for Tess, and in this, she succeeds. But *The*

Gingerbread House's problem lies in its architecture: Katia fails to bring the structure together. In opting for such a saccharine frame, it is unfortunate that Beaufoy neglected what is most important about the gingerbread house itself: its heart.
–*The White Bear*

To Bayeux and Beyond

The Comet Seekers
Helen Sedgwick

Harvill Secker, RRP £12.99, 290pp

With a PhD in Physics from the University of Edinburgh and a Distinction in the MLitt Creative Writing from the University of Glasgow, Helen Sedgwick is one of those irritatingly talented people you can't help but admire, particularly when it comes to her shining debut *The Comet Seekers*. The novel follows four main characters: Róisín, a stargazer and scientist who dreams of travelling the world; Liam, her cousin who owns a farm in rural Ireland and with whom she shares an illicit yet intense relationship; François, a French boy with a flair for cooking and a desire to travel outside of France; and Severine, his young mother who longs to escape the small town of Bayeux where she was born but remains, anchored by the ghosts of her ancestors. The novel spans from the creation of the Bayeux tapestry in 1066 right up until the present moment and offers fleeting glimpses into the lives of the characters and their ancestors, who only appear in the novel when a comet is visible in the sky.

Much like the comets themselves, this novel is full of cycles, near-misses and deaths both violent and invisible. Róisín and François exist in an endless cycle of almost-but-not-quite encounters, narrowly missing each other while comet seeking in the same locations throughout the 1990s before finally colliding in the Arctic, where the novel starts and ends. At the same time, the relationship between Róisín and Liam is mirrored subtly but beautifully in the many intertwining tales of François' ancestors- a sentiment which is reflected in François' remark to Severine that "you go back far enough and you can see that everyone in the world is family". It is this interconnectedness which renders the novel so compelling: by weaving the ancestral threads of both characters so tight, it is impossible not to believe that Róisín and François were always supposed to meet. We find ourselves rooting for each of them, knowing that their meeting will change everything, yet unaware of how it will come about.

In addition to this, the use of the Bayeux tapestry as a link between past and present is expertly executed. The 69ft long tapestry hangs in the Musee de la Tapisserie de Bayeux and anchors the characters not only to the small town, but also to the comets. We are told that Ælfgifu, one of Francois and Severine's earliest ancestors, is the one who stitches the infamous Halley's comet to the tapestry on its creation in 1066. Consequently, this is the beginning of the ghosts, the intertwining of stories and the love, fear and awe of the comets experienced by Róisín, François and Severine.

In conversation with Harvill Secker, Sedgwick states that "both scientists and writers are people who love to ask questions". Never has this sentiment rung more true than when discussing *The Comet Seekers*. By drawing on accurate scientific knowledge and an undeniable talent for storytelling, Sedgwick manages to weave the fragile strands of fact and fiction together as skilfully and as intricately as the Bayeux tapestry itself in an attempt to ask questions about destiny, faith, love and life, leaving the reader to ponder the answers. The strength of the storytelling, however, only serves to help us along the way: in the novel, destiny is real, faith is strong, love is bittersweet and life is fleeting. Only the comets are consistent, a lonely yet reassuring reminder of the universe and our place in it.

— *The Dog in the Night-Time*

'slightly / synthetic and in a state / of indecision'

Aiblins: New Scottish Political Poetry
Edited by Katie Ailes and Sarah Paterson

Luath Press, RRP £10.00, 132pp

Politics: so much of it just keeps on happening. A lot of it happened back in 2014 – the year of what may retrospectively come to be referred to as 'Indy Ref 1'. It was a time when the binary choice faced by the nation as to what it *might become* cast into stark relief the underlying, historical ambivalence about what Scotland *is*. The title poem of *Aiblins: New Scottish Political Poetry* sums up both the collection and the nation thus; 'slightly/ synthetic and in a state/ of indecision'. The sense of repetition and despair as the nation now again attempts a shift in speech from the future conditional to a present tense is reflected in the final two lines of Calum Rodgers' poem 'Postscript' (written on the evening of 18 September 2014) in which he predicts 'I'll probably cry and never vote again/ I'll probably cry, and never vote again'.

The exposure of the nation's political ambivalence has proved fertile ground for the arts to both respond to present political circumstances and to contribute towards an imagining of what might be. The 'cultural front' played a vibrant role in the independence referendum and *Aiblins* fulfils an important service in capturing poetry which editors Katie Ailes and Sarah Paterson recognise would otherwise have had 'only a fleeting, ephemeral existence', 'performed live or lost in private notebooks or social media sites.' The editors make clear that they left the definition of both 'Scottish' and 'Political' intentionally broad, taking their cues from the featured poets' own understandings.

As a result, a range of perspectives emerges in the collection. Some, like Harry Giles' poem 'All the verbs…' delineate the structures of language and power that govern everyday life. The poem demonstrates that the sheer proliferation of verbs in a local policy document can be politically overwhelming. Many of the poems in the collection are internationalist in outlook, such as David Cameron's 'Korean Letters', Henry Bell's 'Alice Coy Told me How' and Arun Sood's 'Divali in Kessock'; all reflecting a sense of national identity conscious of its porous political contours. Other poems such as Jim Carruth's 'Let Truth Tell Itself' make apparent voices being erased from contemporary Scottish culture, articulated only through their own negation, 'Never will you live the heft and carry'. The linguistic diversity of contemporary Scottish culture is also captured, with poems in English, Gaelic and Scots. In a reversal of the standard practice, four of the English poems are translated into Gaelic with the Gaelic left untranslated to provide 'an opportunity to reflect upon the political and social role of translation in today's cultural economy'. For the non-Gaelic speaking reader, this flips the privilege customarily enjoyed by being an occupant of the destination language. Other poems including John Bolland's 'Thin Ice', AC Clarke's 'Territory' and Gavin Cameron's 'Crossing the Road' unsettle understandings of boundaries – whether of geography, gender or politics – and convey a sense that the ground in Scotland is always shifting.

A consideration behind the selection of poems included, the editors argue, is a concern 'not to let the politics overwhelm the poetry'. The referendum can be understood as an example of politics overpowering the imagination, as Robert Crawford argues in his afterword that all 'those attempts to sing a new Scotland into being, were almost, but not quite, enough'. This rich and varied collection performs the function of affirming a particular, pluralist understanding of Scottish national identity and contributes to the political project of realising Scotland as a fully imagined community. As we approach Indy Ref 2, perhaps the imagination will yet overpower the political status quo.
— *Karen Veitch*

Devil You Know

The Mauricewood Devils
Dorothy Alexander

Freight Books, RRP £8.99, 225pp

In 1889, fire ripped through the Mauricewood coal pit in Penicuik. Rather than mount a rescue operation, the owners shut the pit so the fire would burn itself out. Of the sixty-five men and boys working that day, only two survived. *The Mauricewood Devils* tells the tale of a little known episode of Scottish history, an event known to locals for decades afterwards simply as 'The Disaster'.

Dorothy Alexander's debut novel begins a week after The Disaster takes place. She opens with the nightmares of Martha, a seven-year-old girl whose father died in the pit, and goes on to explore the lives of other women left behind. Martha and her step-mother Jess are the main narrators, their stream of consciousness reactions punctuated by folk stories and interludes of historic research. Presented in 50-word chunks of ballad metre text, these factual segments provide a stark counterpoint to the more human aspects of the narrative.

Writing about how she approached the text, Alexander has said she began with "vignettes, possible scenes imagining the child Martha's childhood." This makes sense of the structure, which at times does feel slightly fragmented – it reads as a series of recollections and documentary evidence about an event rather than a linear narrative. This approach helps create the illusion that you are reading real oral histories, which is particularly impressive when you consider that the starting point for the story was the barest snippet of information from her great-grandmother, the inspiration for the central character of Martha. "As was the way with her generation, she never said much about the tragedies of her childhood," Alexander explains in her author's notes. All she had to go on was a twiddled button and a lost piece box.

These recollections may be vague, but nevertheless gave enough of a jumping off point for a novel meticulously researched. Historic fiction, and social history in particular, walks a difficult line between info dumping and including enough detail to feel real. Alexander negotiates the balance particularly well, with only very occasional extraneous detail in Jess's narrative.

The novel also explores the complicated ways hardship impacts people differently through the character of Martha's formidable grandmother, a martyr to her own grief and a poor caretaker of small children. She is very much the villain of the wee girl's story, and her wicked stepmother air complements Martha's many flights of fancy. These include regular internal re-tellings of the day they heard the news, daydreams in which she is able to save her dad. Of all the realistic points in the novel, this feels like one of the most recognisable and human responses.

The cover blurb hints at a proto-feminist campaign for justice by the wives and mothers left behind, and Alexander invokes the sense of fury and injustice they must have felt. But what comes across far more strongly is a sense of how the community banded together to look after one another. The source material of *The Mauricewood Devils* is a bleak but important moment in history, one worth reading about. In her debut, Dorothy Alexander has come up with a fitting tribute to the men and boys who lost their lives, as well as the women who survived them.

— *Ali George*

Lyric in the language of the intellect

Moon for Sale
Richard Price

Carcanet, RRP £9.99, 72pp

You should expect a librarian to take particular care in organising poems in a collection, and Richard Price, who has a big job at the British Library, is exemplary. He is a poet with a huge range of styles, for whom no subject matter is outlawed, and his sequencing (I want to say 'shelving') of the poems lets us experience them as a well-told story. He clusters similar poems so they sing to each other – a group of nature poems, a medley of songs – and the opening, penultimate and final poems are gracious, gentle and pleasing. We're never in any doubt that we're in the company of an unusual intelligence, but he is clever in a generous way.

He establishes early on, in a long, funny poem called 'The Price', that he's a nerdy archivist who has been working hard in the poetry workshop for years and years, and who doesn't take himself too seriously. 'Remember when a poem could be banned / for beginning with the word 'Remember'?' He notes various other sins, including 'deploying 'marram', / 'palimpsest' or 'shard'', and then, in the first of what will lead to a refrain. 'I loved those years. / I am a Trading Standards Officer./ There should be a price on every word.' He sends himself up beautifully with interjections that remind

me of W.S. Graham. ('I feel we'd better have a word like 'heft' in this well-crafted poem./ We all need a guarantee, the reassurance of heritage vocabulary.') I'd trust Richard Price to be my union rep. Does anyone know better the standing orders of the poetry institution, and how to bend every one of its rules?

While often smart and playful, Richard Price also gives us genuinely beautiful lyricism and there is grief among the pages: 'a pang the weight of the sun's fist'. Here's a demonstration of his artful use of repetition and sound-patterning, from the opening of 'A Quiet River.'

> "Melancholy knows
> the interior of slow. Melancholy
> knows
> what it wants to know,
> inertia yearning, waiting, longing,
> a quiet rivers' stepping stones,
> a quiet river's undertow."

The poems often seem to be striving towards a communication beyond words. Touch is at the heart of the book, with its messages that 'transmit a very short distance'. The central sequence of poems begins with flirting, a liaison that feels secretive, perhaps even illicit. It's delicious to read someone who plays so deftly with words. 'Let's improvise our intimate lives, perfect an intricate duet.' In 'A Little Trouble', the relationship becomes erotic, 'a finger/tracing a tattoo// on soft skin.' Tattoos are a repeating motif in the love affair. Here's a 'taku' (cross between a haiku and tattoo), 'Between the Shoulders'.

> "Zone I can't see: texts
> only you can read. Speak! Read
> my back back to me."

In 'Late Enough' the tattoo butterfly comes alive, flitting about, mobile as touching fingers. Interesting things happen inside parentheses (as if between sheets), adding to the sense that we are being let in on secrets. Yet this is overtly, self-consciously, a publication, perhaps even a public performance, and the erotic culmination is a 'dainty opera', intercourse with an audience, which of course becomes funny. 'Will your tongue be dwelling/on the nub of my question?'

This opera is just one of many song-like poems in the collection. The poet makes heavy use of repetition and refrain, sometimes, I have to admit, to a point where the significance becomes obscure and the words seem to become only sounds. Yet he seems utterly foot-sure, and while many of his poems are difficult, they are robust, and you get the feeling you can ransack them as hard as you like and they will pull themselves together again for the next reader. And there are many surprises, and serious work done with humour, such as the hilariously plausible list of made-up plant names for an impossible 'new wilderness', including 'SIM-leaf', 'Brags and droops' and the one you certainly won't find here: 'Sloppy librarian'.
— *Mandy Haggith*

Sex and the Mickey

The Making of Mickey Bell
Kellan McInnes

Sandstone Press, RRP £8.99, 401pp

We first meet Mickey Bell bare-arsed in a sexual health clinic with a Glaswegian nurse administering a routine procedure for someone who is HIV positive. Mickey, as we come to learn, lives a peculiar life. When he isn't sat in a white tank top on the roof of his council estate tenement in Drumkirk ("the smell of Drumkirk is always the smell of burning"), he is attempting to bag his final munros, accompanied by a highland collie, occasional texts from his sociopathic Buddhist ex-boyfriend, and a leather fetish biker named Mr Fuk Holland 2012. Life in post-IndyRef Scotland never seemed so colourful.

Kellan McInnes' *The Making of Mickey Bell* is a dazzling broadside of a character piece. McInnes draws Mickey in touching detail, bringing out such moments as remembering a homophobic assault while spotting a scar on his chin, or watching the Milky Way "blaze a ribbon of white muslin" across the sky with his new collie. It would be easy for a lesser writer to imagine Mickey as an infirm cliché, debilitated by his HIV status. McInnes is able to avoid these tropes, and touches on the important reality for over 5,000 Scottish citizens. Notably, the spectre of CD4 and viral load counts lurks as an ever-present note at the end of chapters, with the air of mundanity and threat.

Despite Mickey's attempt to bag his final munros serving as the culmination of the novel, it is the moments of human spirit that grab the reader. Mickey's description of anxiety, diarrhoea and fatigue in order to claim Disability Living Allowance is a touching and painful sequence. This humiliation gives later sequences a tinge of bleak heroism, a particular highlight being the honey trapping of a misogynistic mountaineering fraud from Skye. Even a notable subplot of Nigel, the belaboured civil servant, attempting to navigate a survivalist retail store in order to spy on Mickey is blackly heart-warming; "it had never occurred to him cooking stoves would range in price from £27 to £399."

Some of the more experimental sections of *The Making of Mickey Bell* fray around the edges. The sequences written from the perspective of Tyke the Highland Collie grate the nerves as Tyke, a dog, tells the reader, in case they missed it, "I'm the dog I'm the dog I'm the dog." There are other exercises at experimentalism that feel like misjudged tautologies, such as a description of dripping water shaped as a water droplet, or the chapter that starts with "the texting had started again. TBH it had never really stopped."

Yet, at times, McInnes' stylistic passages add a special texture to the novel. The retreating glaciers licking munros into shape in a vision of deep time is one such example. The interplay of human and natural movement feels light and easy to grasp, while at the same time situating the reader with "the sense… of Scotland the island floating on a blue planet in dark space." It is at those moments that a reader can forgive McInnes' peculiar decision to specify that door locks are Yale door locks.

The Making of Mickey Bell is an exciting imagining of gayness, Scottishness, and humanity. It feels contemporary, albeit sometimes heavy-handed. But its moments of pleasure are able to give spirit to a portion of society that is so readily made pariah. That, and the moment when Mr Fuk Holland 2012 empties his bag of sex toys onto the A9 is blisteringly funny.

— *Frederick Rea*

Artful Accessible Poetry

Abbodies
Nicky Melville

Sad Press Poetry RRP £6.00, 40pp

Nicky (nick-e) Melville has long been a wonderfully experimental voice in poetry in Scotland. His work explores political and personal concerns artfully and accessibly with wry, ironic humour. 'Abbodies' looks at the author's childhood of the late 1970s and early 80s through the lenses of pop megaband Abba, science fiction and D. C. Thomson's Oor Wullie.

Melville's title combines the word 'Abba' with the end of the Oor Wullie by-line: 'Oor Wullie! Your Wullie! A'body's Wullie!' That last part, 'A'body's Wullie!' was always likely to invite sniggers, shock, perplexity, surprise and comment from many a Scottish child.

This is an autobiographical narrative poem which reflects upon itself, Scottish, British and European identity, and what it means to be a human being living in the world now. Each page is like the miniaturised chapter of a novel only with far fewer words and highly adept technical and poetical skill. The narrative moves forward until we meet Melville as a father himself, reflecting on what his father means to him, and what might be the way ahead for his own children in order to lead happy and fulfilling lives at a time of great political uncertainty:

> "and Trump is
> master of the scene
>
> can't resist the strange attraction
> from that giant dynamo
>
> look into his angel eyes
> one look
> and you're hypnotised
>
> don't look too
> deep in to
>
> one day you'll find
> out he wears a disguise
>
> a'body's on the line"

What's really interesting here is Melville's uncovering of how deeply the pop-culture of childhood ingrains itself in the memory and the effect it has on the emotional make up of adults. This would be a standard kind of pop-psychology except that it intersects with national and international political questions such as Brexit, the rise of Donald Trump and the so-called 'migrant crisis', producing a poetry that could not be more relevant or up to date.

In its relationship to Melville's other poetry this long poem deploys some of the techniques of 'found poetry' and interplay between sight and sound. 'Abbodies' has fantastic rhythm and pace. It works as a page-poem and extremely well in performance too: it is a poem for both the eyes and the ears and is highly satisfactory on both counts. He plays with lines from numerous Abba songs but takes the refrain 'there's a body on the line' from a translation of Nestor Perlongher's 'Corpses', which has the refrain 'there are corpses'. Melville makes a bold political move in assigning 'corpses' or 'bodies on the line' to the policies of neo-conservatism and corporate capitalism:

> "when the eyes of a Tory
> open in the morning
> there is a body on
> Iain Duncan Smith
>
> it's not so much how
> does he sleep
> but why should he wake up?"

'Abbodies' is a major contemporary poem: it is brave, honest, intelligent and darkly humorous. It is also neatly packaged like a seven inch single with a picture sleeve. Definitely worth buying.

—*Towser*

The Dark Side of Motherhood

The Daughter of Lady Macbeth

Ajay Close

Sandstone, RRP £8.99, 320pp

It's said that in the end, we all become our parents, and this certainly isn't the first novel that explores the tensions of turning into a person that you don't like. Thankfully, despite this setting, *The Daughter of Lady Macbeth* is more about toxic mother-daughter relationships and the desperation for a parent than it is about the desperation for a child, or the pain of becoming one yourself.

The novel switches between the past and the present to tell two stories concurrently. The first is the story of Lilias, an aspiring actress, sent to a farm to wait out her pregnancy out of the sight of her married lover and their mutual social circle. The second is the story of Freya, Lilias' daughter, similarly ensconced in a rural setting to be closer to the fertility clinic through which she and her husband are trying to conceive. Lilias, now elderly and with no flair for drama lost, is as indifferent and cold a mother as she has always been. The fact that she has never disclosed the identity of Freya's father has made the gap between the two women even wider but, as the two stories unravel, we learn that there are more similarities between Lilias and Freya than either might like to admit.

It's refreshing to read a book in which an older female character is given range, history and agency. It's equally as refreshing that neither of the two female protagonists are particularly likeable; they're both interesting and engaging, but neither one is free of moral ambiguities and both have very human faults. The relationship between Lilias and Freya is the strongest in the book, and perhaps the most relatable – the combination of Freya's apparent inability to say what her mother wants to hear and Lilias's unwillingness to embrace her daughter for who she is will be one that many readers can understand.

Yet several of the interactions in the book fail to ring true. The surrounding male characters suffer from being somewhat two-dimensional, or from having inadequately defined goals and desires. Freya's lack of real response to her own actions and their consequences when she finally finds what she's been looking for her whole life, she fails to really *feel* much at all – at least nothing that is indicated to the reader. The psychic distance between the reader and Freya is simply too far.

This isn't to say that the book is underwritten. The plot set-up is fresher than many others, and the physicality of the rural setting is well defined by Close, though at times the prose could stand to be pared back a fair amount; Close is a talented writer and it would be more satisfying to see some of her better descriptions allowed to breathe instead of being smothered by paragraphs full of similar sentences. And yet despite a misplaced linguistic focus, the novel still works. The story is full and explores what is means to be a parent, what it means to be a child and what the desire to be either says about us. Lilias, in particular, stays with you far past the final page and past her final curtain. If only the rest of the characters did, too.

— *Heather Parry*

The Small Things Of Real Life

Things We Never Knew
Hamish Whyte

Shoestring Press, RRP £10.00, 64pp

Hamish Whyte has a lyrical touch to his poetry that is often derided in the modern politicised and performance poetical traditions. This is poetry that needs no grandiloquence, no explanations, no justifications; Whyte is serving up slices of his life in small, almost graceful lyrics that charm their way into your mind.

While these poems may be far from challenging the governing political orthodoxy, or stepping up to injustices they do achieve, very easily, what they set out to do. *Things We Never Knew* is a collection that makes no proclamations other than the simplicity of the memorials painted within.

Published the year before John Burnside's *Still Life with Feeding Snake*, *Things We Never Knew* sits in the same state of mind filled as it is with the lost, missing, and lapsed. These pages have fallen from the almanac of a man who carries a lot of life on his shoulders, but there is a humour and vitality in these pages that outweighs any possible fade into melancholia that could arise.

In a sense, these are poems that one can only write as one ages, as one loses more and more of what was important, and as one's griefs and pains grow larger, or more dominant. As Whyte himself says in 'Out Of Sorts', "We become more and more / the sum of our small ailments".

Never were truer words spoken.

Several of the poems reference the loss of things, whether the death of a father, a theatre changed or the heyday of the 1960s counter culture, but they never tread the shallow path into trite verse. This is a man speaking his own life, in his own words. The vernacular is broadly English, but with hints of Whyte's Scottish patter.

In many of the poems, the location is either irrelevant or at the least, opaque and vague – this lends well to the 'captured moments' feel of the overall collection. These are not full stories, fleshed out in pub retelling details.

This is a collection that is deeply rooted in the specifics of Whyte's own life and experiences, and while this lends several of the poems a strong sense of familiarity and warmth, there is an argument that this can easily distance the reader. Some poems suffer from the fact that they reference people, situations or locations that are too precise, and while I can appreciate the cadence of Whyte's writing, I cannot bring the same enthusiasm that he clearly demonstrates for the subject matter.

However, even with this occasional straying into near solipsistic writing, I was happy to sit back and let Whyte show me these slivers of his life through these small windows. There is something calming in this mad world of political crises and dramatic demographic shifts to just sit quietly and share the visions of a man reflecting on a good life, well lived.

— *Shadowfax*

The Bechdel Test for Books

A Woman of Integrity
J David Simons

Freight Books, RRP £9.99, 307pp

The title of *A Woman of Integrity* is somewhat misleading, as it is equally about two women who struggle with integrity and authenticity throughout. Laura Scott is our modern-day protagonist, once a sought-after Hollywood actress who has been reduced to voicing a crab for a Disney film, before being dumped by her chain-smoking agent altogether. At the other end of the century is Georgie Hepburn, born in the year 1900 with a brief, dazzling career as a silent film actress before leaving Hollywood to become a pilot, then eventually settling down as a world-renowned photographer.

Laura has always been drawn to Georgie's life because of her independence and strength: whilst off flying Spitfires, Georgie refers to herself as "a Spitster, not a spinster". It's this admiration – added to the potential for a career comeback – that leads Laura to put her life on hold in order to team up with the inevitably unreliable Sal Yerksaw to produce a play based on Georgie Hepburn's life. Sal inflates Laura's ego by telling her she's perfect to play Georgie in terms of demeanour and looks, and before long Laura is single-handedly spear-heading all aspects of the play's production.

Georgie and Laura each have to contend with one or both of the following throughout the book: lecherous men, financial difficulty, unfaithful men, unfaithful friends, egotistical men, illegitimate children, gold-digging men, unreliable mothers, emotionally unavailable men, unrequited OBEs, men dying violent deaths and apple-picking. They navigate these elements with as much integrity as each can muster, and with a somewhat detached attitude to where life has taken them. The dispassionate narrative style really works in this novel, with financial betrayals and familial difficulties shrugged off by Laura and multiple deaths or infidelities borne by Georgie with a stiff upper lip.

For all Laura and Georgie extemporise about how much better off they would be without men, their lives invariably revolve around the wishes and memories of men – in work, in love, and even revealing significant truths about genetic relationships. In short, this novel definitely wouldn't pass the Bechdel Test.

A Woman of Integrity is well-paced and nuanced, composed of bite-sized chapters that often end on intriguing cliffhangers that keep the story compelling. The women's stories are told chapter about: Laura's from a third-person perspective that allows for a bird's-eye view of her self-centricity and poor decision-making, and Georgie's through her unpublished memoir entries and a 1982 BBC radio interview transcript, full of what-ifs, regret and acceptance.

The book is driven not by interest in the play being staged but by the potential connection between these two women, and in this regard the book ends on an anti-climax. There's real potential for a revelation that could have nicely linked the two stories together, but J David Simons chooses to end the novel on a more sentimental note uncharacteristic of the rest of the book. The writing style emphasises the parallels of the female characters but less so the distinctiveness of their undoubtedly disparate worlds. It's a novel full of questions of integrity and authenticity, and whilst well-researched and crafted, its world – and character depth – are not quite as authentic.

— *Mrs Tabitha Twitchit*

A Poetic Wunderkammer

From The Wonder Book of Would You Believe It?
Jane McKie

Mariscat Press, RRP £6.00, 36pp

From *The Wonder Book of Would You Believe It?* is Jane McKie's much anticipated second pamphlet collection from Mariscat Press. However, this pamphlet has more of a book-like presence in length and feel to it in its harking back to the days of adventure and lushly illustrated encyclopaedias of the natural world. The poems within are like items in a cabinet of curios, or *Wunderkammer,* all brought back to life by the poet's craft. But McKie does much more than play gallery-attendant, cataloguer or collector in a 'wonderland of physical science' – she sets out to show the primacy of the natural world instead of many poets who might seek to render the natural world in personified human terms.

The strongest poems in the pamphlet are, as suggested by the Ernest Haeckel drawings on the cover, poems about bats and to highlight the difference of McKie's approach to other poets, it's worth comparing D. H. Lawrence's famous 'Bat' poem to McKie's. In Lawrence's poem, all of the images are drawn first from the human world – Lawrence's vision is a deeply patriarchal or paternal one where the core images originate in the man-made world: thus a bat is a 'black glove' or a 'black piper' or merely 'bits of umbrella'. In 'Old Inhabitants of Our Home', the speaker's Nan makes it clear that they must respect the bats as they are the original residents – even human laughter must be flung into the alcoves where the bats live, and as such human activity is shaped and influenced by the natural world, and not the other way round. 'Not Like Us' attempts to answer the question 'What is it like to be a bat?' and again the essence of the bat, or 'batness', comes first:

> "[...] One minute hunger, the next
> a snap of jaws around a fizzing whit
> of insect life that, to a human, might
> taste of white peach or ice-cold Prosecco?
>
> [...]
>
> Batness is impossible to name
> as what it is to be the friend I love –
> the one who, unaware of my feelings,
> leans in drunkenly at a party to
> whisper, 'that girl looks sexy in half-light."

Into the precision and order of the natural world, this pamphlet introduces the difficult and sometimes messy lives of humans and instead of suggesting that both worlds stand apart, completely othered from each other, McKie urges us to begin to see parallels between both. Her eye for the dazzling poetic image seems to belong to that natural world – like the bats that hunt to 'pick off noise' in 'Strange Ears and What They Hear' – and it is a skill that could easily be domesticated out of existence if people ceased to look at, and treat, the natural world as something wondrous. In 'Creatures that Emit "Cold" Light', the ground fireflies used in Caravaggio's paint are a tribute to the creative human world being enhanced by an engagement with the animal kingdom. In the luridly titled 'Nightmare Denizens of an Unexplored World' McKie shows us that the only way to understand the natural world is to be an engaged and inspired part of it, not a competitor, tamer or destroyer of it:

> "Dead crabs float by, bleached out
> and translucent:
> she picks one up and puts it on
> her tongue.
> It tastes of salt and the newly
> greased hairs
> of a cello's bow. It tastes of ideas."

— *Richie McCaffery*

Contributor Biographies

Rizwan Akhtar is Assistant Professor in the Department of English, Punjab University, Lahore, Pakistan. He has published poems in well-established international poetry magazines.

Lin Anderson is best known for her long running series of forensic thrillers. She is co founder of Bloody Scotland and a screenwriter.

G. Armstrong grew up amidst North Lanarkshire's gang culture. This debut novel was written whilst studying English at the University of Stirling.

Karen Ashe, 2016 SBT New Writer's awardee, was highly-commended in the Bridport prize (twice!), published in Mslexia (twice!) and is writing a novel.

Rachelle Atalla is a prose writer and is the recipient of a Scottish Book Trust New Writers Award.

Andrew Blair is the co-producer of the Poetry as F*ck podcast. His debut collection is out through House of 3 press.

Dmitry Blizniuk is an author from Ukraine. His most recent poems have appeared in Dream Catcher (UK) and River Poets Journal (USA).

Dan Brady Keeps wirting. Word attrition. Don't give up. You've just not found the right desk for your work to land on.

Jenna Burns (22) has been published by Zoetic Press and The Retired Beekeepers of Sussex. Find her on Twitter @Jenna_221b

Ken Cockburn is an Edinburgh-based poet and translator. His new collection, Floating the Woods, is published by Luath in 2018.

David Crews is author of the poetry collections High Peaks (Ra Press) and Circadian Rhythm (Paulinskill Poetry Project). davidcrewspoetry.com

Rob Currie lives in Dundee and writes fiction and drama. He is a Scottish Book Trust New Writers Awardee (2013).

Jim Ferguson lives in Glasgow. Forthcoming poetry collection when feeling fully at home in the drifting living room of time due early 2018.

Lily Greenall is a writer from the Isle of Lewis. She is currently working on a PhD at Aberdeen University.

George Gunn lives in Thurso. He has been a deep-sea fisherman, a driller for oil in the North Sea, a journalist, playwright and poet.

Anne Hay has written short fiction and comedy for BBC radio and published poems in Northwords Now, Orbis and Umbrellas for Edinburgh.

Noëlle Harrison's sixth novel The Gravity of Love will be published by Black and White Publishing in May 2018. www.noelleharrison.com

Lars Horn is a writer, mixed-media artist, and translator.

Alex Howard is a poet and novelist from Edinburgh. His debut book Library Cat has been translated into Italian and Korean.

Vicki Jarrett is a novelist and short story writer from Edinburgh. Author of Nothing is Heavy and The Way Out.

Brian Johnstone has published six collections, lately Dry Stone Work (Arc, 2014) and a memoir Double Exposure (Saraband, 2017). www.brianjohnstonepoet.co.uk

Loll Jungeburth studies at the University of Glasgow and is the founding editor of RAUM poetry magazine.

Judith Kahl is a writer and translator working in Edinburgh, Munich and Shanghai. Find her at poetickindness.wordpress.com

Jackie Kay is Scotland's third modern Makar, A poet, novelist and writer of short stories, she has enjoyed great acclaim for her work.

Stephen Keeler writes and teaches in the north-west Highlands. He received a Scottish Book Trust New Writing Award in 2015.

Rached Khalifa teaches literature at the University of Tunis El-Manar. He has published critical and fictional works. He's currently working on a novel.

Chris Kohler is a writer who lives in Glasgow. He is trying to write a book.

Marjorie Lotfi Gill is a founder of The Belonging Project. Her poems have been widely published and been performed on BBC Radio 4. www.marjoriegill.com

Claire MacLeary gained an MLitt from Dundee University. Cross Purpose, her debut novel, was long-listed for the 2017 McIlvanney Prize.

Martin Malone lives in Gardenstown. He has published two poetry collections: The Waiting Hillside (Templar, 2011) and Cur (Shoestring, 2015).

Iain Maloney is the author of three novels, a poetry collection and "The Only Gaijin in the Village" column. @iainmaloney

Richie McCafferty's first collection was called Cairn. His second collection is due out in 2018 from Nine Arches Press.

Alan McFarlane is a poet and short story writer with an interest in the sound and delivery of everyday language.

Colin McGuire is one of Scotland's most exciting poets. His page and screen delivery is serious, urgent and sharply funny. www.colinmcguirepoet.co.uk

Alex McMillan grew up in Livingston and now teaches in Lima. He writes poems sometimes.

Hugh McMillan is a poet from Galloway. His new collection Ghost Dancers in the Gallowgate is due out in 2018.

Scott McNee is currently a first year PhD student in creative writing at the University of Strathclyde.

Elizabeth McSkeane is an award-winning poet, (three collections) short-story writer, novelist. Liz's first novel, Canticle, will be published by Turas Press early in 2018.

Ian Newman lives in Kirriemuir. He enjoys cooking and climbing trees. At thirty-nine he does one more than the other.

Hannah Nicholson is from Shetland, and recently graduated from the University of Aberdeen with an MLitt (Distinction) in Creative Writing.

Helen Nicholson lives in Cupar, completed a St Andrews MFA in poetry (2016) and is a trustee of Magma poetry.

Rebecca Parker is based in Fife. She is a writer, copy-editor, and a member of the publishing team at Tapsalteerie.

Fiona Rintoul is an author and translator. Fiona wrote The Leipzig Affair, which was shortlisted in the Saltire awards and broadcast on BBC R4.

Elizabeth Rimmer has published two poetry collections with Red Squirrel Press. Her third, Haggards, will be out in 2018. www.burnedthumb.co.uk

Stewart Sanderson wrote both of the poems printed here while on a 2016 Robert Louis Stevenson Fellowship in Grez-sur-Loing, France.

Finola Scott was mentored by Liz Lochhead on the Clydebuilt Scheme. A performance poet, she is proud to be a slam-winning granny.

Max Scratchmann is a writer and illustrator. His work appears internationally and he runs the performance poetry company, Poetry Circus.

Graeme Smith holds an MLitt from Dundee University and recently finished his first novel. He teaches English and creative writing in a prison.

Shane Strachan's work has appeared in New Writing Scotland, Northwords Now, Stand and others. Find out more at www.shanestrachan.com

Samuel Tongue's first pamphlet is Hauling-Out (Eyewear 2016). He is co-editor of New Writing Scotland and poetry editor at The Glasgow Review of Books.

Louise Welsh is the author of eight novels including Death is a Welcome Guest. She is Professor of Creative Writing at Glasgow University.

Jim C Wilson's latest poetry collection is Come Close and Listen (Greenwich Exchange). Much more information at www.jimcwilson.com